# $L$_ADY_ ı

Driven by fierce patriotism to ~~England~~ uess of Haverstock will do anything to reclaim the money his best friend lost at cards, money that was to purchase battle plans from a French official.

The bewitchingly beautiful but illegitimate Anna De Mouchet agrees to give the marquess back the money she "won." On one condition: that he marry her.

From this forced marriage rises a love as powerful as the canons of the war which tears them apart.

***With His Ring*** (The Brides of Bath, Book 2)
"Cheryl Bolen does it again! There is laughter, and the interaction of the characters pulls you right into the book. I look forward to the next in this series." – *RT Book Reviews*

***To Take This Lord*** (The Brides of Bath, Book 4)
"Bolen does a wonderful job building simmering sexual tension between her opinionated, outspoken heroine and deliciously tortured, conflicted hero." – *Booklist of the American Library Association*

***The Bride's Secret*** (The Brides of Bath, Book 3)
"What we all want from a love story." – *In Print*

***One Golden Ring***
"*One Golden Ring*...has got to be the most PERFECT Regency Romance I've read this year." – *Huntress Reviews*

Holt Medallion winner for Best Historical, 2006

***The Counterfeit Countess***
"This story is full of romance and suspense. . . No one can resist a novel written by Cheryl Bolen. Her writing talents charm all readers. Highly recommended reading! 5 stars!" – *Huntress Reviews*

"Bolen pens a sparkling tale, and readers will adore her feisty heroine, the arrogant, honorable Warwick and a wonderful cast of supporting characters." – *RT Book Reviews*

Daphne du Maurier award finalist for Best Historical Mystery

***Protecting Britannia***
It's fun to watch the case unfold in this nonstop action adventure...Graham and Britannia's second chance at love adds dimension to the story. – 4 STARS *RT Book Reviews*

**By Cheryl Bolen**

**Regency Romance**

House of Haverstock Series
  *Lady by Chance* (Book 1)
  *Duchess by Mistake* (Book2)
  *Countess by Coincidence* (Book 3)

The Brides of Bath Series:
  *The Bride Wore Blue* (Book 1)
  *With His Ring* (Book 2)
  *The Bride's Secret* (Book 3)
  *To Take This Lord* (Book 4)
  *Love in the Library* (Book 5)
  *A Christmas in Bath* (Book 6)

The Regent Mysteries Series:
  *With His Lady's* Assistance *(Book 1)*
  *A Most Discreet Inquiry (Book 2)*
  *The Theft Before Christmas (Book 3)*

Brazen Brides Series:
  *Counterfeit Countess* (Book 1*)*
  Book 2 coming in late 2015
  Book 3 coming in 2016

*The Earl's Bargain*
*My Lord Wicked*
*His Lordship's Vow*
*A Duke Deceived*

Novellas:
*Lady Sophia's Rescue*
*Christmas Brides (3 Regency Novellas)*

**Romantic Suspense**

Texas Heroines in Peril Series:
  *Protecting Britannia*
  *Capitol Offense*
  *A Cry in the Night*
  *Murder at Veranda House*

*Falling for Frederick*

**American Historical Romance**

*A Summer to Remember* (3 American Historical Romances)

**World War II Romance**

*It Had to be You*

**Inspirational Regency Romance**

*Marriage of Inconvenience*

# $\mathcal{L}$ADY BY $\mathcal{C}$HANCE

## (House of Haverstock, Book 1)

### by

## Cheryl Bolen

Copyright © 2011 by Cheryl Bolen

*Lady by Chance* is a work of fiction. Names, characters, places, and incidents are the products of the author's imagination or are used fictitiously. Any resemblance to actual events, locales, or persons, living or dead, is entirely coincidental.

# $\mathcal{P}$rologue

**London, 1808**

Anna de Mouchet studied the deck spread face down in her hands. It was remarkable that no one ever noticed how the birds' eyes varied on the back of the cards. Narrow eyes were face cards. Cards of lower denominations featured regular eyes. And the birds on the aces had round eyes. Of course, the men who had played at her mother's tables would have been more engrossed in the beauty of the dealer than in the etchings on the cards that assured her mother's winnings. Anna flipped over a king and smiled as she heard her chamber door smoothly open.

"Mademoiselle!" the maid screeched as she lightly kicked shut the door behind her and nervously scurried into the room, balancing her young mistress's breakfast tray. "Your mama would be most furious were she to know you still play with her cards. She desires nothing but to make a fine lady of you, *cheri.*"

No one was closer to Anna's mother than Colette, who had accompanied Annette when she fled the Terror more than fifteen years ago. Had it been discovered Annette de Mouchet was a noblewoman, Colette could have lost her head.

"But I don't want to be a lady," the girl protested. "I don't want to go to that fancy school.

Unlike Mama, I know I will be treated with no more civility at Miss Sloan's School for Young Ladies than we have received from our hostile neighbors here on Grosvenor Square."

"But your mama wants you to make friends with the daughters of the *ton*. After all, are you not one of them?"

Anna thrust out her chin and spoke through compressed lips. "I can never be one of them and well I know it."

Shortly after breakfast Anna was surprised to see a crested barouche in front of her house. The crest did not belong to any of her neighbors on Grosvenor Square, and her mother had not entertained noblemen since they moved here from Marylebone a year ago.

Anna walked to the morning room to see who was calling but found the doors closed and heard angry shouts from within.

"I will not have the illegitimate daughter of a French whore at school with my own daughters," an angry male voice said.

"My daughter has just as much right to be there as yours," Annette said defiantly. "Even more, for her father was more exalted than you, my lord."

Proud of her mother's fiery retort, Anna listened, fury pounding in her chest, as the man spoke.

"You schemed to get money that should have gone to Steffington's duchess, but you can never buy rank for your bastard."

Annette's voice quivered. "I took not a farthing from Steffington while he lived. Only his love. That is why I receive your rancor. Because of me, he would not bed your wife's sister. Now his money has come to his only child." Her voice cracked. "If it takes every shilling I own, our daughter will be a fine lady."

"Not by going to Miss Sloan's School for Young Ladies," he countered angrily. "I have a letter from the headmistress. She regrets to inform you there is no room for Anna de Mouchet."

The door suddenly flung open and a portly man in fine clothes swept past Anna without looking at her.

Anna scurried across the room to her Annette, who collapsed on a silken sofa, sobbing into her hands.

"Mama, please don't be upset," Anna soothed, leaning so close to her lovely mother she could smell her rose water. She gently hooked an arm around her. "I will be much happier here with you, and not with daughters of that horrid man. Pray, who was he?"

Sniffing, her mother gazed toward the doorway and spoke softly. "That was the Marquess of Haverstock."

# $\mathcal{C}$hapter 1

**London, 1813**

The Marquess of Haverstock dismissed his butler and firmly closed the doors of his library himself before showing his friend to a comfortable club chair near the fireplace and pouring two glasses of port. He settled in a broad chair before the fire where the smell of burning coal was strongest. "Our necessity for utmost secrecy cannot be stressed enough," Haverstock said in a voice much lower than his usual commanding style. "I have to be particularly cautious in this house filled with wretched females."

Ralph "Morgie" Morgan took a rather large swig of port. "Don't know how you tolerate it, my good man. Five sisters." Morgie shuddered as if the port had been poisoned.

"There are only four left, now that I've married off Mary."

"Oh, jolly good. Only four," Morgie said good naturedly.

Now the marquess shuddered. By the time he had provided four more dowries, he would not be able to afford to get married himself. Not that he wanted to, but still he cursed his father for leaving them so lean of pocket.

As if reading his friend's mind, Morgie said, "You really aren't bound to provide hefty dowries for the gels. Got to leave something for yourself."

"Then I'd be no better than my father."

Morgie swallowed and cast a glance at the painting of the marquess' brooding father over the fireplace. He loosened his cravat. Even from the grave, the former marquess could render one uncomfortable. Diverting his gaze from the intimidating portrait, he said, "I say, you'd have pots of money if you'd spend more time on your own affairs and less at the Foreign Office."

"Duty to one's country must take precedence over personal gratification. Which recalls me to the matter you and I need to discuss."

"Ah, yes." Morgie glanced at the door, then lowered his voice. "Came straight away to inform you the loan has been approved. Thank the bloody good Lord my father approved it before his recent demise. Otherwise, I'd have the devil to pay to get a shilling before his estate is settled." He looked pleased with himself when he announced, "I'll have the money in the morning."

The marquess's eyes brightened. "Excellent."

"Excellent for you. And even for England, but bloody bad for me. Since we could not disclose the clandestine nature of the loan, I had to say the whole bloody fifty-thousand pounds was to pay off my gaming debts. I feel like an utter baboon."

"Come now, Morgie. Your heavy gaming is a matter of public knowledge in London."

Morgie took another drink. "Never lose more than I can afford."

"That may be, given that every member of your family has more money than a nabob. And it is my good fortune that my closest friend is a member of the renowned Morgan banking scions."

Haverstock quietly studied his friend as Morgie slightly loosened his expertly tied cravat. Morgie, as Haverstock had referred to Ralph Morgan since their days at Eton, might not possess the keenest intellect, but he displayed impeccable taste. Perfectly tailored clothing – with extra padding over his slim shoulders – set his figure off to distinction, and his dark brown hair always appeared portrait perfect in the most fashionable, understated style. In addition to his exemplary physical appearance, Morgie's manners were above reproach. Because of his vast wealth, he was accepted everywhere despite that several members of the *ton*, including Haverstock's deceased father, quietly snubbed Morgie because of his Jewish lineage.

"If you get the money in the morning, we should be able to leave for France the following day," Haverstock said, fingering the cut crystal glass from which he had yet to drink. He did not share his friend's excessive fondness for liquor. "It's imperative we're in France by the twentieth."

Morgie nodded, patting his chest. "Had my tailor make a special coat lined with several inside pockets to hold a large portion of the money."

Haverstock sat up straight, his black eyes flashing with anger. "You didn't tell the man you'd be carrying large sums of money?"

"Course not, Haverstock. What do you take me for? I'm not a bloody idiot. Told the tailor I'd be traveling and had to carry documents, snuffboxes and hordes of medicinals."

Haverstock relaxed his large frame and smiled. "It's just that except for a select few who work with me at the Foreign Office, no one is to know we will be traveling with the money."

"And none of them know either your destination or the recipient of the cash. Correct?"

"Only me. And only because I speak French as a native. I've received excellent information from our French official in the past, and I completely trust his validity."

"How can you trust a man who sells his own country's secrets?"

Haverstock steepled his hands in thought. "It's because he's a patriot he wants to thwart Napoleon. Too many Frenchmen have spilled blood for Boney."

"Right he is about that Corsican monster, but does this Frenchman have no conscience about his information leading to the slaughter of more French?"

"He's been able to assuage his conscience by convincing himself the emperor's armies now consist mostly of foreigners who've been conquered by the French."

"Can't fault that, either."

Rising, Haverstock blew out a nearby tallow. "You must stay here tomorrow night so we can get an early start the following morning."

* * *

Anna pulled off her drab brown gloves and carefully placed them on her silken bed before untying her equally drab bonnet and depositing it next to the gloves for Colette to put up when she returned from her half day off. Of course, Anna was in for a thorough scolding from her life-long abigail. First, Colette would be angry because she had gone to the East End without her protection. Anna smiled, amused at the unlikeliness of the thin old maid preventing even the harmless fleecing of a street urchin.

Next, Colette would chide Anna for going out in such unfashionable attire.

"You must always dress as the grand lady you are," Colette recited daily.

But despite the last wishes of her mother, Anna knew she would never be a lady, nor would she ever be welcome in the fine homes of Mayfair. She dropped onto the chaise and lamented the dreariness and hopelessness of her life. She was eighteen years old, the owner of a large fortune, not at all unattractive, yet she had no hope of being presented. And even less hope of marrying a gentleman.

In her loneliest moments she gave way to a deep, aching longing to share her life with a man who would accept her as an equal, someone who would love her and give her the children she so desperately wanted.

Even more than the partnership and the children, she hoped for a love as powerful as her parents', a love so strong they had happily deflected society's scorn. But her parents' imperfect union had created a daughter who could never belong to either of their worlds.

Anna cast her head heavenward. Oh, Mama, I'm sorry to disappoint you.

The most social situation Anna ever encountered was her Sunday morning church service where the ladies enviously eyed her exquisite clothing while the men endeavored to make her acquaintance.

She stretched out her legs and sighed. *It is I who is so unfortunate I need the people of the East End more than they need me.* In the five years since her mother's death, the trips to the East End had provided her only joy. She had no friends. No male admirers. Her solicitor was her only caller. She had long since dismissed her dancing master over Colette's objections, for Colette still harbored illusions that Anna would go to fine balls and dazzle the young men as her mother had done in France so many years ago. The devoted Colette would never concede the futility of Annette's dreams for her daughter.

While Anna was engaged in her morose thoughts, Perkins rapped forcefully at her chamber door. "A caller for you, Miss de Mouchet."

Anna sat upright, startled by the announcement. Her solicitor had been here yesterday, so he would not be calling again. Who could her caller be? Walking to the door, Anna asked, "Pray, who is it?"

As she opened the door, Perkins handed her a gentleman's card.

It was Sir Henry Vinson's.

"Tell the gentleman I will be down in ten minutes."

Even if she had never been particularly fond of Sir Henry, she would meet him in one of her most fashionable morning dresses. Colette might contemplate murder otherwise.

As she removed the old East End garments, Anna wondered why Sir Henry would be calling. She had scarcely seen him since her mother's funeral. She had always suspected he had been in love with her mother, but Sir Henry was far too selfish to marry. He must be fifty now, and she had yet to hear of him marrying.

She felt a stab of fear at the fleeting thought that perhaps he wished now to marry. To marry her for her fortune.

She would never be that desperate.

* * *

Sir Henry gazed out the window at Grosvenor Square. He was surprised over his own nervousness at facing Annette's daughter. Of course, his very future could depend on the outcome of the meeting. He hated to admit a mere girl held his fate in her inexperienced hands, but he remembered her deft hands effortlessly shuffling and dealing cards as one born to the task. Smiling, he knew it was in her power to bring him the riches he had sought for so long.

Twenty-five thousand pounds now. And later, the promise of a ministry in France. Bonaparte himself had offered the Palais Vendome to Sir Henry if his activities here in London met with success.

How he despised these arrogant English aristocrats! Especially the straight-laced Haverstock. Though the young marquess avowed disdain for his deceased father, he very much reminded Sir Henry of his sire. Both men had been decidedly cool toward Sir Henry, and the son shared no confidences with him though they worked in the same department at the Foreign Office. He was every bit as haughty as his father had been.

Sir Henry's back was to Anna when she entered the room. He turned when he smelled the rose water. Annette's scent. He froze as Anna greeted him. It was as if he were being transported back in time nearly thirty years, to the Recheaux Chateau, recalling a time of lavishment that was now as buried as the pharaohs and as unlikely to ever be resurrected. A time before the revolution.

If it weren't for her very English voice, Anna de Mouchet would be an exact copy of her mother, he thought, his heart racing even now as he remembered his devotion to Annette. No woman had ever been more beautiful. Yet, this girl before him was. He noted her dark brown locks which glistened golden in the late afternoon sunlight. Her creamy, petal-soft skin with natural pink in her cheeks set off her spectacular eyes. They were large and almond shaped and the color of rich coffee beans. God's teeth, but they were beautiful! Even her figure was perfection.

And, he noted appreciatively, she had inherited her mother's taste for what was the finest a modiste had to offer. She wore a pink gown of exquisite cut, just low enough in front to reveal her ivory chest and to display the promise of a woman's full breasts. His eyes traveled down the length of her, resting at her satin slippers that were a perfect match to her dress, both of them accenting the blush in her cheeks.

"Ah, Anna, you are the very picture of you mother."

"I perceive that as a compliment, Sir Henry." She indicated a settee. "Do have a seat. Will you have tea?"

He lowered his tall, thin frame on to the settee. "No, my dear. Just looking at you will be enough nourishment for me." He reminded himself not be a glutton, reaching for the whole larder at once. He would take his bounty a little at a time by manipulating the girl with steady doses of prevarication.

She blushed and sat in a chair several feet away. She knew she should tell him how very good it was to see him, but Anna deplored lying.

Instead she said, "I trust you have been well? I've not heard from you in a very long while."

"Since your mother's funeral," he said, his expression grim. "You are probably wondering why I have come."

"Old friends don't need a reason."

"Ah, Anna. You make me ashamed I have not come sooner. Actually, I have been thinking about your mother – and you – a great deal of late. A situation has arisen which Annette would have been able to effortlessly handle. I think, though, you are the very one I need."

"You need me?" Was the wretched man going to offer for her hand?

He resituated himself on the settee and met her gaze squarely. "I have a business proposition to make."

Thinking only of his balding head and long nose, she refused to look him in the eye, sincerely hoping his proposition wasn't matrimony. "But, I assure you, I am quite well off." She tried to sound mature.

"No one ever has enough money, Anna."

"But I live quietly and my needs are not great."

"There is no one who could turn down twenty-five thousand pounds."

It was a very great sum, indeed. She would be foolish not to listen. Leaning forward, she asked, "What do you want from me, Sir Henry?"

"I remember how well you played cards as a child."

She stiffened. "I haven't played in years."

"Ah, but one of your skill never forgets."

Her eyes narrowed. "Does your proposition have something to do with me playing cards?"

"Indeed, it does."

"Then I can listen no more. My mother abhorred the idea of my playing, and I respect her memory too much to disregard her wishes."

"Anna, I'm offering a vast sum for one night's play."

She wasn't tempted, but she was curious. "Pray, what do you wish of me?"

"I know a very foolish man who will come into possession of fifty thousand pounds in cash tomorrow. I intend that half of it will go to you and half to me. For reasons I cannot disclose, I cannot relieve him of the money. That is why I need you. I plan to bring him to your parlor where you will make sure he is plied with the liquor for which he has a great fondness. Then, you will suggest a game of cards. You will suggest simple wagering and allow him to win at first. Then, as the stakes are raised, you will begin to win – using skills learned from your mother."

Anna sprang to her feet, fully intending to show him the door. "What you suggest, Sir Henry, is not only cheating, but stealing, and I will have no part of it."

"Sit down, Anna, and hear me out."

"There's nothing you can say that will change my mind."

He stood up and walked to her. "Who is the man you hate most in this world? Who is the man you blame for your mother's death?"

Without hesitation, she answered, "The Marquess of Haverstock."

Sir Henry's cool green eyes glinted. "Just so. My plan will ruin Lord Haverstock." Sir Henry lifted her chin. "Wouldn't that make you happy, my dear?"

"Nothing would make me happier. I loathe the

man. But I cannot do it. To do so would be breaking a solemn promise to my mother."

"For God's sake, Anna, she's been dead five years," he said harshly, then softened. "Trust me. Annette would be proud of you for making twenty-five-thousand pounds in one day. She knew that large fortunes open many doors."

"I will not change my mind."

A frown on his narrow face, he strolled to the window and stood there pondering his next move. He would have to reveal more of the true scope of his plans. More carefully fed lies. But he had confidence he could persuade her to do what would be far more repugnant to her than cheating at cards.

# $\mathcal{C}$hapter 2

"Come, let us sit together," Sir Henry said, walking to the damask sofa. "I have much to tell you."

They sat down, Anna leaving a wide gap between herself and her caller.

A solemn expression on his face, Sir Henry turned to Anna and spoke in a voice barely above a whisper. "Since the money didn't tempt you, I'm going to have to take you in my confidence."

She eyed him warily.

"Were my superiors to know what I'm about to tell you, I could be in serious trouble." He took a deep breath. "You see, I work at the Foreign Office – as does Lord Haverstock. The two of us are directly involved in French espionage." A pained look crossed his face. "Sadly, we suspect Lord Haverstock is in the employ of the French."

"How could such a man ever have been given a position of importance?" Anna asked, dismay and disgust in her voice.

"Actually, it is Lord Haverstock's son I'm speaking of. The father – the one you despise – is dead."

"Then I have no complaint against the son. I know too painfully the injustice of branding the child for the sins of the parent."

"But I assure you the son is equally loathsome.

He must be thwarted. Through his greatest friend – Ralph Morgan of the Morgan banking family – the marquess is secretly securing a loan for the French. Mr. Morgan believes the loan is for the English to purchase information from a French official.

"The money is to be ready tomorrow. It had been my hope to have you win the money from Mr. Morgan to keep the French from getting it."

Anna's eyes widened. "That, sir, is a horse of a different color."

He nodded with satisfaction. "It was your mother's desire that you become thoroughly English. Are you telling me you consider yourself an English patriot?"

"Can you doubt it?" Anna challenged.

A smug smile curved his lip. "How far would you go to prove your loyalty?" He got up and paced the floor. As much as he hated the thought, Sir Henry knew what he was about to propose would cost him the twenty-five thousand pounds for which he so keenly hungered. But if this new plan came to fruition, Anna could be his goose who continued to lay golden eggs.

"Could you marry for the love of your country?" he asked.

Her brows shot up. "What do you mean?"

"Marry Lord Haverstock. Become a spy for England. Get close to him. Learn his secrets. Pass them to us."

Anna laughed. "I assure you, Lord Haverstock would rather swing from the gallows than marry me."

"You underestimate your own charms, Anna." Sir Henry came back and sat next to her. "Consider this. Say you played cards with Mr.

Morgan before he can get the money to his friend. You win the fifty-thousand pounds Haverstock borrowed. Haverstock could fear for his neck since he has no personal fortune from which to replenish the money. I am persuaded you could wrangle a marriage proposal from him in exchange for giving him back the money.

"But then the money would go to the French!"

Sir Henry's eyes sparkled. "Yes, but the English would have you in Haverstock's house. Think what you'd be able to learn as his wife! You could be a wealth of information to us." To himself, Sir Henry hoped she could learn the identity of Haverstock's contact in France. Napoleon would surely pay a hundred-thousand pounds to learn who the treacherous informant was. Any number of lucrative possibilities presented themselves to Sir Henry. He cocked his head and studied Anna, a smile twisting his lips. "Lady Haverstock. Think, Anna, how much your mother wanted you to be a lady."

Her eyes stared vacantly for a while. The very thought of becoming the wife of the horrid marquess repulsed her, leaving her with a deep melancholy, a futile longing for a mate to whom she could give her heart. If she went along with Sir Henry's plan she would have to bury her hopes for a loving husband. She would have to welcome to her bed the son of the rotund Lord Haverstock. The son was most likely as disgusting as the father. The thought made her cringe.

But to go along with Sir Henry's scheme might not be so great a sacrifice. Her life was utterly empty. As Haverstock's marchioness surely she would at least have entry into society, not that she craved the balls and social whirl. But how wonderful it would be to have friends to share a conversation with, to have someone to ride with in the park.

Then, too, if she were to become Lady Haverstock, she could fulfill the deathbed promise she had made to her mother.

Her feelings hardly mattered when weighed against England. For the first time since her mother's death, Anna felt needed.

"I will win the money from Mr. Morgan," she said.

\* \* \*

It was very distasteful to Sir Henry to dress so innocuously, but he could take no chances he would be recognized by Ralph Morgan. He had watched, unobserved, as Morgan entered the bank. What was taking the man so deuced long? Sir Henry yanked in his fob and noted the time on his watch. *The fool had been in there for an hour.* As he placed the watch back in his pocket, he saw Morgan leave the bank, his step jaunty as he carried a small leather valise to his barouche where half a dozen liveried men assured his protection.

So the man wasn't half the fool Sir Henry had thought. Still, Sir Henry was puzzled. Fifty thousand pounds should be in a portmanteaux, not a small valise. Nevertheless, Sir Henry mounted his horse and followed at a discreet distance.

Assured that Morgan was home, Sir Henry hurried to his own house to change and prepare for his next step. In less than an hour, he was being shown into Morgan's opulent parlor.

"My dear Mr. Morgan," Sir Henry said, "I was

passing by and decided I must pay you a call. You and your friend Haverstock have been much on my mind of late." He watched Morgan as he sat down. He seemed heavier than Sir Henry remembered. That was it! He carried many of the sovereigns within his coat. Sir Henry's respect for Morgan's intellect increased.

"Pray, why is that, Sir Henry?"

Sir Henry took out his snuff box, withdrew a pinch and inhaled. Then, smiling mischievously at Morgan, he sat down in a tufted chair and said, "The female conquests of you two are rather well known. I believe there is a certain rivalry over which of you can escort the loveliest women."

Morgan's face colored. "More often than not, Haverstock wins the beauties."

"Alas, it is hard to compete with a title."

"Oh, it's not just his title. Given the choice between a man small of stature like myself or one as huge and rugged looking as Haverstock, most women prefer the bulk."

"That may be, but if a beautiful woman were to see you first, I am sure you could win her over with your elegance of person."

Morgan blushed again.

"That's why I'm here. There is a great beauty who has recently come to London. Since it's too early for the season, none of the bucks have made her acquaintance. Take my word on it, there is not a lovelier woman in all of England. And I propose to introduce you to her today."

Morgan's eyes narrowed. "Why are you not interested in her for yourself?"

Sir Henry shook his head. "I've long since given up young maidens as well as the thought of marriage. Fifty is much too old to change my bachelor ways."

A slow smile crossed Morgan's face. "Got a bit of time on my hands. Where do we meet this nonpareil?"

"We will present ourselves at her house on Grosvenor Square."

Morgan lifted a brow. "Then she's not – -"

"Not a lightskirt. She's a gentlewoman. However, have no fear she will try to grip you in parson's mousetrap. She has quite a fortune of her own."

Rising, Morgan said, "If it's all the same to you, old chap, I prefer to take my barouche. Feel a lot safer with my able men surrounding me. So much crime of late, you know."

Getting his greatcoat from his regally liveried butler, Morgan announced that he was going to Grosvenor Square.

* * *

Wearing a soft white gown that revealed her ivory neck and decolletage, Anna presided over the tea table, engaging Mr. Morgan in talk of the campaigns in the Peninsula. Then, telling him she knew men much preferred port, she began to fill and refill his glass with the Portuguese liquid. It was at that point, Sir Henry took his leave.

Since Anna had neither a parent nor a companion to chaperon, for the sake of propriety she had arranged for a maid – the one closest to her size – to don one of her fine dresses and sit in the parlor doing needlework.

Despite that Anna was tired from having practiced her card playing with Sir Henry throughout the night, she charmed Mr. Morgan as the future of England depended on it.

After the liquor began to relax him, Anna said,

"I cannot pretend that your reputation has not preceded you, Mr. Morgan. Your every activity merits scrutiny from the *ton*. Even I have heard a great deal about you. For instance, I know you are in possession of a large fortune."

"Sir Henry tells me you, too, have vast wealth."

"Yes. It seems we have that in common," she said. "I have also heard that in one night you can win or lose sums large enough to dower half the ladies coming out in any given year."

"Kind of you to mention winning. Seems I do much more of the opposite."

She lowered her impossibly long lashes and favored him with a bewitching smile. "I do not believe that for a moment, Mr. Morgan. I am sure a man such as yourself possesses great skill."

"You are all kindness, Miss de Mouchet."

"I adore playing cards though my skill is sadly inadequate."

"We shall have to play sometime."

She looked up hopefully. "Should you like to play a few hands of vingt-un today?"

"Capital idea."

Anna summoned her servants to set up the card table while she and Mr. Morgan established the rules. She easily persuaded him to wager. Then, they decided to change the dealer with each game and to allow the dealer to win double the wager for having a pontoon.

For the first half hour of play, Anna consistently lost but insisted on increasing the amount of the wager with each new game.

After they had played an hour, Anna's winnings amounted to ten thousand pounds.

Patting his coat laden with money, Mr. Morgan said, "I say, my luck had better change. Don't care to face Haverstock when he's in a rage. Such a large man."

Anna shivered, remembering the elder Lord Haverstock's rage, though she had no recollection of him being excessively large. "Pray, why should Lord Haverstock care what you do with your money?"

"He, ah," Mr. Morgan stammered, "He holds a strong dislike for gaming."

As Mr. Morgan's consumption of liquor increased, his skill decreased. Relieving him of his very considerable funds was as easy as blinking, Anna thought. Even without the marked cards, she could have effortlessly plucked her winnings from the drunken man.

"Devilishly bad luck I'm having," he uttered, throwing down his cards. "Better cut my losses and leave."

"Pray, do not get discouraged," Anna coaxed. "I just know you will win the next hand."

With Anna's help, he did win the next hand. "'Pon my word, my luck is most decidedly changing," Mr. Morgan said happily while Anna dealt the next hand. He had a seven showing; her visible card was an ace.

She had a king face down and could tell that Morgan's bottom card was a number between two and ten. She declined a hit; he took one. It was a four. He took a swig of port and smiled broadly, proudly flipping over his cards. They added up to twenty-one.

Then Anna revealed her pontoon and scooped up the money on the table and an additional fifteen thousand.

For the next hand, the wager was twenty thousand. He dealt Anna a face card down, himself an ace down. His next card was a nine, hers an ace.

He smiled broadly. "Can't possibly have two pontoons in a row."

"I am sorry to say I can, Mr. Morgan," Anna said, watching him utter an oath before he began to scrawl an IOU.

* * *

When night fell and Morgie still had not called, Haverstock's anxiety grew. He decided a visit to Morgie's town house was in order. There, he discovered Morgie had gone out with Sir Henry Vinson. Haverstock arched a brow. He did not know Morgie was acquainted with Sir Henry. Having a rapport with Morgie's servants from the frequency of his visits, Haverstock's gentility did not prevent him from asking where Morgie had gone.

"He's gone to Grosvenor Square, my lord," Morgie's butler replied.

Haverstock rode his gig directly to Grosvenor Square, where the presence of Morgie's barouche indicated which house his friend visited.

The marquess surveyed the stately four-story house approvingly before mounting the steps and rapping on the door. After presenting his card to the butler who greeted him, Haverstock said, "I have an urgent need to see Mr. Morgan."

The butler looked nervous, but since he was unaccustomed to callers, showed the marquess to the parlor.

Haverstock was horrified at the sight he beheld. There, Morgie lazily stretched out in a chair at a game table, a glass of port in his hand. But it was the table which drew Haverstock's attention. On it stacked crooked towers of gold sovereigns. Hundreds of them.

And sitting opposite Morgie was a young woman of exquisite beauty.

Haverstock strode up to her, bowed and said, "Charles Upton, the Marquess of Haverstock, at your service."

A puzzled look on her face, Anna sputtered, "But you cannot be the marquess. You look nothing like your father."

"You knew my father? May I have the honor to make your acquaintance, Miss – -?"

She extended her hand hesitantly. "Miss de Mouchet. Anna de Mouchet."

That name! He had heard not only his father but also his mother speak of the de Mouchet woman in the most demeaning way. It was the de Mouchet woman who had deprived his Aunt Margaret of the fortune due her as Steffington's duchess. It had been said the de Mouchet woman had presided over a gaming establishment. And it was the de Mouchet woman who had borne the old duke's child out of wedlock while Haverstock's poor aunt went to her grave barren. This woman he now gazed at must be that child. And she had obviously inherited her mother's evil ways.

He looked at her beauty only with contempt now. "How much has he lost?"

"A very large sum, my lord," Anna said smugly.

"How much?"

"I believe it is about fifty-thousand."

"Pounds?"

She nodded, slipping the marked cards in the false bottom of a drawer of the table. A perfectly legitimate deck remained on the table.

Since her hands were under the table, Haverstock had not seen her action. He grabbed the deck that remained. "I will have a look at the cards, Miss de Mouchet."

"Please, do. I have nothing to hide. You will find I won the money fairly."

Mr. Morgan made an attempt to straighten his spine. "I say, Haverstock, bit rough on the girl. I take full responsibility for my losses."

Haverstock ignored his friend as he examined the cards for several minutes. Then he looked around the room. "No one else has been here while you played? Someone who could have been observing my friend's hand and passing the information to you?"

"No one," Anna snapped. "Unless you count my companion who has not moved from her chair on the other side of the room."

He turned to observe the young woman who sat sewing at least twenty feet away. "May I ask who the dealer was?"

"The deal changed with each hand, my lord," Anna said calmly.

He flung the cards back on the table as Morgie began to slide from his chair.

"Deuced fool. He's passed out," Haverstock said, lifting Morgie effortlessly and carrying him to a nearby sofa.

Then, Haverstock turned back to Anna, malice on his face. "I don't know how you did it, but I submit that you are a cheat and a thief, like the French whore who was your mother."

Her face growing hot with rage, Anna rose. "Get out of my house at once!"

Fury flashed in his eyes as he glared at her icy beauty. "I will not leave until I have my friend's money back."

"That, my lord, is impossible."

He knew Morgie would make up the losses within the next few months, but that would be too late for his meeting with Monsieur Herbert.

By holding back his anger and negotiating with the woman, perhaps he could get the money by tomorrow. Drawing a step nearer to her, he said, "Forgive me. I spoke rashly. It's just that it's imperative that I have the money tonight."

"As I said, that is impossible."

"I will give you a promissory note to return the entire sum with ten percent interest before the end of this quarter. That's another five thousand pounds for you."

"My answer is still no."

In silence, he stared at the lovely creature for what seemed like several minutes, phrasing the words that gathered in his mind. "I know you to be a woman of fortune. May I ask why you cling so obstinately to this money?"

She lifted her defiant gaze to him. "It is because I have no love for the House of Haverstock. Your father treated my mother cruelly and unjustly, and my mother was the kindest, most loving woman I've ever known."

From the way he had heard his father talk of Anna's mother, he could well believe his father's treatment of the woman. And he knew only too well how cruel his father could be when dealing with those he felt were beneath his rank.

"Surely you cannot blame the son for the sins of the father?" he said in an apologetic voice.

Her eyes as cold as Sienna marble, she challenged, "Does his blood not run in your veins?"

He spoke slowly and almost with a gentleness. "I am not my father."

"But you also insulted me. For that you will pay."

\* \* \*

Anna looked up into Haverstock's piercing black eyes. She had never stood so close to such a large man before. He had to be several inches over six feet. Everything about him was large from his broad shoulders to his deep, resonant voice. He neither looked nor acted like the man she remembered as his father. Whereas his father had been fair, the son was dark. His thick black hair crept slightly further back on his forehead than she guessed it had a decade earlier. And a fleshiness around his square chin added to his maturity without detracting from his good looks. His somber face featured a full mouth and fine aquiline nose. She found him quite handsome, and his presence had a disturbing effect on her. She wanted to detest him but found she could not, particularly after he had so humbly said *You cannot blame the son for the sins of the father.* Without speaking unfavorably, he had acknowledged his parent's meanness.

As if in defeat, he lowered his huge frame into a chair. "Is there nothing I can do to get back the money?"

"Perhaps there is," Anna said, her voice decisive. She walked to the window and stood looking out on the square, her back to him. Finally, she turned to him and smiled. "I can think of no better revenge against your father than for you to marry me, the daughter of a French whore."

# $\mathcal{C}$hapter 3

Had his deceased father walked into the room, Haverstock could not have been more shocked. He opened his mouth to protest, but no words came. He merely looked upon the temptress who glared at him with a challenge in her eyes. The woman must be mad to make so ridiculous a suggestion.

Yet he found himself contemplating her proposal. He had given marriage little thought, largely because he had no money to set up his own household. He had known he would someday have to marry a woman of fortune. And here was a woman of great fortune whose beauty was unmatched. But he could not give serious consideration to her demand. He could not marry a woman of such low morals.

After a long silence, she crossed the room to him. "You said you had to have the money tonight. My way is the only way you will gain possession of it, my lord."

"Can you not give me a fortnight to contemplate the matter?"

"Certainly. If you can wait a fortnight for the money."

"But I leave tomorrow on a trip and must have the money then."

"Then you must marry me tonight."

"God in heaven, woman, I cannot marry you tonight! We have no license."

She hovered over the card table, her hands raking through the gold coins. Lifting her eyes to his, she spoke casually. "With your rank, I am sure you could ride to Lambeth Palace tonight and secure a special license from the Archbishop himself."

He rounded the table and planted his feet in front of her. "And who, pray tell, would marry us tonight?"

A flicker of triumph flashed in her eyes. "I can take care of that matter, my lord."

He had less than forty-eight hours before his meeting in France. What was he to do?

He decided to shock her. "Do you mean to say you would bed a man you despise?" Surely the thought of making love with him would repulse her into changing her mind. "I would insist on it, you know."

Her eyes widened. After a moment, she whispered, "Yes, I could do that for I want children very much."

He lifted a brow. "Children of Haverstock blood?"

"They would also have the blood of Annette de Mouchet," she countered.

His eyes traveled over the soft curves of her perfect body and, against his will, he wondered what it would be like to have such a woman beneath him in bed. He felt himself wavering.

Then he thought of his mother's reaction to the match. He would rather throw himself beneath a runaway coach and four than tell her. She had loathed Anna's mother. And like her husband, his mother would never be able to think of Anna as anything but the illegitimate daughter of French whore, certainly not of the breeding to be the Marchioness of Haverstock.

"I doubt my family would ever accept you," Haverstock challenged.

She threw her head back and laughed. "Do you think I care? I know very well what your family thinks of me. Which makes my revenge all the sweeter. I want to hurt your family as your family hurt mine."

His voice softened. "What is it my father did to cause such loathing?"

A flash of anger leapt to her eyes. "He killed my mother."

Haverstock's brows lowered. "Come now, I know my father was no saint, but he did not kill anyone."

"Oh, he didn't lift a finger against her, but he killed her as surely as if he'd fired a musket ball through her heart."

A look of concern swept over his face. "How so?"

"It is a long story, and I do not have time to tell you tonight. Another time, perhaps."

"You don't have time because you plan to marry tonight. Correct?"

She nodded.

Why did the prospect of marrying the doxy leave him with a gnawing emptiness? Surely he had not harbored hopes for a loving marriage. His own parents clearly had not married for so sentimental a reason.

Marriage to a wealthy woman did have its merits. Anna de Mouchet possessed a large fortune and uncommon beauty. He could bring worse to his bed.

God, but the woman balanced his honor and his ruin in her delicate hands, and he hated her for it. She had the power to unravel four years of his relentless labor to restore the good name of Haverstock his father had so thoroughly soiled.

Haverstock got to his feet. "I am a defeated man. I go now to Lambeth Palace."

* * *

Anna, a generous benefactor to St. George's, scribbled a note begging the curate to come at once to Grosvenor Square. She then set about selecting a wedding gown. She chose a gown she had never worn, an elaborate dress of white sarcenet, suitable for a presentation gown. She had known she would never be presented to the queen, but nevertheless had commissioned the gown to please Colette.

As much as Colette wanted Anna to be a fine lady, she was not at all pleased over this marriage, protesting when Anna informed her of the vows that would be exchanged that night. "Not the man most despicable!"

"He is the son of that man," Anna defended. "He's nothing like the father." She hated not being able to confide in Colette the real reason for marrying the marquess.

Tears glistening in her eyes, Colette had asked, "What of *amour*?"

It was a question for which Anna had no answer.

Once Colette had fastened Anna's silken buttons, Anna stood back to gaze at herself in the looking glass. Her bare ivory shoulders curved into tiny puffs of sleeves. The neckline was much too low for a young maiden, but now she would be a married lady. Gossamer layers of silks softly gathered below her bosom, falling along the smooth curves of her body. In the back, the dress flowed into a train edged with pearls. The queen herself could not have a lovelier gown, Anna thought approvingly.

She slipped her feet into dainty beaded white satin slippers and pulled on long, opera-length gloves.

Dismissing Colette, she walked back and forth to the window. What could be taking the man so long? Was the archbishop not at home? Had Haverstock changed his mind? The second prospect more likely. The Marquess of Haverstock did not seem to be a man who would allow himself to be forced into marriage. Especially to her, *the daughter of a whore.*

She heard the clopping of hooves on the square and hurried to her window. A gig with a lone rider approached her house. Haverstock had come. She pulled away from the window and tried to calm the rapid beating of her heart. Was she doing the right thing? Was she being foolish?

A moment later, Perkins rapped at her door. "Lord Haverstock has arrived, Miss de Mouchet. And the clergyman is also waiting."

She opened the door. "Show them into the par – -" Then, remembering that Mr. Morgan was stretched out, dead to the world, on the sofa, changed her mind. "Show them to the salon, Perkins. I will be right down."

She was unable to take the next irrevocable step, the step that would indelibly alter her future. She had to remind herself that she would not only be helping her country but also granting her mother's last wish. She pictured her lovely mother, wasting away on her deathbed, meekly whispering, "Promise me, Anna. You will show them all. You will be a grand lady."

Tears streaking her face, Anna had replied, "Yes, Mama. For you, I will be a lady."

If only she could satisfy her own wishes for a loving partner. Raising her head proudly, Anna strode from her room and descended the stairs.

* * *

Haverstock and the curate were sorting out the matter of the license when Haverstock smelled the rose water and turned to gaze at his bride-to-be. Her head held high, she regally glided into the room. A sense of unreality shook him. It was as if he levitated from his own body looking down upon her ethereal beauty. She looked so angelic in her flowing white gown, she seemed framed in a radiance, like a Madonna in an old Italian painting. No mortal woman had ever appeared more flawlessly beautiful than this woman he was about to marry.

The curate spared them the awkwardness of a greeting. "Will there be any attendants?"

"Only the two of us," Anna said softly. "If you have need for witnesses, my servants can oblige."

The clergyman nodded, then stood the bridal couple in front of him. Standing between them, he began the ceremony.

Haverstock found himself taking Anna's delicate, gloved hand in his own. Her touch was devastating. He cursed the swell of life in his groin. He was responding to beauty, not goodness.

Anna recited her vows in a voice barely above a whisper.

Then it was his turn. Would he love, honor and cherish her until death? the clergyman asked. If only he could, he thought, a deep, sinking feeling of hopelessness engulfing him. He promised to forsake all others. Perhaps he could honor that one pledge, provided she satisfied his sexual needs. Then he felt coarse and cheap. She was a brood mare, he a stud.

When it came time to place a ring on her finger, he took off his signet ring and slid it over her gloved finger. It could have fit over two of her slim fingers. "When I get it from my mother," he whispered, "the Haverstock ring shall be yours."

After the ceremony and after Haverstock thrust a handful of guineas into the curate's palm and dismissed him, the two of them faced each other in the suddenly chilly salon and found themselves at a loss for words.

"I will make arrangements with my solicitor in the morning, my lord," Anna said. "You will find me generous."

Anger rose within him. Did she think he was to be bought like a horse at Tattersall's? "I do not want your bloody money!" he snapped.

She faced him calmly. "Nevertheless, my lord, it is yours. Whatever I have is now yours. And, of course," she said bluntly, "your title is now mine."

"Yes, it is, Lady Haverstock," he said, malice in his voice. "Bought in an unfair manner."

Stinging under his rebuke, she fingered the large signet ring and shot her husband a perceptive gaze. "Tell me, my lord, is your mother in London?"

He looked at her warily. "Yes."

"Yet you chose not to get her ring tonight. Am I correct in saying you would rather not inform your mother of our marriage?"

He walked around the pianoforte, avoiding her

gaze. "I shall notify her. But since I will be gone these next two weeks, I find the idea of conveying the information by means of a letter much less confrontational. I shall pen the letter tonight. She will receive it tomorrow and will have two weeks to prepare Haverstock House for you. I give you my word, you will be mistress there."

"Do you know, I have no notion of where your seat is."

"It's in Devon."

"I've never been there," she said, moving toward the pianoforte and forcing him to meet her gaze. "Is it quite lovely?"

"Quite. But Haymore needs much work."

"If you don't want my fortune for yourself, then perhaps you can put it to use restoring Haymore."

Had the cursed woman invaded his very thoughts? How could she have known how strongly he wanted to bring Haymore back to its former glory, before his father squandered his money at the gaming tables?

"I may consider that," he said coolly, erecting a barrier between himself and this woman, his wife. He must not let her get too close. Stiffening, he addressed her: "Madam, I go to my town house now to ready for my trip. Do me the goodness to have one of your servants rouse my friend, Mr. Morgan, at four in the morning." He turned his back to her and stepped toward the door.

The ceremony had been legal enough, Anna thought. Haverstock had even addressed her as *madam*, but she did not trust the man. In the eyes of the law, she was still not his wife. And if the marriage were not consummated, he could easily dismiss her with an annulment once he had spent the fifty-thousand pounds. Though she did not desire him, she knew what she must do.

She strode to him and laid a gentle hand on his arm. "I know you are in haste to prepare for your journey, my lord, but you forget this is our wedding night. I would have the marriage consummated before you leave on your journey."

His eyes lingered over the perfection of her face and once again cursed her touch that brought the swelling in his breeches.

# $\mathcal{C}$hapter 4

If consummation was what the woman wanted, then she would have it, Haverstock vowed angrily as he paced the masculine chamber adjoining hers. He would take her swiftly, with no allowances for pleasuring her. Wife she may be in name, but name only. He would satisfy her legal whim and be gone. He had other matters to see to tonight.

After an adequate amount of time for her to ready herself, he rapped at her door, then entered. The room's only light came from a fire glowing in the hearth and a single taper beside her gilded bed. She was in the bed, propped up on mounds of lacy pillows, her freshly brushed hair hanging loose around her lovely face. She wore a white lace gown buttoned to the neck and looked impossibly innocent. He held back a snort, doubting her innocence. The woman was the daughter of a whore and was herself most likely a cheat and a thief. Certainly no innocent.

He would not accord her gentlemanly courtesies. "You are to remove your clothing, madam," he said, his voice as clear and cool as an icicle.

Her eyes widened for a hint of a second, then she moved to the edge of the bed, blew out the candle and began to unbutton her gown.

"I want the candle lighted," he said harshly. "I am your husband, and I want to see what I'm getting." He scooped up the candle, strolled to the fireplace and relit the wick from the flames. Walking slowly back to her bed, he watched her lift the gown over her head, then clutch the coverlet to hide her breasts, her face flaming.

He set the candle on the marble top of her bedside table and leaned over her, lifting her chin with his finger. "I cannot believe the former Miss de Mouchet blushes over the prospect of displaying her lovely body."

"It is just. . ." Anna whispered, "I did not know this act was performed . . .totally naked?"

His laughter shook the room. "Yes, my dear, we shall perform the act totally naked. I pity your former lovers if they were denied the pleasure of your entire body." His hand moved from her chin, down the slope of her chest, where he flicked off the covering and cupped a full breast while his thumb plied her pink nipple.

"There have been no lovers, my lord," she said in a shaky voice.

He removed his hand and met her bewildered gaze. "Do you mean to tell me you're a virgin?"

All he saw were her huge, brown eyes staring at him like a frightened doe as she nodded.

"So you say. There are ways a man can tell if a woman has been with a man."

She lifted her chin and spoke in a voice now devoid of shakiness. "I'm very happy to learn that. Then I will be exonerated of at least one odious deed."

"Oh, but my dear," he said, sitting beside her on the bed and stroking her breast, "there is nothing at all odious about the deed."

"Then you've done this before?"

He guffawed. "God in heaven woman, I'm two and thirty years old!"

Softly, she asked, "How old were you the first time?"

He remembered the fair Denise at Oxford and smiled. "Eighteen."

She spoke in a whisper. "I am eighteen, too."

He struggled with himself not to feel sympathy for her. He would soon know if she was a whore.

Her eyes flicked to his hand as he kneaded her breast. "I suppose this a ridiculous question to ask one's husband, but what is your first name, my lord?"

A smile curved his lips. "Charles."

"Have you ever had a mistress, Charles?"

"That is no concern of yours, my dear. I vowed to your priest tonight that I would forsake all others, and I intend to keep at least that part of my vows, provided you satisfy my bedroom needs."

"I will endeavor to try," she said softly. "Oblige me by being a good teacher."

He got up from the bed and blew out the candle. She was either a damned good actress or truly a virgin. If she had never seen a naked man before it was no wonder she was shaking. He began to remove his own garments, determined to end this charade of her virginity. His breeches fell to the floor and he climbed on the bed beside her.

"Wife," he said formally as she moved to make room for him beside her, "Let us begin to discover a few things about each other."

He could hear the lonely howl of the wind outside the casements as he pulled her to him, slipping one arm beneath her and wrapping his other around her. He felt her warmth as his chin nuzzled in the hollow of her neck, the fragrance of her rose water mingling with the softness of her loose hair. God's teeth, but she smelled good and felt good! His manhood throbbed.

He would not kiss her, not yet. She wanted consummation. She would get that, and only that. She was stiff as a poker. He forced her thighs apart, and she quickly clamped them back together.

Entry would not be easy with such resistance. He could see he would have to relax her. He began by stroking her back, and as he sensed an easing in her tension, his large hands slid along the smooth flesh of her bare hips, pressing into her roundness, nudging her closer with his hands, establishing a rhythm that continued when he ceased to pull her toward him.

While their bodies rolled into one another with a lulling, hypnotizing motion, his hands kept up their fluid stroking of her satin skin.

With unexpected pleasure, he felt her body mold into his, and he took delight in hearing the shortening of her breath. Virgins and wives, he had been told, lay rigid while their husbands took their pleasure. That Anna was no ice maiden brought relief mingled with disappointment.

He eased her back flat to the bed and leaned over her, his lips finding her breasts and closing around a nipple. She began to softly whimper.

Once again, he forced her thighs apart, and this time she widened even further. When his fingers found her wetness, her whimpers turned to moans as she raised her hips toward his stretched out body. He lowered himself into her and felt himself sheathed in her tight slickness. In a frenzy matching his movements, he called out her name once. Twice. Three times.

As he sunk deeper into her sweetness, he felt her stiffen and cry out in pain. And he knew he must be gentle with her. For she was indeed a virgin. As well as his wife. Holding her tightly and whispering her name, he heaved a gasp as his seed spilled into her.

He lay very still, loosening the tightness of his hold, staying within her, brushing the moist hair from her brow, kissing her forehead, her cheeks, her nose, and at last pressing trembling lips over hers.

He had never before called out a woman's name as he had with Anna. But, then, he'd never had a woman like Anna. He had always avoided deflowering virgins. And there was no shred of doubt that Anna had brought her virginity to this bed tonight. The thought softened his anger and hatred for her.

Yet as his wife's name had tumbled almost reverently from his lips, her blatant enjoyment of their intimacy made him want to curse her and the long line of cyprians whose blood ran in her veins.

Why couldn't this sexual encounter affect him as all the others in his past had? He had always been able to take his pleasure with commitment of nothing more than a few pounds. But tonight was so different. The physical pleasure, he must admit, had been, indeed still was, intense. By far the most intense he could remember. But there was something more. Something that seemed to envelop his mind and his emotions like nothing he had ever experienced. An alien tenderness toward the mere girl who shuddered beneath him, bereft of her innocence, nearly overpowered him.

He cursed himself for his weakness. And for the first time in his life he wished he could have been more like his heartless father. Why couldn't he have taken his pleasure from Anna without feeling? Why had he bent like a spring shoot and blown out the blasted candle? He had treated her with the same compassion he would have shown were she his own chosen bride and not a scheming chit who would stop at nothing to gain his title.

Yet against his will, his arms closed around her even tighter, and her feel and her scent swamped him with an odd sense of tenderness.

\* \* \*

Now that it was over, Anna willed herself not to stroke the supple muscles of his body. Now that she could gather her thoughts somewhat clearly, she wanted to die of shame. Years of careful grooming to act like a lady, to look like a lady and to think like a lady had come unraveled like a cheap ball of yarn. All because her body betrayed her.

She had thoroughly succumbed to the intoxicating love making of the selfish traitor who was now her husband.

She had acted like a whore. Like the woman everyone thought her mother was. But Anna had never believed what others said of her mother. Her mother had told her that what happened in privacy between her and Anna's father was beautiful because they loved each other.

At least Annette had her own self respect in the knowledge that her body belonged to the man she loved.

Anna could not even say that.

She must be a whore. That's what the English said of beautiful French women. Perhaps they were right. Perhaps there was a curse over French women that caused them to be slaves of the flesh.

Two things kept her from gathering up her things and fleeing: the knowledge that she was helping England, and the fact that the marquess would be the only person who knew of her shameful weakness.

\* \* \*

Removing himself from Anna's bed while she slept started a perplexing quandary in Haverstock. He would have enjoyed staying with her all night and taking her again when she awoke. He would like to awaken with her beside him, the morning light displaying her youthful voluptuousness.

He quietly dressed, collected a small valise containing gold coins, then braced the cold and took himself to his house on Half Moon Street. There, he packed for his journey. Not only did he not wish to wake his valet, but he did not want even Manors to know of his mission.

Once he had packed, he sat down to pen a letter to his mother informing her of his haste to marry before his business journey. He would tell no one the circumstances under which he and Anna married. He told his mother the clandestine marriage was necessitated by his mother's dislike of Anna's family. Now that the act was done, he wrote, his mother would have to accept his choice for a bride. "I beg you will welcome my wife and accord her the respect she deserves," he concluded, after telling her Anna would be mistress of Haverstock House within a fortnight.

Next, he wrote to Anna.

Lastly, he left a letter requesting his secretary inform the newspapers of the nuptials between Miss Anna de Mouchet and the Marquess of Haverstock.

With those duties done, he personally walked round to the stables to collect his horse for the ride to Morgie's town house. As Haverstock had instructed Anna's servants, they had roused Morgie and taken him home.

When Haverstock arrived, Morgie awaited him, fully dressed in riding clothes and packed for the journey. Hanging his head rather shamefully, Morgie asked, "Is France still our destination, or do you take me to Newgate?"

"We will discuss your indiscretions once we are on the boat for France," Haverstock said sternly as the two men mounted their horses and rode off into the early morning's darkness.

On the ship, though the two men shared a private cabin, little conversation occurred. Their dialogue consisted of Morgie, who unpleasantly expelled the contents of his stomach, insisting that he was dying and Haverstock assuring him his discomfort was the result of the ship's motion or an overabundance of liquor.

Once in Bordeaux, they took rooms at an inn near the waterfront. Over dinner, which Morgie barely touched, he ran a thin hand through his hair and said, "I say Haverstock, I'm bloody ashamed of losing the deuced money. How'd you get it back?"

"I won it back," Haverstock lied.

Morgie appraised him admiringly. "Thought you detested high-stakes gaming – because of your father."

Haverstock washed down his bread with the

wine this region was famous for. "What else had we to lose?"

"Right you are," Morgie said cheerfully. "By the way, did you not find Miss de Mouchet quite the loveliest creature you've ever beheld?"

Haverstock's heart quickened as he remembered Anna's lovely, pliant body beneath him. "Indeed I did. In fact, she is no longer Miss de Mouchet. The next time you see her, you may address her as Lady Haverstock."

Morgie spit out his wine. "The hell you say!"

Haverstock's black eyes shone mischievously. "How could I possibly leave for a minimum of two weeks and hope she remained unattached when I returned? There was only one thing to do. I rode to Lambeth Palace for a special license."

Morgie pursed his lips. "You're teasing me. I don't believe you for a minute. You've never done an impulsive thing in your life."

"Ah, but my dear friend, I never before met the ravishing Miss de Mouchet." Remembering Anna's extraordinary beauty, he almost believed his own words.

* * *

Exhausted from playing cards with Sir Henry throughout the previous night, Anna slept for ten hours. When she awoke, warmed by the sun that directed through half dozen windows, she felt something else, too. Between her thighs a deep soreness reminded her of what had occurred between her husband and her.

Her eyes snapped open and she turned to see if he were still beside her, knowing by the light outside that he would have left hours ago. She wondered if he had departed as soon as he had taken his pleasure or if he had slept all night within her arms.

She saw the indentation on her satin sheets where he had lain and experienced a feeling of loss. A chill settled deep in her bones. She pulled the covers around her snugly. How much more reassuring it would have been to awaken with him beside her, pressing soft kisses on her, letting her know their lovemaking had been acceptable, that she was a wife, not a whore.

Enveloped by her eternal loneliness, she now felt bereft and soiled by his seed which still moistened her sheets. The Haverstock seed, she thought, her heart pounding painfully.

# $\mathcal{C}$hapter 5

Later that afternoon, a page from Haverstock House brought Anna a letter from her husband. She carried it to her chamber, now their chamber, and quickly broke the seal with trembling hands and stood beside the bed to read it.

*My Dear Wife, By the time you read this I will be far away. I disliked taking my leave without saying good-bye to you, but you slept so soundly I knew you needed the sleep too badly to be awakened. My mother has now been informed of our marriage and has been instructed to make Haverstock House your home. I will call upon you when I return to London, and I look forward to continuing your instruction. Yours, Haverstock*

Anna held the letter to her breast, a warmth blanketing her. The letter was an unexpected pleasure, coming from a man who fully intended to honor his vows. This dark lord was indeed not his father's son. This man she had married – this man who had taken complete possession of her – intended to honor his vows.

If only he could be honorable toward his country, she thought bitterly.

She tied the letter in pink satin ribbon and placed it in a drawer of the table beside her bed.

In bed that night, she had difficulty falling asleep. She wondered if Haverstock had given the money to the French by now. She rued his treachery. Inexplicably, she wondered if he had given a thought to her.

\* \* \*

During the next two weeks Anna attempted to keep so busy that Haverstock would not intrude upon her every thought. At the beginning of each day, she dressed meticulously in the latest fashion, expecting a call from her mother-in-law, whom she knew was informed of the marriage. But that call never came.

Anna and Colette – with outriders in addition to their already formidable assortment of attendants – visited the East End and distributed clothing, coins and food to the unfortunate.

Anna kept busy at a number of other tasks. She started fancy work of her own complicated design. She portioned off each of her servants and oversaw the packing of her most essential possessions. She made arrangements for letting her house on Grosvenor Square.

When two weeks had passed, Anna found herself running to the window with each clop of horse hooves, checking to see if Haverstock had arrived. With every breath she took, she thought of him. And cursed herself for doing so.

\* \* \*

With an armed Morgie standing watch, Haverstock met with his French contact at a farm house on the outskirts of Bordeaux. The meeting went well. Monsieur Herbert presented Haverstock with several pages of dates and descriptions of shipments to troops in the Peninsula as well as their locations. In exchange for the information, Haverstock handed over the fifty-thousand pounds.

"My necessity for the money grows urgent," the fleshy Frenchman said. "Soon, I will be forced to leave France."

Haverstock cocked a brow. "How so?"

"Our government has been informed that a traitor is passing information to the British. As yet, no one knows my identity."

"I have told no one your name," Haverstock said.

"Are you aware that someone who works in your Foreign Office is a spy for the French?"

Haverstock experienced a sinking feeling. "Are you sure?"

The Frenchman nodded. "Just as he does not know my name, I do not know his. But I must warn you to be very cautious."

During the journey home, Haverstock was thankful he could keep busy reading, translating, and memorizing the documents. For the first time since he left London, he was too busy to think of his strange marriage and the unwanted attraction his devious wife solicited in him.

He was pleased to learn some of the documents even sketched out battle plans and enumerated French troops. All in all, England had struck a good bargain by paying Monsieur Hebert for the information.

Near the end of the journey, Haverstock translated a great deal of the information into code and burned the originals, keeping the coded papers on his person at all times.

As he and Morgie approached London, Haverstock faced a dilemma over whom to see first: Anna or his mother. He had written to Anna that he would see her immediately upon his arrival, but he also wanted to smooth things out with his mother before bringing Anna home.

In the end, his impatience to once again look upon Anna won out. Was she really as lovely as he remembered? He could still remember how it felt standing before the cleric holding her slim gloved hand within his own and placing his signet ring on her finger. Her recalled how small her voice had sounded when she recited her vows. And he would never forget the picture of her sitting in the bed, attempting to cover her exquisite body while declaring her innocence in a shaky voice. Most of all, he remembered the feel and smell of her naked body against his own. As he drew near Grosvenor Square, he felt like a schoolboy in the flush of his first flirtation.

# $\mathcal{C}$hapter 6

Morgie accompanied Haverstock to Anna's house. Haverstock brought his friend along to prevent himself from raising her skirts and taking her on the floor of her parlor. For when it came to Anna, he was consumed by lust.

When Perkins answered the door, Haverstock said, "Please announce me to my wife."

Perkins showed the two gentlemen into the parlor, and a few minutes later Anna glided into the room. Haverstock's mind had not embellished her extraordinary appearance. If anything, she was even more beautiful than he remembered. He had not seen her by the light of day before. She wore a soft white morning gown sprigged with violets, with purple velvet ribbands at the edge of the three-quarter sleeves and at the flounce at the hemline. Her skin above the low-cut bodice was as smooth and white as he remembered and her face as flawless. In the sunlight he could see deep brandy-colored highlights in her rich brown hair.

He took her hand and kissed it. "I trust you have been well these past sixteen days, Anna."

Her face colored ever so slightly when she assured him she had enjoyed good health.

Remembering his companion, Haverstock indicated Morgie and said, "You remember Mr. Morgan, my dear?"

Morgie swept into a deep bow. "Your servant, Lady Haverstock."

"Do sit down," Anna told them as she sat on a rose brocaded settee, "and tell me of your journey. Where did you go?" Haverstock took a seat on a French chair that looked much too small for his large body. "We had to check on various investments around the country."

"The investments you needed the money for, my lord?" she asked.

He pursed his lips and frowned. "Have I not instructed you, my dear, not to address me as *my lord*?"

"I am sorry, Charles," Anna said.

"Yes, my dear, we needed the money for the investments."

"Have you seen your mother?" she asked.

"No. I came here straight away. How soon can you be ready to move to Haverstock House?"

"I am ready now. I have made arrangements to let this house."

"Very good," Haverstock said. "By the way, has my mother called?"

"No, but I did not expect her. I cannot blame her for being disappointed in the match. She has no doubt decided I am completely unsuitable," Anna said in a confident voice. "Beside your mother, who else is in your family?"

"I have five sisters and a brother. I bought James colors, and he is now in the Peninsula." He shook his head. "Worry like the devil over him." Sighing, he added, "My sister Mary married last year and lives in Cornwall. The sister closest to me in age and in temperament is Lydia. She's thirty and has no prospects of marrying. Unfortunately for her, she resembles me very much. I fear she is much too tall and too broad to attract suitors – which is a loss for them for she is quite the most agreeable woman I have ever known. But, then, I might find her so because she thinks and acts more like a man."

"Bruising rider," Morgie added. "And a capital whist player."

"It's easy to see that Lydia is your favorite," Anna said.

Haverstock thought for a moment without responding. "I suppose you're right. Lydia, too, is probably the most loyal to me, because of the closeness of our ages, I expect."

"What about the other three sisters?"

"I'm sorry to say they are a pack of empty-headed females who will all marry quite well. They are tolerably good looking and think of nothing except the latest fashions and hair arrangements."

"And what are their names and ages?"

He thought for a moment. "I am not particularly good at remembering that sort of thing. I know Charlotte is the youngest. She's seventeen and will come out this next season." He skewered his face in thought. "Let me see, Cynthia came out last season and turned down several offers. I believe she's holding out for a peer. I think she's nineteen. Then there's Kate. She's a year older than Cynthia."

"The three youngest seem very much of my own age," Anna said.

"And I am sure they will adore you, for you possess that which they hold above all else – an enviable wardrobe."

"Then outfitting them in all new clothes will be very enjoyable for me."

His eyes narrowed. "I told you I don't want your money, Anna."

"In most matters, my lord, I will abide by your decisions, but when it comes to my money, I will spend it as I like, and providing your sisters with beautiful clothes will give me great pleasure."

He rose and paced the room. With his back to her, he said, "I go to make sure Haverstock House is ready for you, madam. If all goes well, I will collect you later this afternoon."

She offered her hand first to Morgie, then to her husband, who kissed it softly before he took his leave.

\* \* \*

Lydia was the first to meet him when he entered Haverstock House. She wordlessly pulled him into the morning room and spoke quietly. "I don't need to tell you how distressed Mama has been over the news of your marriage. She's taken to her bed. What's come over you? You've never done a rash thing in your life."

He placed his hands on her broad shoulders. "When you meet her, you'll understand."

"Knowing you as I do, I cannot believe you would enter into a gross misalliance. I will endeavor to make your wife welcome in every way."

He kissed his sister on her cheek. "You are the best of sisters." Then he swept from the room, mounted the stairs and found his mother in her bed in the marchioness's chamber.

His face flushed with anger, he said, "This room was supposed to have been made ready for my wife, Mother."

Tears seeped from her eyes. "I have been much too upset over your marriage to do anything."

"You have had sixteen days to get over the shock. You are to remove yourself at once from this bed. My wife moves in this afternoon."

"Charles, you are heartless."

"I am not throwing you out on the streets. You will merely move down the hall. I am thirty-two, Mother. Did you think I would never take a wife?"

She sniffed. "It is just that I thought bans would be posted and I would have more time to prepare for the changes." Bursting into fresh tears, she said, "And I never in my wildest nightmares thought you would marry so far beneath you."

"My wife is the daughter of a duke, and her mother was a member of the French aristocracy. I hardly think that is beneath me."

"Her mother was a  – -"

"You will not speak ill of my wife or her mother," he interrupted angrily. "Ever! Is that understood?"

"Can I not even hope that you will change your mind about the marriage?"

"No, you cannot."

"Then the marriage has been consummated?"

His jaw stern, his lips a straight line, he replied, "Indeed it has."

She observed her first born. "You are exactly like Steffington. He was totally obsessed with the de Mouchet woman. Just because she possessed an extraordinary beauty. Is the daughter also beautiful?"

"You will have to judge for yourself. I am of the opinion that her beauty is unrivaled."

She shook her head. "You're breaking my heart just as Steffington broke my poor sister's heart."

"Aunt Margaret is dead," he said sternly.

"Steffington is dead. Annette de Mouchet is dead. You need to put the past behind you, Mother. Don't blame Anna for the circumstances of her birth. And let us hope she does not blame us for the cruelty she and her mother received from Father."

                    * * *

Late that afternoon, the Haverstock women gathered in the saloon to meet the new marchioness. Anna had selected an impeccably cut dress of deep gray wool with matching pelisse. The pelisse was trimmed in claret velvet and a claret-dyed ostrich plume jutted from the fashionable gray hat which sat askance on her head. She carried a huge fur muff dyed in the deep claret and wore gray leather boots. She felt rather like a fine horse being trotted before bidders at Tattersall's as Haverstock escorted her into the salon where the awaiting females unabashedly took in her every feature and cast envious glances at her exquisite attire.

One by one, Haverstock introduced her first to his mother, who offered a cool greeting, then to each sister before taking a seat beside his wife on the sofa.

Haverstock strongly resembled his mother, Anna thought. The dowager was a large woman, more in height than in weight, though she carried a good bit of matronly padding. And, like her son, her eyes were black and her hair still a dark brown.

Lydia shared the coloring and stature of her brother and mother, and Anna thought she looked even older than her thirty years.

The three younger sisters bore little resemblance to the others, though they looked remarkably like each other. They were small, though not as small as Anna, and were fair and blonde.

"I understand you have a rather large staff," the dowager said to Anna.

"I bring only my abigail with me," Anna answered. "She has been with me my entire life and with my mother before that."

Anna noted Haverstock's mother stiffened at the mention of her mother.

"I suppose I should have checked with you these past two weeks to determine how many you would bring so we could ready quarters for them, but I have been indisposed," the dowager said.

Lydia got up and rang for a servant. When the butler entered the room, she told him to instruct servants to ready a room for Anna's maid.

"Thank you, Lydia," Anna said gratefully.

Awkward silence followed before Cynthia asked Anna, "May I inquire as to who is your modiste, Anna? Those are quite the most exquisite garments I have ever seen."

Anna smiled. "If it is agreeable to you, I will take you girls there tomorrow and have Madam Devreaux design gowns for each of you."

"My wife is possessed of a great fortune which – above my objections – she is determined to shower upon my family."

"I do not find that objectionable at all," Kate said, grinning.

Her mother cast a disapproving glance at Kate. "I think not tomorrow, girls. Remember, there's a rout at the Abernathy's tonight and you will not get to bed until very late."

"Then the day after," Anna interjected authoritatively. She had decided to exert her authority from the start. The dowager would not be given the opportunity to undermine her.

Her face grim, Haverstock's mother turned her attention to her son. "You and your wife will accompany us tonight?"

Anna noted her mother-in-law had refrained from referring to her by name.

"I think not, Mother," he said. "I wish to enjoy a quiet evening at home with my wife. You forget, we have been apart for over two weeks."

# $\mathcal{C}$hapter 7

The two of them sat before the fire in Anna's chamber and partook of a light dinner in near total silence. After the servants took away the dishes, Haverstock poured two glasses of brandy he had brought back from France, giving the snifter to Anna, then sitting beside her on a settee in front of the fire.

She took a sip and grimaced. "I have never had brandy before, my – -, Charles."

His eyes flashed mischievously. "What! A French woman who does not appreciate excellent brandy?"

"I am not a French woman," she said defiantly. "My mother held a great bitterness for her country, and her greatest desire was that I be thoroughly English. I was baptized in the Church in England, my mother spoke only English to me – though Colette spoke only French – and my sympathies in this awful war are entirely with the English, I assure you." Her chest tightened as she ruefully remembered her husband did not share those sympathies.

"So I have married a thoroughly English woman," Haverstock said gently. He took her hand in his.

His touch had a profound effect on her. "There was just one area where my mother did not succeed in Anglicizing me," she said, trying to retain her outward composure while inside she fairly sizzled from the feel of his huge hand clasped about hers. "It was her fondest wish that I be educated at Miss Sloan's School for Young Ladies. I had no desire to leave my home, but Mama was insistent." She stopped and gazed into her husband's obsidian eyes. "It was your father who kept me from the school."

"Surely that's not why you hold him accountable for your mother's death?"

"It broke her heart," Anna said softly. "After he left that day, she cried inconsolably. It was a bitter cold January day and she left the house without even a shawl. She walked for hours in the square. I didn't know she had gone out. She came home when night fell, blue with cold." Anna's voice lowered. "She took lung fever and was dead a month later. At her death bed, she made me promise I would be a lady."

Haverstock released her hand. "So that – more than revenge against my family – was your reason for coaxing me into marriage."

"You are very kind to use the word *coaxing* when you know very well I forced you," Anna said lightly, her lips curving into a smile.

"'Tis my fate to be shackled to an authoritative female," he said teasingly. "I shall not be master in my own home."

Was it the brandy or her husband's presence that spread a liquid ease to the core of her body? She almost laughed over her mind-numbing desire for this man she had been prepared to stoically tolerate. She had come to crave the very sound of his voice, his powerful body, his ruggedly handsome face. But most of all, she ached to be held by him. With full cognizance, she knew this longing for what it was: an extremely strong physical attraction she could never confuse with love. For she could never give her heart to one who turned against his own country, his own brother.

Her voice husky with a passion she tried to repress, Anna looked up into his eyes. "You will be my master, my teacher, Charles."

Their eyes met and held, that feeling of oneness she experienced on their wedding night enveloping Anna again. She wanted to feel his lips on hers, to feel herself cradled within the comfort of his arms.

He gently touched her face with a finger, and she found herself lifting his hand to her lips. That instinctive gesture removed all barriers between them. His burly arms came around her as she moved into his chest, resting her head against him, listening to the thumping of his heart.

His head lowered, and she lifted her face until she felt the soft warmth of his mouth on hers and slipped her arms around him, basking in the solid feel of him.

After the kiss, he spoke softly. "I have something for you, *my lady*." He reached into his pocket and presented her with a huge emerald ring surrounded by diamonds.

She drew back and looked at it but did not take it from him. "Will you put it on?" she asked.

He slipped it on the third finger of her left hand. "I shall have it cut down for you, my dear."

"I hate to remove it, Charles. It is very beautiful. I feel so. . .so undeserving."

A frown furrowed his face. "It belongs to you, for you have become my wife in every way, or have you forgotten?"

She stared into his black eyes, remembering how thoroughly he had taken possession of her. "I am yours," she said breathlessly.

Over her clothing, his palm stroked her breasts, massaging them with surprising tenderness. The effect on Anna was devastating. Her body came alive at his touch. It was for this moment she had lived the past sixteen days.

With practiced ease, he unfastened her buttons and lowered the top of her gown, then her chemise and stays. Her gaze dropped, and she saw the contours of her own sizable breasts in the glow of the firelight. Though no other man had seen them before, she was not embarrassed.

He reverently lifted a breast in both hands. "Oh, my Anna, you have the body of a goddess." His lips covered her breast, his tongue circling the tip, then taking it deep into his mouth and suckling.

Warmth flowed deep within her. *My Anna.* How magical those words sounded, how blissful he made her feel with every magical stroke.

When he gazed up at her, his face wet and heated, something seared inside of her like flame to parchment.

He stood, his majestic body blocking the firelight. Her breath hitched as he threw off his coat, planting his booted feet and standing tall, the fire to his back. *My dark titan.* Her eyes flitted from his broad shoulders beneath the soft linen shirt, down his v-shaped torso to his flat waist, then rested on his straining groin. She wanted to see his flesh golden in the firelight. She wanted to feel its moistness against her own bare body.

His black eyes hungry, he held out his hands to her, drawing her to a standing position as her gown and chemise pooled on the carpet. She moved to untie his cravat, her eyes never leaving his, then she slipped her fingers beneath the soft linen shirt, stroking his moist flesh. She deftly unfastened his buttons, and he assisted her in removing his shirt.

His eyes devoured every inch of her bare flesh, his uneven breath a catalyst to her own surge of. . .desire. She had finally been able to put a name to this craving she held for this man.

Effortlessly, he swooped her into his arms as if she were paper and carried her to the bed where he gently set her on its silk coverlet and lay down beside her, drawing her into himself. His lips came down on hers in a wet, open-mouthed kiss while his smooth, strong hands moved over her back, down her hips, then her legs. A wet heat gushed between her legs. How could one man have such a nearly debilitating effect on her? She was powerless not to arch into him.

Those magical hands of his moved between her thighs and inched upward until her thighs parted as his long finger slipped into her wetness. With breath labored as if she'd been running, she circled his tongue with her own, windmills of pleasure spiraling through her thoughts, thoughts that were nothing more than pulsing fragments: *Desire. Need. Love.*

He withdrew his finger, trailing its wet path over her stomach, the erotic gesture robbing her of breath.

When he raised his hips to remove his breeches, she almost could not bear the brief separation, almost could not bear the anticipation of his next move.

The glorious spectacle of his skin glowing

golden in the soft firelight was nearly as compelling as drawing a breath. She softly stroked the firm muscles of his chest and its mat of soft black hair, moving toward the swell of his manhood. Her hand curled around him as a deep groan escaped his throat. That she could solicit such a primeval noise from her giant exhilarated her.

His hands began to work their magic on her again, first one finger, then another sliding into her warmth as she widened herself even more. All thoughts now obliterated from her mind save for this meeting, this melding with her dark giant.

She initiated a hungry kiss, then a series of feverish, wet kisses as she arched her body into his, her breath even more labored. She felt his heat, his warm breath on her, his manhood brushing against her. And she parted her legs and guided him into herself. He plunged deeply as her whole being rocked with the numbing pleasure he gave her. His motions quickened, her body trembled convulsively. He kept saying her name, and she reveled in it.

Their chests heaving together as if one heartbeat united them, Anna's hands dug into her husband's back. Where dream left off and reality began Anna couldn't say. All she knew was this was what she lived for, these dreamy moments when nothing else intruded on their world of two. She savored the feel of him within her and lovingly stroked his firm body.

He rolled back to his side. She moved, too, to keep from disengaging him. His powerful hand lightly touched her temple and brushed away the damp hair, softly kissing her brow. He began to trace her features with a long finger, placing soft kisses on her eyelids, her nose, then came to brush gently on her mouth. She smelled his heat and the brandy and the scent of their sex and was oddly sated by it.

She kept her arms around his rock hard back. Her face rested on his chest, his harsh, heavy breathing reassuring. She lay in the peace of him, a deep contentment washing over her.

\* \* \*

His mind in a drug-like stupor from the sensations she had aroused and the overpowering emotions she touched, he held her close, delighting in her rose water scent and the feel of her smooth skin against his own. When the sensual fog began to clear from his brain, he remembered everything clearly. The way he languidly kissed her mouth and her extraordinary body. The way he had been more intent on giving her pleasure than in seeking his own. The way he called out her name repeatedly. In a lifetime of vagrant passion, he had never done these things with a woman before.

He held her close, stroking her satiny flesh with a gentleness that surprised himself. Soon, her rhythmic breathing told him she was asleep. While his own body craved sleep, his mind fought it, his thoughts racing with exhilaration brought on by the fragile beauty of the woman he held in his arms. The unnamed yearnings of the past sixteen days, he knew now, had been his deep hunger for Anna. His own Anna.

His arms cradled her. He reveled in the bliss of his possession. He remembered his vow to cherish her, and he knew that whatever lay ahead, he would protect her until his dying breath.

When he awoke in the morning, Anna's huge brown eyes peered into his own and a sweet smile lit her lovely face. She had pulled up the sheet to cover her nakedness.

He trailed a single finger along her cheek and the slope of her chest, then down further, to gently follow the contour of her breast. "Your aptitude for learning exceeds my expectations."

He stifled her smile with a heavy kiss. "Now, to continue your instruction."

# $\mathcal{C}$hapter 8

It was well past dark when Haverstock came home the next day. Anna had been watching from her chamber window and scurried down the broad staircase to greet him.

She watched warily as he gave his greatcoat to the butler. His step slow, his hair tousled, Haverstock looked tired enough to have performed yeoman's work at great length. Her heart caught at his haggard appearance. He looked to be twice her age. Then, she realized his secretive post at the Foreign Office was what drew all his strength, and a bitter anger welled within her.

At the foot of the stairs, she remembered Sir Henry's instructions to play the adoring wife. She held out her hands and forced a smile. "My lord, you look so very tired."

A flicker of pleasure passed over his face as he gazed at her. "That I am, my dear."

"Please bring a fresh pot of tea to my chamber," Anna instructed Davis, linking her arm through her husband's and mounting the stairs. "You must come warm yourself before my fire, Charles. A cup of tea is just what you need."

Haverstock collapsed on the settee in front of her fireplace. She bent over him, tenderly loosening his cravat. "There, now, get comfortable and relax." Their eyes met, merging them, driving the anger from her. She stroked the shadows of his beard. "You have worked far too hard today." She told herself she was merely playing the role Sir Henry demanded of her, winning her husband's confidence through her feigned devotion. The problem was, she feigned little where Haverstock was concerned. When she was with him, he earned an unpretentious affection.

Only when they were apart did she recall his traitorous deeds. Because then she was not drawn to the depth of his black eyes and not seduced by the nearness to his tall, golden-skinned body.

He took her hand and brought it to his lips. "Sit by me, Anna."

She obliged.

"It is so very good to be home. I will be fine now," he said. "It occurred to me today that I should like to possess a miniature of you so that I might look at it when I am away."

"I am greatly flattered," Anna said, hoping her voice did not reveal the leaping excitement in her pulse. She squeezed his hand and shot him a concerned glance. "Now tell me what is it you work yourself so hard for?"

He ran his large hands through his hair and sighed. "When my father died, I learned that he had foolishly lost most of the family's fortune. Since that day, I have contrived to restore the money as well as the Haverstock good name – neither of which have I been particularly successful."

"Oh, Charles, I would so very much rather you take my money and not work so hard. Your companionship, I find, far preferable to this house full of females." She had felt so alienated and lonely at Haverstock House without Charles. Though one day was no gauge of how well she would get along with his family, this first day brought bitter disappointment. Her mother-in-law had not come out of her chamber all day. Anna longed to get away from this house, to go to Haymore. "Could you and I not go to Haymore?" she suggested.

"Nothing would give me greater pleasure, my dear, but I cannot consider it at this time for I have far too much work."

The butler entered the room with a tea tray and set it on a table in front of the settee.

"Thank you, Davis," Anna said as he bowed and departed.

Haverstock watched Anna as she poured tea into a gilded cup. "It distresses me that you are so unhappy here, Anna. Has my family not made you welcome?"

"It is not that," she said, handing him is tea. "It is just that they kept to their rooms most of the day, except for Lydia, who has been quite wonderful. She gave me a tour of the house and explained the various family portraits and even showed me the butler's pantry."

"How do you like Lydia?"

"She is the most wonderful of sisters. I count myself very fortunate." Anna poured herself a cup of steaming tea from the silver pot. "She tells me she does not like town life. Perhaps that is what has me longing to go to the country. She described the green hills and country lanes. She's quite enamored of horses, isn't she?"

He laughed. "Yes, it's an enthusiasm not shared by my other sisters. Lydia very much enjoys the outdoors. When we were reduced to just one gardener at Haymore, Lydia actually took to working side by side with Benton trying to restore the park there to what it had once been – another futile effort, I'm afraid."

"I should love to see Haymore."

He took her hand in his and warmly pressed it. "And so you shall. I promise as soon as the war – I mean, as soon as I'm finished with my work, I shall take you there. It can be a honeymoon."

"You are so very good to honor your marriage vows when marrying me must have been extremely distasteful to you."

"Oh, yes," he said mischievously, "it is such a burden to be shackled to such an ugly woman." He cupped her breast. "I have to force myself to make love to the old dragon." His other hand began to unfasten the buttons on the back of her dress. "Such dreadful unpleasantness."

She ran a hand along the rigid planes of his face."Don't force yourself, my lord."

"In truth, I'm powerless to deny myself when I'm with you, Anna," he said in a low, husky voice.

* * *

Sated by his wife's compliant body and feeling her smooth warmth against him, Haverstock held her close long after they made love. Her touch had the power to free him from the discomfort of the day's long hours of writing down all the maneuvers Monsieur Herbert had painstakingly written in French.

Haverstock wanted nothing more than to trust Anna and felt guilty that he had not been honest with her about his duties. A marriage should be built upon truth and trust, and he fully intended this to be a real marriage.

But he did not really know Anna. He had been with her but three days. Three days that had reoriented his world. Nothing would ever be the same again. No woman had ever consumed him as engagingly as Anna. He could not be near her without experiencing an overwhelming rush of possessive tenderness, and more than that, an urge to make love to her until there was no breath left in his body.

Like the purity and passion Anna brought to their marriage bed, this wife of his was a paradox. It seemed inconceivable that the woman who likely cheated and schemed to gain his title could be the same gentle lover who offered herself so completely.

With thoughts of Anna circulating in his mind, he gave way to his exhaustion and fell to sleep.

He was awakened an hour later by Evans rapping at the door. Haverstock started up, then saw a fully-dressed Anna standing near the door.

"What is it?" she asked, her amused glance shooting from the closed door back to her naked husband.

"Her Ladyship asks if you plan to join the family for dinner."

"Tell her we will be down presently," Anna replied with authority.

Lighting a taper, she strode to the bed and leaned down to kiss her husband. "Shall I perform your valet's duties, my lord?" she asked with mirth.

"I beg that you don't." He climbed from the bed. "Your touch has a very devastating effect on me, I'm afraid. I would never make it to dinner were you to offer me assistance, and I fear my mother's wrath excessively."

Anna set down the taper and bent to pick up her husband's clothes that had been rapidly discarded in his haste to bed her. "Do you think your mother knows what we've done here?"

He took the breeches she handed him, stepped into them and cast her a bemused smile. "Most certainly."

Anna blushed.

"It's nothing to be ashamed of, my dear," he said, lightly touching her chin. "All married people do it. Do not forget my mother gave birth to seven children, so she most certainly has done it any number of times."

* * *

The dowager and her daughters were already seated at the long dining table when Haverstock and Anna came down. He glanced at his mother, sitting at the foot of the table. "I see you still sit at the marchioness's place, Mother. How very kind of you to encourage Anna to sit by me." He slid out a chair for Anna beside his own at the head of the table.

She took a seat, casting a quick glance at her mother-in-law, who glared at the couple. Once again, Anna felt like a horse being trotted out at auction as her sisters stared at her.

"That is a most becoming dress, Anna," Charlotte said.

"Thank you," Anna said as a footman uncovered salvers and heaped buttered crab on her plate. "I am blessed to be the owner of a fine wardrobe. The only thing I lack is lovely ball gowns. For reasons which I am sure you are aware, I have not been in society."

Charlotte lowered her eyes.

"We shall remedy that soon, my love," Haverstock said. "It will be my good fortune to escort the loveliest woman in London to all the balls this season."

"If she hasn't been in society, how did you meet her?" the dowager asked her son.

Anna's insides crumbled. She wondered how Charles would answer.

"Actually, Morgie knew her first," Haverstock replied truthfully, then took a bite of French beans.

Anna's pulse returned to normal, but she still felt slighted that her mother-in-law chose to address Haverstock instead of her.

Turning to his wife, Haverstock said, "With the Season just a few weeks away, I suggest you commission gowns, Lady Haverstock."

"Yes, my lord. I should like to pay Madam Devreaux a call tomorrow." She turned to the sisters. "Would you like to accompany me? No one can turn out the lot of us better than Madam Devreaux."

"Mama once had a gown fashioned by the modiste," Kate said. "It was quite the prettiest gown she ever owned. That was before Molly had to start making our clothes."

"Then you all must come with me tomorrow and select wardrobes for the season," Anna said, smiling. "We'll send the bills to Charles. Whether he wants to admit it or not, he is quite fat in the purse now that he has married me."

"Now that I have you as a sister," Lydia said to Anna, "I will not need to provide propriety for the girls. I would far prefer not to attend all the balls, and I care nothing for clothes."

Anna threw a dubious glance at Haverstock.

"I understand perfectly, Lydia. My marchioness can take your place, and you can be spared the tediousness of attending the functions I know you find so very unpleasant." Turning to his wife, he added, "Lydia would far prefer to sit home reading."

"Then I am happy to be of service," Anna said. "But should you need a new dress, please go to Madam Devreaux and send your dear brother the bill."

All of them, except for the dowager, laughed.

After dinner, they retired to the parlor where Haverstock and his mother played Anna and Lydia at whist while the other girls perused fashion magazines and discussed the various gowns they would request on the morrow.

The whist game was evenly matched, with both sets of partners displaying uncommon skill. The lead zig zagged until Anna and Lydia prevailed as the winners.

"I may have to take my wife as my partner next time, Mother," Haverstock said. "She possesses remarkable skill at cards."

"Of course she does," the dowager said, a sly smile on her face. "Look who her mother was."

* * *

As the family members prepared to go to their bedchambers, the dowager said, "A word with you, Charles."

Anna met his gaze, then began to mount the stairs.

"Of course, Mother."

Once Anna was upstairs, the dowager said, "I find your conduct most inappropriate. You must be sensible to the fact that you have four maiden sisters in this house who do not need to be exposed to your lust."

"I presume you are referring to the fact I have spent much of my time in my wife's chamber."

"Yes," she said, her eyes cold.

"I must ask that you not use the word *lust* when you talk about anything that occurs between my wife and me. It is expected that a newly wed man enjoys the company of his wife. Granted, a husband and wife wanting to be with each other is a novel experience for our family," he said curtly.

She gasped as he turned his back to her and began to climb the wide staircase.

# $\mathcal{C}$hapter 9

Anna was hard pressed to determine if the three sisters or Madam Devreaux were the more excited over the flurry of measuring and ordering of dozens of dresses and gowns. Kate, Charlotte and Cynthia had timidly entered the shop bearing dog-eared copies of fashion magazines and brimming with ideas – all of which the French modiste was only too happy to accommodate. Madam Devreaux grew even more accommodating when she learned her long-standing patron, the exquisite Miss de Mouchet, was now the Marchioness of Haverstock. Anna could tell from the gleam in the French woman's eye, she was already planning on the commissions that would come her way when the Haverstock women were seen in society wearing her gowns.

Anna's ideas for her own ball gowns met with appreciative compliments from Madam Devreaux.

When they finished at the modiste's, the four young ladies happily stepped into the Haverstock barouche, Anna casting a dubious gaze at the grey skies as she allowed the coachman to assist her into the carriage. She hoped the rain that saturated the ground that morning would not return. Haverstock had promised to take her to the park this afternoon, and she wanted nothing to interfere with the outing.

Anna directed the coachman to the milliner's on Conduit Street.

"This has been so very much fun," Kate said.

"Especially for me," Anna responded. "I cannot tell you how delightful it is to finally have sisters. I do not at all recommend the life of an only child."

"I am sure you'll never be lonely again," Charlotte said. "It seems Charles can hardly bear being without you."

"Such a difference has come over him since his marriage," Kate added. "He is most certainly not the brother we have always known."

"Oh, not at all," Charlotte agreed. "What ever happened to that stern, tight-fisted brother of ours I am sure I cannot say."

"I beg you not speak ill of your brother," Anna said. "If he seemed parsimonious, it was because he worried excessively about providing well for all of you."

"It is so sweet to see how devoted you two are to each other," Charlotte said. "I hope the Season brings me a man as besotted over me as Charles is over you."

"He is indeed that," Cynthia concurred.

Anna wanted to protest. Charles certainly was not besotted over her. If he were, he surely would be with her every day instead of trudging off to his office. She had to admit she satisfied his. . .what had he called it? His sexual needs. But nothing more.

When the coach stopped in front of the milliner's, Anna urged, "Do hurry, girls, for I must be back in time to ride in the park with Charles." She fully intended to dress to perfection, hoping she could make him proud, fondly recalling his words the night before. "This will be my first opportunity to display my lovely wife," he had said.

"Do you mean to say Charles is actually going to stop working to take you to the park?" Kate uttered in shocked tones.

"He must be besotted," Cynthia added as she stepped from the coach.

The three girls purchased nearly every bonnet in the shop, so many that the coachman was obliged to make another trip after depositing the ladies at Haverstock House.

*  *  *

Colette's deft hands fashioned ringlets about Anna's face as Anna watched the artistry in her looking glass. From time to time, Colette would be seized by a coughing spell and have to stop.

"That's a terrible cough, Colette," Anna said, concern in her voice. "You've never been susceptible to taking a chill."

"Never before have I slept in so cold a room," Colette said, sniffing.

Anna spun toward her abigail. "Surely you don't mean there is no fire in your room."

Colette nodded.

"Come, show me your room," Anna instructed, her eyes flashing with anger as she leaped to her feet and headed toward the door.

Colette led Anna to a tiny, dark chamber on the fourth floor. Anna looked over the musty smelling quarters with dismay. The floors were of cold stone, with no rugs. A tiny straw bed took up most of the small room, which had just one casement, where cold air whistled through a jagged crack. There was no fireplace.

Her lips compressed in anger, Anna said, "This will never do."

Amidst a flurry of French protests from Colette, Anna stormed toward the dowager's royal blue chamber, where she found Lydia joining her mother, doing needlework before a crackling fire. The dowager directed a frosty gaze at Anna as her daughter-in-law entered the room unannounced.

"My lady," Anna said breathlessly, "I must speak to you about an important matter."

The dowager did not ask Anna to sit. She merely cast cold blue eyes at her, then continued with her sewing. "And what is that, pray tell?" She ran her needle into the linen as she spoke.

"Of the sadly inadequate room that has been allocated to Colette."

"To whom?" the dowager asked calmly.

Anna, knowing very well the dowager knew to whom she referred, bit back a derogatory retort. Honey, not vinegar, Anna cautioned herself. She would use honey to get what she wanted. "My dear maid, my lady. I fear I have spoiled her excessively these many years. She is unused to staying in a chamber where there is no fire. Her constitution is rather delicate. If you cannot find a servant's room with a fireplace, then I may have to insist on moving her into the guest room down the hall."

An amused smile crossed Lydia's face at this announcement, Anna noted, but Lydia stifled it before her mother noticed.

The dowager raised her brows at Anna's suggestion. "I am unused to French customs. Your servants mingle with their betters?"

Anna fought back her seething anger. "I am *not* French, Mother. I merely want to provide my maid what she is used to."

Avoiding Anna's eyes, the dowager said, "I am ignorant of the fourth floor, but there must be some rooms with fireplaces. What do you know, Lydia?"

Lydia got to her feet. "There are several. I will see to it that Colette is moved into better quarters."

"And, please," Anna said to Lydia, "see to it there is a rug on her floor."

* * *

Dressed in a deep, rose velvet pelisse trimmed in soft white fur at the collar and cuffs and down the front, Anna glided down the staircase, her hand tucked into a fur muff while her bonnet dangled from the other hand. Haverstock and Morgie watched her from the foot of the stairs, admiration in their gazes.

"How lovely you look, my dear," Haverstock said, bowing over her hand and pressing it to his lips. "Do me the goodness to entertain Morgie while I change into more suitable attire."

He mounted the stairs as she turned her attention to Morgie, whose well cut coat of dark blue superfine represented the understated elegance for which Morgie was noted. "Won't you come with me to the morning room, Mr. Morgan?"

As soon as they sat down, Morgie said, "Good effect you have on Haverstock. Don't know when I've seen him leave that office while it was still light outside. Man works too deuced hard."

"I agree with you most emphatically. I'm attempting to persuade him not to work so hard, but I fear it is a losing battle, Mr. Morgan."

He nodded. "Please call me Morgie. Everyone does."

"Very well, Morgie."

"I must apologize for intruding on your ride. Newlyweds and all that. But Haverstock insisted."

"Of course he did, and glad I am of it," Anna said. "Charles has told me how you are his dearest friend, and I am grateful that he means to advance my friendship with you."

He cast his eyes downward, turning his hat in his hands. "I must also apologize for my state of inebriation that day on Grosvenor Square."

Stung by her guilt over that day's events, Anna spoke gently. "You have nothing to apologize for. In fact, I should apologize to you for forcing so much liquor on you. I shall have to plead ignorance of the world. You see, I am not only an orphan but also an only child and have not been at all in society. I had no idea how a gentlewoman was to act. Then, too, I was rattled over having so eligible a gentleman in my parlor."

Morgie colored at this.

"I hope we will become friends," Anna said as her husband opened the door.

Haverstock said, "That, too, is my most sincere hope." Anna felt a pang in her chest as she gazed at his virile good looks.

"Sorry to learn she's an only child," Morgie said, rising. "Was hoping she had a sister."

Linking her arm to Charles's first and then to Morgie's, Anna said, "I don't, but Charles has four. I am sure he would be most happy to make you a brother."

"Never thought of that," Morgie said as they reached the front door that was held open by a footman. "Course those three little ones are rather young for me, and Lydia is. . ." he cast a quick look at Haverstock.

"And Lydia has no desire to marry," Haverstock finished.

In the phaeton, Haverstock took the ribbons. "How did your morning go, my dear?" he asked.

"Oh, very well. The girls will unquestionably be the best dressed on the Marriage Mart this year. I feel so very badly, though, that Lydia got nothing. You know Charles, I've been thinking. . ."

"Better watch out, old chap," Morgie interjected.

Anna smiled at Morgie and continued. "Being city-bred, I know nothing about horses, but couldn't you select a mount for Lydia? The two of you could take morning rides in the park. I think she would love that."

She watched as a smile brightened Haverstock's face. "I believe she would. I'll go to Tatt's tomorrow."

"I say, wouldn't mind tagging along." Morgie turned to Anna. "Haverstock's noted for his knowledge of horseflesh."

"No doubt Lydia was heavily influenced by her older brother," Anna said.

The entrance to Hyde Park was a great bottleneck where conveyances of all kinds politely took turns at entering. Haverstock and Morgie tipped their hats to any number of minor acquaintances.

From beneath hooded eyes, Haverstock cast a quick glance at Anna. The white, fur-lined brim of her rose silk bonnet provided a perfect frame for her lovely face and its fringe of dark ringlets. Her rose scent seemed far sweeter than all the flowers lining the beds of Hyde Park. He was very glad indeed to be here with her today. Though wished it were sunny, he was grateful for the absence of rain.

With pride, he introduced his bride to several acquaintances along the way but avoided long conversations that might snare the procession of equipages.

"I say Haverstock," a voice called.

Haverstock looked ahead a short distance and saw his old friend John Thornton, whose gig was mired in a muddy track just ahead.

"Could you and Morgie give a hand?" Thornton asked. "Can't seem to budge this old hack."

Haverstock reined in. "Only too happy to." He gave the reins to Anna and leaped, along with Morgie, from the gig.

Paying no heed to the mud, the marquess and his friend got behind Thornton's gig and put their shoulders to it until it advanced, the men shouting their approval as it did so.

The sudden movement of Thornton's gelding caused one of Anna's horse to bolt. As it leaped forward, the ribbons were pulled from her hands. She screamed.

Haverstock looked up to see the phaeton careening off at great speed. *God in heaven, what was I thinking?* Hadn't she just told him she didn't know anything about horses?

He cursed and ran after the gig, able to think of nothing, save Anna's body crushed from a horrible spill.

He sprinted after the runaway carriage, but the gray only gained ground on him. In bitter futility, he stopped and tried to catch his breath, his eyes never leaving the phaeton and the terrified woman in rose velvet.

As the gray came to a wood, it turned as if it were rounding a track and headed back to where

Haverstock stood. He stood his ground in the horse's path and heard Anna scream at him to get out of the way. As the gray's pounding hooves came upon him, Haverstock stepped aside and leaped at its neck, grabbing both neck and mane and trying to pull himself on the beast's back. He was dragged several feet before he could throw a leg over the horse's back and mount it. All the while he heard Anna's horrifying wail.

Within seconds, he brought the phaeton to a stop. He slid off the horse and in two long strides was in front of Anna, reaching for her with his huge outstretched arms. She threw herself into his protective embrace. He held her trembling body tightly to him, then set her down and spoke in a voice more calm than he felt. "Are you unhurt?"

Her face ashen and voice quivering, she replied, "My lord! You could have been trampled!"

He smiled. "Madam, it appears I need to teach you a thing or two about handling horses."

Morgie ran up. "God's teeth! I was bloody worried about both of you! You could have been killed, Charles. Never should have given her the ribbons, old boy. Fool woman – -" He shot an embarrassed glance at Anna. "Beg your pardon, my lady."

Anna smiled weakly. "It's quite all right, Morgie. I am quite the fool when it comes to horses."

The news of Haverstock's heroics spread rapidly, and he proceeded to be complimented several dozen times, all of which he found so excessively tedious he cut the ride short and left the park.

# $\mathcal{C}$hapter 10

The day after Anna was introduced to London society as the bride of the Marquis of Haverstock via their well publicized romp in Hyde Park, a dozen ball invitations arrived by morning post. Anna and her sisters perused them at the breakfast table where, for the first time since Anna had moved in, the dowager joined them.

It was also the first time the dowager spoke directly to Anna. "The best thing about your and Charles's marriage is that it ensures the two of you escort the girls to the season's balls, releasing me from that chore. Having already presented four daughters, I am much too old to keep such late hours. The older one gets, the more the comfort of one's bed beckons." The dowager added another spoon of sugar to her tea. "And I know Charles is chomping at the bit to display your loveliness to all of London. He obviously wasted no time in commissioning your miniature."

That was as close to a compliment as Anna suspected she would ever get from her mother-in-law.

"It turned out quite nicely," Lydia said. "Though one must admit the artist had a lovely subject."

Feeling uncomfortable, Anna changed the

subject. "Mother, you must instruct me on which invitations we are to accept."

The expression on the dowager's face softened as she reached for the invitations, eyed them hurriedly, then discarded five that would have to be turned down. The others she handed to Anna with instructions that Lord Haverstock would attend these.

Though her mother-in-law assured Anna that Haverstock's secretary could handle the correspondence, Anna personally wrote notes of regret after breakfast to the rejected five, explaining there were previous engagements for those nights.

* * *

Colette's happy anticipation of the Wentworth Ball reminded Anna of a child excitedly awaiting Christmas. The old abigail smiled and hummed as she swept back Anna's dark hair, allowing a halo of ringlets to fall around Anna's face. "If only I could see how you outshine all the others, *cheri*," Colette said.

"You are most decidedly prejudiced." Anna peered into the looking glass, quite satisfied over Colette's artistry.

When Colette finished fashioning Anna's hair, she assisted her in dressing.

"Pray, how do you like your new quarters?" Anna asked.

"*Tres bien*," Colette said as she removed the dress from its hanger. "It is not dreary like the other because on a corner it is, and sunlight comes through windows on two sides."

"I am very happy to hear that," Anna said.

"And lovely new carpet is now on the floor."

Colette helped Anna into the dress, then

fastened the satin buttons which ran down the back.

Anna stood back to observe her appearance in the cheval glass. The gown's sarcenet overskirt split down the front to reveal the contrasting silk of the underskirt. Where the overskirt split, wide gold bands gave the impression of an inverted V. The same gold banding edged the train that flowed from the back.

Colette fumbled through Anna's drawer and brought out long white satin gloves which she handed to Anna before standing back to admire her charge in full length. "Oh, *mon cheri*, you are most beautiful."

The last touch was to fasten in Anna's hair a gold band from which three white ostrich feathers swept upward.

"If only your mama could see you," Colette said. "She would be so happy."

With a poignant smile, Anna whispered, "She sees."

Anna sat down before her dressing table to slip on gold and white slippers as a tap sounded on her door, and Haverstock entered the dressing room. He wore a well cut royal blue velvet coat with diamond buttons over a white shirt and white knee breeches.

Anna smiled at her husband as she thanked Colette and dismissed her.

Haverstock moved toward Anna, unable to take his eyes from her. Her loveliness never failed to captivate him, whether it be watching her sleep under dawn's hazy glow or admiring her in promenade attire as she chatted merrily with his sisters. When he was close enough to smell her rose water, he felt a sense of heady intoxication.

He trailed a finger along the satin smoothness of her shoulder.

"I have brought you something," he murmured, holding out a velvet box the size of a loaf of bread.

She took it and opened it. Dozens of diamonds sparkled in the candlelight. "It's the most beautiful necklace I've ever seen."

"It's yours for a lifetime. My mother has reluctantly relinquished the jewels to the new marchioness." He reached to unfasten the necklace. "Allow me to clasp this on your most exquisite neck, Lady Haverstock."

When he finished, he said, "Now, if you please, rise so that I might determine if you will do."

"I am sure I will do, my lord, for your mother herself cast approval on this gown," Anna said with false confidence as she stood.

Haverstock circled her. "I can see I will be the envy of every man at Lord Wentworth's tonight."

Her amused eyes met his. "I hope I don't bring you embarrassment."

"I beg that you avoid the card room, my dear," he said teasingly. "It wouldn't do at all for Lady Haverstock to relieve my friends of their money."

"I shall endeavor to obey you, my master."

He looked down into her laughing eyes and kissed her softly.

\* \* \*

Her husband's obvious pride in her did much to relieve Anna's fears over her reception at the Wentworth's. For apprehension had made her sick all week. Details of her background by now trickled off the tongues of the *ton*, she knew. She kept remembering the scathing words she had heard her husband's father utter behind closed doors on that cold January day half a decade earlier. *The daughter of a whore will not attend school with my daughters.* Would others also wish to avoid tainting their women with her presence? Would she be snubbed at the Wentworth ball?

As they sat in the dark carriage waiting for the queue in front of them to unload their finely dressed ladies and gentlemen at the Wentworths', Charlotte said, "I am so very nervous."

"You will do well," her brother assured. "I have never seen you more lovely." His eyes traveled over her virginal looking white gown.

"Charles never said such kind words to me last year when I came out," a pouting Cynthia said.

Kate answered, "Oh Charles is much kinder and more appreciative of beauty since he married."

"The three of you are quite beautiful," Anna added, trying to instill in her sisters the confidence she lacked.

As Charlotte proceeded to voice her fears of being a wallflower, Anna's thoughts turned to her own fears – fears far greater than the embarrassment of not having a dancing partner.

Finally, their barouche pulled in front of the stately house where footmen posted like sentries on every other step all the way to the opened doorway. Anna's apprehension accelerated, as did her heartbeat, when she gave her hand to her husband and alighted from the carriage.

They passed through the doorway into a brightly lit room. Her eyes flitted to the flickering chandeliers laden with rings and rings of tapers. In this room alone, Anna guessed, over a thousand candles burned.

At the opposite end of the massive hall, Lord and Lady Wentworth greeted their guests. While

Anna and Haverstock waited in the reception line, Anna felt certain her husband could hear the rapid pounding of her heart. The next few minutes were critical. A smile and a kind word from Lord or Lady Wentworth assured Anna of an acceptable reception. Coldness sealed her doom.

Soon, she was face to face with her host and hostess, whom she judged to be old enough to be her parents. Anna found herself staring at Lady Wentworth's diamond necklace, oddly wondering how the woman's slender neck was not misshapen from the weight of the spectacular jewels.

"It is my great pleasure, Lord and Lady Wentworth, to present you to my wife," Haverstock said.

Anna shyly stepped forward and curtsied.

"You did well to marry her before the season," Lord Wentworth said in a fatherly voice to Haverstock, "for one of her beauty would not have lasted long."

"I am aware of my good fortune," Haverstock said.

Lady Wentworth took Anna's hand. "London is abuzz with the story of Haverstock's heroic rescue of you in the park. We are very happy to meet you at last, my dear."

"Thank you, my lady. Being here tonight is very special, not only for me but also for our sister, Lady Charlotte. This is her first ball." Anna reached for Charlotte and presented her.

With the dreaded introduction behind her, Anna squeezed her husband's hand as they climbed the marble staircase. Haverstock introduced her throughout the upstairs ballroom.

Had Anna not been so confident in her

appearance, she would have been mortified at her reception. Men and woman alike stopped conversations and stared at Anna as she walked by on her husband's arm.

It took nearly an hour to make their way across the crowded room. Anna stiffened when she saw the bald head of Sir Henry Vinson amidst a group of men against the far wall. He met her gaze and smiled, walking toward Anna and Haverstock.

"My dear Anna, how lovely you look," Sir Henry greeted.

Haverstock looked puzzled. "You know my wife?"

"Yes, we are very old friends. I have known her since she was but a baby," Sir Henry said, "and I must tell you, Haverstock, she was beautiful then, too."

Anna detected an uneasiness in her husband in Sir Henry's presence. Haverstock soon directed his gaze a bit farther away and excused himself and his wife, saying he had to speak to a friend.

Haverstock found seats for his wife and sisters and left them to get ratafia.

As he passed Sir Henry, Haverstock invited the man to have a smoke with him on the balcony of the adjoining room.

On the balcony that faced Berkeley Square, Sir Henry accepted a cigar Haverstock offered, and the two men stood smoking in the chilled air.

"You are wondering why I wanted a private word with you?" Haverstock said, blowing out a pungent puff of smoke.

"Yes."

"It pains me to admit I have not been completely truthful to my very satisfactory wife,"

Haverstock said. "Anna does not know of my post in the Foreign Office."

Sir Henry took a long drag on his cigar. "I see."

"I beg that she will not learn of it from you."

"The nature of our work makes secrecy a necessity, my good man," Sir Henry said.

Haverstock tossed his cigar away. "I am glad we agree on that."

* * *

When he returned to the ballroom, Haverstock found his wife and sisters surrounded by admiring men clamoring for dancing partners. "I claim my wife for the first dance," he announced, holding out his hand for Anna.

Though conversations hummed from every part of the room, Anna felt as if her every footstep echoed on the wooden floor as she followed her husband to join the other dancers. The pounding in her chest returned. Dancing with a dancing master in her own drawing room was altogether different than doing the quadrille with a host of strangers and an even greater host of onlookers. But Haverstock put her at ease, teasing her about the flock of men who had already begged to stand up with her. She was so relaxed in his company she did not even have to think about the dance steps. They came naturally. And not once did her feet betray her.

Her feet did begin to hurt after an hour of non-stop dancing. She was most thankful when she could finally sit down. She sat alone, fanning herself rapidly in a vain attempt to displace the room's heat while tying to spot her sisters on the dance floor. But it was her husband – so much taller than all the others – who stood out most as he danced with Kate. Anna felt a flash of pride as she watched him. His manliness made all the elegant dandies look like fops. And though he did not warm to the social whirl, he performed satisfactorily at every level from dancing to conversing.

A man smelling of sandalwood came and sat next to Anna. She turned and saw it was an exquisitely dressed Morgie. "How very good it is to see you here," she said with pleasure.

"I confess to holding no great fondness for such events," he said, "but Haverstock demanded I come. Seems he wanted to guarantee his sisters would be assured of dancing partners."

"How very sweet of him, though his fears were completely unnecessary. The girls have danced every dance."

Morgie watched the dance floor. "Terrible cravat on Weatherford," he murmured. "Wonder how much Tolivar paid Prangle to dance with his fat sister?"

"Morgie, you are so very wicked."

"Not wicked. Just honest."

"And critical. Pray, what would you say about me if I were on the dance floor now?"

"Don't criticize friends – not that I could find anything disparaging to say about you."

"I am glad we are friends."

"I see Kate and Charlotte and Cynthia. Where's Lydia?"

"She did not wish to come."

"I've always said she was the smartest of the lot."

"You are quite honest. And correct."

Sir Henry's voice broke in. "Ah, Lady Haverstock, how good it is to find you seated. I beg you will grant me this dance."

Anna excused herself to Morgie, stood up and took Sir Henry's proffered hand, limping slightly because her left foot had blistered.

"Are you all right, Anna?" Sir Henry asked.

"It is just that my feet are unused to the dancing."

"Then we must sit this one out," he suggested, leading her from the room, down a cool marble hall and into an asparagus green library.

Seeing that there was no one else in the room, Anna came to an abrupt halt. It would do her reputation no good to be found alone with a man who was not her husband. "I beg that we return immediately to the ballroom. My husband would not approve of me meeting with another gentleman here."

Ignoring her request, Sir Henry moved to close the door. "But, my lady, an authority much higher than your husband demands that you hear what I have to impart."

Trembling, she sank into a chair.

# $\mathcal{C}$hapter 11

His eyes narrow, Sir Henry watched Anna gaze up into her husband's face while they danced. Only when the marquess was her partner did Anna come alive with laughing eyes and a relaxed grace. Sir Henry noted the way she tenderly caressed Haverstock's broad shoulder, the way their hands locked in a familiar clasp, the way she casually brushed a stray lock of dark brown hair from her husband's forehead. *Damn. The woman's fallen in love with her husband!*

After hearing of Haverstock's heroic rescue of Anna in the park, Sir Henry suspected the marquess was excessively fond of his wife. But now he knew Haverstock's feelings toward Anna far exceeded fondness. Even when she danced with others, Haverstock's eyes followed his wife with every beat of the music as she glided through throngs of richly dressed dancers.

What a fool he had been not to have anticipated this unwanted complication. The girl would be far less pliable now. He would have to be very careful how he manipulated her. At this point, it wouldn't do at all to suggest any harm could befall her husband. Just simple revelations about his supposed activities would suffice. When Anna helped him uncover the identity of Haverstock's accomplices, a tidy sum could come his way.

Later that evening, Sir Henry found her and quietly escorted her from the ballroom to the library. He lowered his voice. "You must find out the identity of your husband's contacts in London. Information your husband's passed has cost thousands of British lives. We must stop them."

"Even my husband?"

He shook his head. "He's far too valuable."

"I have learned nothing at all in these weeks we've been married."

"You must find a way, my dear. And soon. Despite that he and I – both of us being fluent in French – oversee espionage operations, your husband fiercely protects his contacts, even from me. He's obsessed in his drive for success. Few men trusted him – because of his father. The former marquess's arrogance cost him dearly. He always had to be superior to everyone, had to have the best, bet the most, lose the heaviest. It came to the point where he refused to pay his gaming debts. The son has been driven to clear the tarnish from his family name even at the cost of his country. His coldness extends to everyone. He trusts no one, except Ralph Morgan."

"Did Morgie accompany Charles to France?"

Sir Henry nodded. "Those two are closer than most brothers. I've heard that Haverstock came to Morgie's defense when the two were just boys at Eton. Seems Morgie suffered greatly because he descended from Jews. As the story goes, Haverstock saved Morgie as he was undergoing a vicious beating by several chaps. The fellows all looked up to Haverstock. He was a viscount then and a full head taller than all his classmates. To this day, Morgie fairly worships your husband. Were Haverstock desirous of using his friend's head for target practice, I have no doubt Mr. Morgan would oblige."

"Yet you don't believe Morgie knows about Charles's treason?"

"I think not. The Morgans have a deep hatred for the French, particularly since Boney robbed them of their Prussian holdings."

Sir Henry rose abruptly. "We must return to the ballroom," he said, offering her his hand, "before your husband misses you. From now on we will meet at noon every Wednesday at Hookam's."

The library door burst open, and Anna saw the dark giant who was her husband standing in the doorway, his mouth an angry grim line, his eyes flashing. She felt as if the air had squeezed from her lungs.

Haverstock directed a steely gaze at Sir Henry. "I wish to speak privately with my wife."

"By all means. I've been regaling Lady Haverstock with tales of her youth." Though he was a tall man, Sir Henry seemed small as he swept past Haverstock to exit the library.

* * *

Haverstock had been pleased when he was dancing with his sister to observe his wife and Morgie engaged in conversation. When he looked back a minute later, he noticed her gone. A deep frown etched Haverstock's face as he spotted the back of Sir Henry's bald head and saw him leading Anna from the ballroom.

He had never warmed to Sir Henry, though he was forced to work closely with him. Haverstock could not fault Sir Henry's efforts. Despite that the man had spent much of his life in France, he was a true patriot to the English crown. He was accepted everywhere, including in the beds of half the matrons in London.

Perhaps it was Sir Henry's treatment of women that rankled Haverstock. He cast off mistresses without even a small settlement, and he divulged intimacies about married women that no man of honor would countenance.

That Sir Henry directed his attentions on Anna displeased Haverstock excessively. His concern mounting, he could hardly wait for the dance to be over so he could go to his wife.

When the dance finished, he looked for Anna and Sir Henry at the refreshments table but did not find them. With growing concern and anger, he searched for them on the empty balcony.

Blast the woman! He had let her impeccable taste and cultured voice fool him into thinking she was every inch a lady, when at her first ball she behaved as a strumpet.

Now that he had found her in Lord Wentworth's library, Haverstock itched to crash a fist into Sir Henry's face and drag his errant wife from the house. But he refused to give fodder to the gossip mongers.

His face rigid, Haverstock closed the library door and spoke with controlled anger. "You have conducted yourself in a totally improper manner, Lady Haverstock. Closeting yourself alone in a room with any man is a breech of propriety, but to do so with a bachelor who is noted for his dalliances with married women is inexcusable."

"But, surely – "

He cut her off. "You and I both know there was no love on your part when you schemed to become my wife, but since you are my wife, I will expect you to give every indication of being a faithful mate. Is that clear?"

Anna nodded. "I see now that my behavior was deplorable." Her voice cracked. "I will endeavor to conduct myself in an acceptable manner if you can only forgive me."

She could portray innocence most convincingly, he thought as he led her from the library.

The remainder of the ball, Haverstock hovered possessively over his wife, attempting to appear jovial to counteract any unpleasant rumors that could have resulted from his wife's tete-a-tete with Sir Henry.

But on the carriage ride home, he dropped the artifice. While his sisters chatted merrily, he sulked.

"Did you not find Captain Smythe to be quite the most dashing man at the ball, Kate?" Cynthia asked.

"Indeed. A pity he's only a second son."

"La!" Cynthia said. "I would not care were he to show a preference for me for I think he's positively the most handsome man I've ever seen." Turning to her younger sister, she said, "I vow, Charlotte, you danced every dance and not twice with anyone."

"I did dance twice with Mr. Hogart," Charlotte said quietly.

"Was that the man with the terribly ill-fitting coat?" Kate asked.

"You cannot judge a man merely by his clothes," Charlotte defended.

"But really, he stood out like a sty on the eye," Kate said.

"I've never heard of Mr. Hogart," Cynthia added. "What kind of family is he from? Do you know anything of him, Charles?"

Haverstock snapped to attention. "Who?"

"Mr. Hogart," Cynthia chided.

"Never heard of him," Haverstock said gloomily.

"Well, I can tell you all about him," Charlotte said, her eyes sparkling. "He has neither money nor family, but he is wonderfully kind. He is quite pious and plans to become a minister."

Kate rolled her eyes. "Charlotte, my dear, you can do far better. Pray, do not encourage the poor man."

"If he should do me the goodness of calling, I assure you I will be all that is amiable to him," Charlotte said with spunk.

Anna applauded Charlotte's deep goodness but deemed it wisest to keep her own views private for fear of angering Kate or Cynthia. Besides, she did not feel like talking. She still stung from her husband's words. *Schemed to become my wife. No love on your part.*

With those thoughts – and Sir Henry's instructions – keeping her awake, Anna was unable to sleep. She heard Charles in his dressing room, but he never came to her. It was the first night since she had been at Haverstock House that Charles did not share her bed.

* * *

Lydia and her brother, fresh from riding in the park, joined Anna in the breakfast room the following morning.

"Oh, Anna," Lydia said excitedly, "the chestnut Charles bought me is undoubtedly the best piece of horseflesh in London. Charles said she was your idea, and I do most gratefully thank you."

"Seeing your face so lively is thanks enough," Anna said. Davis entered the room and directed his gaze at Haverstock. "Her ladyship requests your presence in her chamber, my lord."

* * *

"You sent for me?" Haverstock asked, striding into his mother's gilded chamber where she took a breakfast tray in bed. He noted the grim set to her face. Even in her youth, his mother had not been a beauty. But she possessed what his father wanted in a wife. She was the daughter of an earl who settled a generous dowry, and she bore him seven children while maintaining a cool detachment from her husband.

"Sit down," she commanded, her voice sharp.

He did as bid.

"I have been delivered a letter this morning – never mind who sent it. It informs me of your wife's deplorable conduct last night. You have brought me untold disappointment in your choice of a wife, Charles. Once a whore, always a whore."

Overcome with rage, Haverstock rose and towered over his mother. His voice quivered with anger. "I will not allow you to speak of my wife in such a manner. She is a total innocent. If she behaved with impropriety last night, it was because she is ignorant in the ways of the *ton*."

"She has bewitched you," the dowager said with disgust. "We cannot have the daughter of that horrible woman bear the title Marchioness of Haverstock. Divorce her before she can become the mother of the future marquess. Don't you see, Charles?"

"I see that you are dangerously close to breaking the bond of my filial duty, Mother. My wife made an innocent mistake. Do not speak so of Anna again."

He turned on his heel and left the room.

# $\mathcal{C}$hapter 12

Today, more than any time since her mother's death, Anna was in a blue funk. A terrible one. She had not slept at all the night before.

Over and over she had remembered the harshness of Charles's words spoken in anger – anger she richly deserved. She wondered how she could learn from Charles the truth about his activities when he refused even to share her bed. At the core of her misery was fear over what would happen to him if she betrayed him.

Perhaps by going to the East End she could purge herself of self-pity.

On her way back to Mayfair after her visit to the East End, Anna lacked her usual feeling of satisfaction. She had brightened one day in their lives but had done nothing to improve their lot. Poverty bred poverty. These people had no skills, no knowledge. They were locked in a never-ending cycle of misfortune. If only they could learn trades to earn a living wage. But how could they?

She had an idea. She and Colette were skilled at needlework. Perhaps they could provide fine fabrics and threads and instruct the women. As their skills increased, the seamstresses might even be able to get commissions to sew for the upper classes. Her idea snowballed, and Anna's gloom shed like layers of an onion. Some of the women – with her assistance – would be able to open shops. A modiste. A milliner. A tailor. Glove maker. Purveyor of fine christening gowns.

Her eyes sparkling, Anna turned to Colette. "You and I are going to open a school for seamstresses in White Chapel."

An understanding smile lifted Colette's weathered face. "*Tres bien.* That is an idea most good, my lady."

* * *

Haverstock stifled a yawn as he attempted to decode a message from one of his men in the field. He had fitfully tossed and turned throughout the night, unable to sleep, fighting the yearning to go to Anna. Yet, his anger stopped him. No, anger was not the right emotion. Disillusionment was closer to the mark. His wife was an enigma. On the one hand, she was the loving innocent with whom he shared a touching intimacy; on the other, a scheming hoyden who got Morgie drunk and most likely cheated to take possession of his substantial funds. This same hoyden had conducted herself like a trollop at Lord Wentworth's.

As he had done so many times before, Haverstock wondered why Anna so fiercely wanted Morgie's money when her own fortune supplied everything she could ever need. Perhaps his mother had been right. Something about Anna's innocence did not ring true. While he cherished the maidenhead she brought to their marriage bed, he questioned her scruples. Was she a scheming seductress who delighted in manipulating men? Was he, indeed, bewitched by the daughter of Annette de Mouchet?

The thought disturbed him. Until last night

when her actions enraged him, he had been totally smitten with her. Did she know what power she held over him? What a weakling he had been for a lovely face and soft, compliant body. Well, he would show her! He would have to resist the temptation of her lovemaking and free himself of the bonds of her entrapment.

He could never free himself with the divorce his mother so eagerly sought. After all, Anna was his wife. She could be carrying his child at this very minute. Lord knows they had ample opportunities to conceive. He would always be responsible for her.

He vowed to devote himself so much to his work he would have little time to dwell on Anna and her bewitchment. If he did not have to behold her loveliness, he could resist her and maintain his dignity. He would be safe from her charms while he continued to take her into society, but he would not himself be alone with her. And she would never again have the opportunity to humiliate him as she had done with Sir Henry.

His thoughts turned to his work, still troubled over Monsieur Hebert's announcement that a traitor lurked in the London office. Who could it be? If only he could learn the wretched creature's identity.

* * *

The posies began arriving at Haverstock House long before the gentlemen sending them started calling on the lovely sisters, putting the household in a flurry of excitement. Abigails scurried about with freshly pressed dresses and hair combs in an effort to render the ladies suitably attired to greet their bevy of admirers.

It fell to Anna to provide chaperonage, since

the dowager had made known her own refusal to leave her chamber. As Lydia conveyed her mother's message to Anna, she blundered. "I declare I do not know what has come over Mother these past weeks. She seldom leaves her room. Why, since Charles's marriage – "

Anna's stricken face halted Lydia in mid sentence.

"Oh, I am so very sorry, Anna," Lydia whispered, her face flaming.

"I daresay your mother cannot help but resent me."

Lydia walked to the dressing table where Anna sat and embraced her sister-in-law. "Give her time," Lydia said. "When Mother knows you better, she will accept you as she does her own daughters."

"Forgive me for saying I do not find that comforting, given what I perceive as your mother's lack of maternal affection."

Lydia sank on Anna's bed, her brows plunging together. "You are right. Mother has never been overly affectionate to her daughters. I believe it was because her own mother died when she was but a toddler. She had no example of motherly devotion. All of her love was directed at her sister, Aunt Margaret. You know Aunt Margaret was your father's wife?"

Anna's eyes widened. "I did not," she said softly. "It explains so very much."

"Mama and Aunt Margaret were like two bodies sharing one heart. When Aunt Margaret suffered in her marriage, Mother felt it just as keenly. I believe it is because of your mother's role in Aunt Margaret's unhappiness that mother resents you."

Anna nodded solemnly and did not speak for

some time. "You said your mother has shown little affection to her daughters. What about her sons?"

"Though you have probably observed little evidence of it, Mother has always been terribly wrapped up in Charles. He always had to have the best. He had to be at the top of his class. And Charles being Charles, he endeavored to please. Only in his choice of a wife was he not guided by her. She has always made it clear she wanted him to marry Lady Jane Wyeth." Meeting Anna's pensive gaze, Lydia added, "I don't think the woman has been born who would be good enough for Charles in Mother's eyes."

Anna's chamber door whipped open, and Charlotte came flying into the room, wearing a posy of wilted pansies. "Oh, Anna, Mr. Hogart is downstairs as we speak. Can you please accompany me now?"

Though Anna wanted to know more about Lady Jane Wyeth, this was no time to ask. She rose from the dressing table, giving a last fleeting glance into her looking glass at her peach-colored muslin. "Of course." Turning to Lydia, she asked, "Do you accompany us?"

"I wouldn't think of missing the opportunity to meet the paragon, Mr. Hogart."

By the time the three ladies entered the saloon, several other expectant young bucks awkwardly occupied chairs throughout the room. As hostess, Anna greeted them first, then ordered tea. Within minutes Cynthia and Kate – both dressed to perfection in Madam  Devreaux's creations – sailed into the room with smiling faces.

To Anna's astonishment, Kate fixed her attention on a Mr. Reeves, whom Anna judged to be forty years old. He possessed neither title nor good looks. He squeezed into clothing he must have worn when he weighed two stone less. His fleshy chin sunk into his highly starched cravat, and the top of his balding head reflected the afternoon sun that shafted into the room.

Anna watched with interest as Cynthia singled out the dashing Captain Smythe, who appeared to appreciate Cynthia's fair beauty as much as Cynthia was attracted to his handsomeness. Anna appreciated Cynthia's taste. Captain Smythe's broad shoulders filled his red coat with its highly polished buttons. He was tall and dark with a ready smile and elegant manners.

Though Anna knew with certainty four men now in this room had sent flowers to Charlotte, Charlotte chose to wear the pitiful bouquet sent from the modest Mr. Hogart. Anna observed that no one except Charlotte spoke to the common-looking man and was reminded of Kate's remark that he stuck out like a sty on the eye. Indeed, the poor man was as out of place with these pinks of the ton as a briar patch at Kew Gardens.

Except for his limp white shirt, he dressed entirely in black, in clothing that had long ago fallen from fashion. A slight man of medium height, he looked much younger than the other men in the room. His hair was still a pale blond, framing a too-earnest face. Despite his lack of fashionable clothes, Mr. Hogart, with his clear blue eyes and fine nose, exuded an elegance of person. Anna decided she quite liked the boy.

"Charlotte tells me you plan to be a minister," Anna said to Mr. Hogart as she handed him his tea. "Church of England?"

He clumsily took the cup. "No, my lady. I am a

Methodist."

The banter of a dozen young people suddenly stopped and all eyes riveted to the ill-dressed Mr. Hogart. Had he said he was a Buddhist, they could not have been more repelled, Anna thought.

"How very interesting," Anna said, forcing a smile. "I confess to having found Mr. Wesley's tracts rather thought provoking."

"If only my parents were as enlightened as you," Hogart said. "They do not approve of my choice."

"What is it they wanted for you?" Charlotte asked timidly, admiration in her eyes.

"My father had hoped I would take over his farms."

"He is a squire?" Anna asked.

He nodded.

Turning her attention to Captain Smythe, Anna asked him to tell the gathering about his activities on the Peninsula, which he did, fully enrapturing Cynthia. Even Kate, who scorned him as a second son, seemed to hang on his every word.

As darkness began to fall, Haverstock entered the salon, his eyes meeting Anna's first, then addressing the visiting gentlemen.

Anna noted with pride that he did not scorn Mr. Hogart as the others had. She scooted over on the sofa so Charles could sit next to her, but he remained standing, pacing the room. He refused Anna's offer of tea and seemed preoccupied with his own thoughts.

After the callers took their leave, the sisters queried Haverstock.

"Did you find Captain Smythe to be possessed of all that is agreeable?" Cynthia asked.

"Though Mr. Hogart is much reserved, I could

tell you liked him," Charlotte said. "Didn't you, Charles?"

Haverstock stroked his sisters with the responses they desired. Meeting Kate's gaze, he said, "Did I detect a preference on your part for Mr. Reeves?"

She nodded, her lashes coyly sweeping downward.

"How can this be?" Charlotte asked. "You spurned the man two seasons ago."

"But that was before it was known that he stood to succeed Blassingame's dukedom. It seems His Grace of Blassingame failed to sire sons," Kate said. "And Mr. Reeves is his nephew," she announced brightly.

Cynthia whirled at her elder sister. "Do you mean to say you would marry Mr. Reeves solely to become a duchess?"

Kate held her shoulders regally, her eyes dancing. "Why should I be content to be a mere lady when I could be a duchess?"

"That is positively irksome!" Charlotte protested.

"You won't find it so irksome when I am addressed as Her Grace," Kate said, strolling toward the doors. "I don't know about you girls, but I for one must select a gown for tonight."

Her sisters began discussing what they would wear as they followed Kate from the room.

Anna turned warm eyes to her husband. "Won't you come to my chamber, Charles?"

"I think not, my dear," he said. "There are matters I must discuss with my secretary."

Swallowing her disappointment, Anna reminded him of the ball they would attend that night.

"Be assured I will escort you, Anna," he said, his eyes cold obsidian. "I dare not leave you alone lest you seduce every blood in breeches."

Blood rushed to her cheeks and she hissed, "That's unfair, Charles!" She lifted her skirts and ran from the room before he could see her cry.

## $\mathcal{C}$hapter 13

A smile fixed on her face, Anna pretended to listen to her sisters' chatter in the carriage ride home from the ball, but her thoughts were on her husband, who now sat silently beside her. She had felt like a fairy princess all night as her Charles, her Prince Charming, lavished attentions on her. He had danced with no woman other than her. He had solicitously procured ratafia for her and her sisters whenever they gave the slightest appearance of being thirsty. He had hovered over her all night, his hands caressing or stroking her in a tender fashion.

But now, with no one but family to observe, he shunned her, brooding in his corner of the carriage, and she knew the entire night had been a sham. In public, he would appear the devoted husband while distancing himself from her when they were alone. Why had this bleeding rift occurred between Charles and her? She had to repair it. How else could she learn the truth about his French activities? It was unthinkable to admit there was any other reason for her deep concern.

The swift rounding of a corner pushed Anna against her husband. She felt the heat of him, the comfort of his sturdiness and yearned to feel the length of him pressed against her. Demurely casting her gaze at his somber face, she swallowed her disappointment over his refusal to look at her. With constricted heart, she studied the grim set to his mouth and achingly remembered a time not so many weeks past when those same lips had the power to make her pulse leap with desire.

* * *

When they arrived at Haverstock House, he climbed the stairs beside Anna and wished her a curt good-night at her chamber door.

"There are some matters I hoped to discuss with you," Anna said. "Won't you come sit in my chamber for a few minutes?"

He gazed into the wide-eyed innocence of her face. Though he had determined to resist her seductive hold on him, he found no power to deny her simple request.

She led him to the settee by the crackling fire and bid him to sit on it next to her.

"I don't want to interfere with your morning rides with Lydia," she began, "but I desire to join you. That day in the park, you did vow to teach me about horses. I would like you to select a calm mount for me and allow me and a groom to accompany you each morning. The groom could instruct me while you and Lydia take a galloping romp."

He remembered the fear that had gripped him when he had heard her screams and watched, terrified, as the furiously pounding grays carried her away. He remembered the desperation he had felt when he thought he was losing Anna. She did need to learn about handling horses. "You can begin tomorrow," he said.

"One more thing," she said. "Will you be taking me back to the park promenade any time soon?"

she asked.

"Not in the foreseeable future for my work is most pressing."

The flicker of disappointment that passed over her face oddly pleased him.

"Then I solicit your permission to ask Morgie to take Lydia and me to the park some afternoons. After my *faux pas* at the Wentworth Ball, I want to seek your permission before I spend a minute in the presence of another man."

"Morgie is not *another* man. You are at liberty to be in Morgie's presence whenever you like, but I do prefer that you take Lydia along." He got to his feet and bent over her, placing a chaste peck on her cheek. "I'll see you in riding habit in the morning, my lady."

When he reached the door, she called his name.

He turned, cocking an eyebrow.

"Are you still angry at me?"

God's teeth but he wanted her! "I was not so much mad as disappointed, my dear," he said, opening the door and leaving the room.

As he tossed restlessly in his big empty bed, he wondered why his power to resist her brought him no joy.

* * *

Dressed in Cynthia's riding habit, Anna met Lydia in the entry hall the following morning, and the two women sailed past the footman who held open the door. Amidst a shroud of fog, Haverstock and the groom held reign to four horses on the cobblestone street below.

Running his eyes appreciatively over Anna, Haverstock said, "That color becomes you, my dear."

She glanced at the deep green velvet. "I borrowed it from Cynthia." Fighting back tears when her husband had curtly taken leave of her the night before, Anna had immediately scurried to Cynthia's room to secure a suitable habit, for the two women were near the same size.

"The bold color suits you far better than Cynthia," he said, cinching his huge hands about the span of her slim waist and lifting her on to the gray.

Displeased over her husband's backhanded compliment, Anna shot him a narrowed glance.

He placed the ribbons in her hands. "The first thing you need to learn is that when you pull on these, the horse will slow." Haverstock nodded at the groom. "Jimmy and I selected this easy stepper for you."

Anna defiantly turned her attention to the groom. "So you're Jimmy." She scrutinized the young man from the top of his curly mop of blond hair to his mud-splattered boots planted firmly on the street. He was tall, though not as tall as Charles, and looked as if his recently sprouted limbs still awaited the meaty flesh that would come with age. She hoped he would suit her plans.

He bowed. "Yes, me lady."

Stroking her horse's mane, she asked, "And what is his name?"

Jimmy stifled a laugh. "'is name is Lady Gray."

"I do hope my ignorance of horses will not try your patience too sorely."

"I have confidence yer ladyship will be riding with the best of 'em in no time," the groom said.

Haverstock's eyes flashed mischievously. "My wife, I have found, is a prodigious student."

Remembering her husband's tutelage on lovemaking, Anna felt the heat rise to her cheeks.

Jimmy gave Lydia a leg up while Haverstock mounted his bay, and guided it alongside his wife. He rode next to Anna all the way to the park, soothing her fears and giving her rudimentary instructions about handling horses.

When they reached the park, Anna urged him and Lydia to go on in their usual manner while she and Jimmy stayed back.

Haverstock would not go until he delivered instructions to the groom. "Jimmy, my good man, I leave my wife in your hands. Please see that she doesn't get herself killed. She knows nothing of horses."

"Really, Charles," Lydia said, "You'll have poor Jimmy afraid to blink his eyes."

Once Haverstock and his sister were no longer in sight, Anna turned to Jimmy. "I must confess to not being totally honest with you, Jimmy. While I do desire to learn to ride, what I desire most is your help in protecting my husband."

"Yer husband is a noted whip, me lady. He hardly needs me help."

"I do not fear he will break his neck. What I fear is that he will stop a musket ball."

Jimmy's eyes widened.

"I'm deathly afraid someone means to kill him, and I would like you to keep a protective eye on him."

"I'll do more than that, me lady," he said through gritted teeth. "If I sees anyone trying to harm me master, I'll kill 'em with me bare hands."

Anna shot an appreciative glance at his large hands. "I shouldn't like to put you in danger."

"Don't fret over me. We both got to make sure

Lord Haverstock stays 'ealthy." He gave her a knowing wink.

She bestowed a warm smile on the young groom. "Whenever you can free yourself, I wish for you to discreetly follow his lordship. Pay attention to anyone he meets, to anyone who looks suspicious."

He nodded.

"There's one other thing, Jimmy. No one else is to know about the danger to my husband."

"I can hold me tongue." Digging his heels into his mount's underbelly and instructing Anna to do the same, he headed off in the direction of Haverstock and Lydia, careful to stay at Anna's side.

As they advanced down the trail, Anna grew used to the feel of a huge horse beneath her and began to relax. She learned how to make Lady Gray turn to the right and left, how to slow down and speed up. As her confidence increased, she did far more of the latter.

Before long, they saw Haverstock and Lydia some distance away, their horses racing neck-in-neck.

"Never mind about me, Jimmy. I'm feeling quite at ease now with Lady Gray. Watch for anyone who looks suspicious."

"Ye mean like hiding behind a tree or the like?"

"Exactly."

Jimmy took to his task like a kitten to warm milk, his attention roused by every man he saw. Keeping Anna close, he cantered off down a shaded lane after a lone equestrian, only to circle back when the well dressed man rode toward the Serpentine.

Presently, Haverstock and Lydia came

galloping from a thicket. Anna watched Lydia tenderly stroke her mount's lathered hide. She watched, too, the lively look of amused affection that passed from brother to sister, and she swallowed hard, jealous that Charles did not share such a bond with her.

Holding her shoulders regally and attempting to appear as if she had been born to ride, Anna rode out to meet her husband.

He slowed and watched appreciatively, then spoke to the groom. "I must commend you. I see my wife is still in one piece."

"Her ladyship is a right fast learner."

Haverstock's eyes sparkled mischievously. "Ah, yes. I have found that to be quite true." He rode alongside Anna. "You will be galloping with Lydia and I in no time."

"I fear Lady Gray is giving me false confidence."

"She'll do well for you. Have you no fears like so many simpering females do?"

She shook her head. "I find riding most exhilarating. Would that we could be riding at Haymore."

He shot her a curious glance. "Why such a strong desire to go to the country when you are city bred?"

They left the park and rode two-abreast along the street.

"It is precisely because I have never been in the country I long for clear skies and vast stretches of green as far as the eye can see." She turned softened eyes on her husband. "And I desire a husband who is rested and given to pleasure seeking rather than one who is determined to work himself to death."

His brows came together. "Have I been such an

ogre?"

She spoke gently. "Never an ogre, Charles. You are almost always all that is kind. I was so very proud of you yesterday when you were the only man who spoke with courtesy to poor Mr. Hogart."

"What manner of host would I be to ignore a guest in my own home?"

"You obviously did not learn your manners from your father."

He failed to take her bait. "You said I was *almost* always kind. Have I hurt you, my dear?"

"I daresay I richly deserved your scathing words at Lord Wentworth's the other night, but they wounded excessively."

He remembered reminding her theirs was no love match, telling her to *appear* faithful. His own foolish anger had caused him to hurt her when, in truth, she had not earned such cruel rebuke. Her only transgression was her total innocence. How innocent she looked now with the early morning light dancing in her dark locks. A fullness expanded in his chest as he thought of her gentle voice and compassion toward the unfortunate Mr. Hogart. She seemed almost childlike in her purity. How it tugged at his heart to know he had caused her pain.

Yet, he had resolved to resist her charms. He had to know who the real Anna was.

* * *

That afternoon Morgie showed up in the Haverstock drawing room, nervously twirling his hat in his hands while begging the marchioness and Lydia to accompany him for the afternoon procession through Hyde Park.

Anna bestowed a grateful smile on him and

silently thanked her absent husband for encouraging his friend to escort her. "Oh, Morgie, how very kind of you to take pity on Charles's neglected wife," Anna said. "I cannot speak for Lydia, but I assure you a ride in the park would be most welcome to me."

Morgie's eyes met Lydia's.

"I thank you for including me," Lydia told him as the two women went to get their bonnets.

The sisters sat on either side of Morgie as he took the ribbons. When they left Half Moon Street, Lydia spoke to Anna. "I must warn you Mama has decided to hold a dinner."

"I am glad she will leave her room," Anna said.

"But it's no longer her place to be hostess at Haverstock House," Lydia protested. "You're the marchioness now."

"I am hardly ready to fill your mother's shoes," Anna said. "If it's her desire to introduce me to her friends I cannot fault that."

"I am sure all of her acquaintances will be there," Lydia said. "And you, too, Morgie."

"Depend upon it," he mumbled. "Promise to be my partner at whist, Lady Lydia." He shook his head. "Never saw a woman who understood the game as you do. Like a man."

"Perhaps that is because you and Charles always treated me as one of the fellows," Lydia said.

A smile curled his lip. "Remember when you were the only girl we allowed in our fort that summer?"

Lydia tossed her head back and laughed. "I suspect, Morgie, you were repaying me for hooking your worm when we went fishing."

He shuddered as he directed his phaeton to

Hyde Park. "Cannot abide those slimy things. Most fortunate to have had you."

"Speaking of fortunate," Lydia said, her eyes sparkling with delight, "have you seen my horse?"

"Was with Haverstock when he bid on her at Tatt's, and uncommon bidding it was, too. Never in all my days saw a beast go for four-hundred guineas."

"Four-hundred guineas!" Lydia clutched her hand to her ample breast. "Why, that's a fortune!"

"Your brother can now afford it."

Anna was thankful he did not elaborate on her wealth.

"Would you like to ride her sometime?" Lydia offered Morgie.

"I should say! That would be jolly good."

"Charles and I ride every morning just after dawn."

He winced. "Too bloody early for me."

"Why, Morgie, I thought you'd be settling down now that Charles has married," Lydia said.

"You know very well, your brother started settling down four years ago. All he thinks of is work."

When Morgie returned his passengers to Haverstock House, Anna asked him, "Is your mind quite made up that you will not ride with us in the morning?"

"Quite sure," he said emphatically. "An afternoon ride is one thing, but rousing myself from slumber to ride in the morning mist is not my idea of pleasure."

"If you would but try it, I am sure you would like it," Lydia said.

Morgie wrinkled his nose and frowned.

# $\mathcal{C}$hapter 14

In the absence of her husband's company, Anna filled the next several days in much the same way. She accompanied Haverstock and Lydia on morning rides in the park. She and Colette worked on establishing their sewing school. And at the fashionable afternoon hour, Morgie would collect her and Lydia for the procession through Hyde Park.

The nights, too, were much the same. Balls and routs with her beaming husband at her side. But in the confines of their home, he ignored her and left her to sleep alone.

As the night of the dowager's fete approached, the house throbbed with preparations. Bouquets of fresh flowers rose from vases everywhere, silver was polished, hundreds of candles jammed into tiers of crystal chandeliers. The dowager roused early from her chamber each day, dressed in colorful morning gowns, and personally supervised all the preparations. She spent days composing her select guest list, for which she neither solicited nor accepted recommendations. She even ventured a trip in the barouche to Madam Devreaux's and commissioned herself a lilac gown.

Haverstock was not so busy he neglected to notice his mother's ministrations. On the morning before the dinner, he stayed behind in the breakfast room to have a private word with her. "It's good to see you have emerged from your chamber and embraced tomorrow's party," he began.

She smiled.

"However, I cannot but feel you are treading on the marchioness's domain."

The smile drained from her face, replaced by a cold stare. "I merely want to assure your wife makes the right contacts."

"I appreciate that, and know Anna lacks the breadth of your acquaintances. But I must remind you this is her home. I beg that you allow her to take her proper place at the table tomorrow night."

"How could I not when you have so plainly reminded me that my old seat is now Anna's?" she challenged.

"Very good," he said through compressed lips. "While you are remembering that, try to remember to treat my wife as if you thought her the crowning jewel in our family coronet."

"Really, Charles, that is carrying it too far."

"I think not. She is the wife I have chosen. I am happy with her, and if you cannot be agreeable to the situation, you can find somewhere else to live.

"That horrible woman is going to drive me from my home – from my own son's affections."

"She is doing no such thing, and she is *not* a horrible woman." Kicking back his chair, he rose swiftly, his face red with anger, and he pointed a finger at his mother. "Not one more word against her. Ever."

\* \* \*

As Anna became more experienced sitting a

horse, Haverstock insisted she ride the trails with him and Lydia, leaving no opportunity for a private word with Jimmy. She particularly wanted to talk with him before her noon meeting with Sir Henry at Hookam's. The opportunity came when Haverstock and Lydia began to argue over the merits of a pair of horses who were to run against each other at Newmarket that day.

"I shall meet you at the stables after breakfast," Anna whispered to Jimmy, who nodded.

After breakfast she found Jimmy outside the mews, and he told her Haverstock had neither been followed nor met with anyone who appeared suspicious. "But if anyone ever threatens Lord Haverstock, ye 'ave my word on it, they'll 'ave to get by me first."

"You're a dear," Anna said sincerely as she stood on her toes to kiss his cheek.

Within two hours Anna was strolling through the book-crammed aisles of Hookam's where she saw Sir Henry, taller than everyone else, perusing a thick volume in the corner that featured books in Latin.

She was pleased he had selected that section because no one else was there. Brushing past him, she whispered, "I have learned nothing."

He turned and followed her, grabbing her arm tightly. "It displeases me excessively that you've been so useless. We'd have been better off to have taken the fifty-thousand pounds."

"Unhand me," she said through gritted teeth, looking around to make sure no one was watching. "I am doing all I can. You forget Charles and I were not at all acquainted when we married. It takes time to build trust."

"How many more will have to die while you

*build trust?*"

"I refuse to take the blame for the casualties of this dreadful war." She glared at him before turning on her heel and stalking off.

* * *

Following the meeting with his mother, Haverstock angrily threw off his riding clothes and paced to the window of his dressing room where he beheld a curious sight. Anna was walking to the mews. Didn't the fool woman know a marchioness did not set foot near a stable? Jimmy came out and a few words passed between him and Anna, then Anna stood on her toes, gave the groom a peck on the cheek and turned to walk back to the house.

Haverstock felt as if he had been kicked in the heart. Until this moment, he had always liked Jimmy. The groom had been in Haverstock service since he was a wee lad. Now he had grown into a fine looking young man. He must be eighteen or nineteen. *Anna's age.*

God in heaven, surely Anna was not – It was too preposterous to contemplate. There must be some reasonable explanation.

Once again, Haverstock pondered the enigma that was his wife. He longed to know which of her personas was the true Anna. But more than anything, he experienced a strange longing to be the object of her complete devotion. And for the first time since he had married her, he felt completely bereft.

* * *

"Did you see my wife this afternoon?" Haverstock asked Morgie, who sat across the table from him at White's that evening.

"I did, and I seem to recall her telling me you

had a fete to attend tonight." He raised a quizzing brow at his old friend.

Haverstock lifted a glass of brandy and drank. "These events grow tedious. I have decided to spend my evening with you, old chap, and get thoroughly foxed."

"Haven't seen you in your cups for the past decade."

"It's this blasted marriage. A smart man you are to stay single."

"Why is it when I see you with Lady Haverstock I have the distinct feeling you're king of the mountain?" Morgie said wistfully. "Makes my own existence seem utterly idle."

"That's the thing about a wife. They can bring you the most complete joy one moment and sink you to utter despair another."

"Can't picture Anna bringing anyone despair. Much too sweet."

"I saw her stand on her toes and plant a kiss on her groom's cheek."

Morgie began to laugh. "So that's what's got you down! You have little knowledge of your wife's character if you don't know of her affectionate nature. Why she's pecked me on the cheek any number of times for what she calls my kindnesses to her. Always she stands on her toes and places a chaste kiss on the cheek."

Haverstock could not deny Anna's affectionate manner. Only with him, her kisses had been more than a brush of lips across a cheek. He seared even now remembering the taste of her sweet mouth open under his. God in heaven, it had been so long since he'd held her in his arms. An intense, physical aching strummed throughout his body.

"Somehow I do not find it reassuring to know my wife goes around kissing all manner of men."

"Be assured her ladyship has eyes for no one but you. Always, it's *Charles this, and Charles that. Poor Charles, he works too hard.* She's positively besotted over you. Lydia teases her all the time about her devotion to you."

My God, Haverstock thought, was she going to be exonerated yet again? Tonight he had determined to make her miserable for being so outrageous a flirt. But he was once more remorseful.

* * *

When her husband did not come home at the usual hour, Anna grew alarmed. She and her sisters dressed for the evening's fete, and still Haverstock did not show. Anna urged her sisters to go on without her. She could not leave until she knew if her husband was all right.

Dressed in a gown of golden and lavender threads, she paced her chamber, surprised she had not worn a hole in the floral carpeting in front of the window. Images of her husband injured or in pain knotted her stomach so tightly so thought she would cry.

At eleven o'clock and still no word from him, she threw on a cloak and left the house, making her way to the dimly lit mews. She entered through a creaking door and began to mount a rickety staircase, softly calling Jimmy's name.

The strapping lad met her on the stairway. "Is something amiss, me lady?" he asked, concern in his voice.

"Oh, yes. I am excessively worried about my husband," she said as she retraced her steps, with Jimmy following her. "He has not come home, nor sent word. I know something has happened to him," she said in a shaking voice.

"What can I do?"

"I would like you to make inquiries. You know where his friend Mr. Morgan lives?"

Jimmy nodded.

"And his lordship is a member of White's on St. James, though he seldom goes there." She closed her eyes and sighed. "If you find him, and he's all right, please protect him."

"Me word on it." He began to saddle a horse.

Anna returned to her lonely room, having sent her maid to bed hours earlier. She languidly removed her cloak and gown and slipped into a sleeping shift with no thought of sleep. She continued to nervously pace the floor, saying every prayer she had ever learned.

It was unlike Haverstock not to have sent word had something prevented him from coming home. Therefore, she grew convinced he had been injured. She became sick with fear. In spite of all the reasons she should dislike him, she could not. She had come to need him as she needed air to breathe. Whatever evil deeds he did, she would love him.

There. She had finally admitted it. *I love my husband.* Despite that he was a traitor.

Several hours later, she heard a light footfall along the hallway and ran to open the door.

"Oh, thank God," she whispered.

Haverstock came to stop in front of Anna's door. "For what are you thanking the good Lord for, my dear?" His eyes swept over Anna from her worried face to the tips of her toes.

"You are all right."

"Quite, and why may I ask was Jimmy waiting

outside White's?"

She thrust out her chin. "I sent him to look for you. I was excessively worried about you."

"You seem uncommonly close to the groom," Haverstock said with disapproval.

"He is loyal to you."

Haverstock reached to stroke her pale cheek. "And you?"

Tears glistened in her eyes. "You need ask?"

Drawn into the depths of her haunting eyes, Haverstock moved closer to Anna, backing her into the room and softly closing the door behind them. He gathered her into the circle of his arms and held her close. "I've been such a brute."

"No you ha-a-a-v" she began to protest. "Well, actually, you have. Could you not have sent round a note tonight?"

His hands stroked her back. "I fear you are shackled to rather a beast."

Anna lifted her head. "How can two people be shackled who are never alone with each other?" she said breathlessly.

"I plan to remedy that tonight, with my lady's permission," he said throatily.

In silent answer, she linked her arms around him and rested her face against his rock-solid chest.

"God in heaven, it's been too long," he uttered softly, drawing her even closer.

She smelled the brandy on his breath and knew by the odd glint in his eye and the unevenness of his words, he was in his cups. It was only the liquor that made him want her, but she did not care. She had yearned for weeks for the opportunity to feel his hands move possessively over her, to melt their bodies together in the most intimate blending and – more than anything – to show him the depths of this intensely physical love she held for him.

His lips came down on hers, softly at first, then nearly bruising from his frenzied hunger. Her own breath was as labored as his, her kisses wet and open. For weeks, she had planned this union and how she was going to abandon all modesty to tenderly offer herself as Charles's instrument of pleasure. But now that the craved meeting was occurring, she had no control over her body. His every touch rendered her subservient to her own betraying need. She could only moan, and tremble and arch against him in a numbing, mindless effort to be thoroughly possessed by her dark giant.

He lifted her, scooping her into his arms as he crossed her chamber and tenderly laid her on the bed. Leaving the candle glowing, he slowly and agonizingly removed her clothing until she lay before him naked, his breath catching as his eyes combed her ivory flesh.

Drawn by the simmering depths of his black eyes, Anna's unwavering gaze united with his as her deft hands reverently stroked the hardness between his legs. She was gladdened by the flicker of pleasure that passed over his face just before his head lowered to her breasts and took one into the warmth of his mouth.

Her hand slipped beneath his breeches so she could feel the length of him. He called out her name and freed himself of the clothes that separated their two willing bodies.

Lying beside her on the satin spread, he drew her into his flesh and held her close. "Oh, my Anna," he whispered breathlessly.

She loved the sound of his words. *My Anna.* If only she could truly belong to him. She lifted her lips to his. He kissed her thoroughly, his hands gliding over her and coming at last to her wet, burning core. She arched and trembled and thought she would go mad with this insatiable need. So much for her plan to seduce her husband. She knew not how long it was before he stretched himself over her and came into her fully, for one action was an extension of another, and all spiraled in an endless whirl of intoxicating pleasure in her foggy mind.

Even when their passion was spent, their wet, sated bodies intertwined and their hearts beat together as one.

Wrapped in each other's arms, they both fell into a deep slumber.

* * *

The sun was high in the sky, its warmth penetrating Anna's room when Haverstock awoke the next day. At first he did not remember where he was, but when the act of lifting his head brought great pain, he remembered the liquor. And much more. All his resolve to resist Anna had vanished like the winter snows in the face of her extraordinarily provocative presence. He shuddered even now remembering the feel of her writhing beneath him. For some inexorable reason, he thought of Morgie's words. With Anna he was *king of the mountain.* Oh, yes. No woman had ever made him feel as he did when he was with Anna. Not just king of the mountain. King of the world.

"Does your head feel as if it came in contact with a brick wall?" Anna asked with mirth.

He opened one eye and gazed at her, lying on

her stomach beside him, her dark hair falling to her milky shoulders. Despite his head, he could get started all over again, he thought, drinking in her loveliness. "It seems my wife has a keen understanding of the after effects of liquor."

"Shall I ring for a servant to bring you tisane?"

"Can't tolerate the stuff." He eased up to a half reclining position, his eyes still on Anna. "I wasn't too. . .forceful with you last night?"

She shook her head.

He sank back to a mound of pillows. "I do not think I will leave the house today."

"Glad I am of that," she said with fervor. "Your mother, too, desires your presence here with last-minute decisions about tonight."

He rolled across the satin spread and brought his arms around Anna. "And what preparations do you tend to today, my lady?"

"Your mother has spared me of all duties," she said, no hint of complaint in her voice.

His lips trailed along her face, the slender column of her neck and to her breasts. "Then you have time for wifely *duties*."

Her arms came around him. "I could be coerced," she whispered hungrily.

# $\mathcal{C}$hapter 15

While her husband and sisters helped sooth their mothers' demands of the servants, Anna and Colette slipped away for their daily trek to the East End. As they did each day, they walked to Piccadilly and hired a hack for the journey to White Chapel. Not only could the Haverstock crest announce their presence to any manner of criminals, but its presence in so undesirable a borough would likely insure the dowager's wrath, Anna thought.

Mindful of their safety, Anna had solicited Jimmy's protection for these afternoon trips. It was highly unlikely that their dependents in the East End would allow a hand to be brought against the former Miss de Mouchet and her French maid. Young and old, the bare-legged, bedraggled females flocked to Number 14 Highberry Street – the building Anna's solicitor had leased for the sewing school.

Anna and Colette had delighted in purchasing spools of every color thread, three dozen pair of scissors and bolts of muslins from the linen drapers. Mr. Wimple had arranged to have tables and chairs delivered, and in a very short time, the free school was filled to capacity, and a waiting list no had twelve names on it.

Though they stayed only two hours a day, the

time passed quickly, with Anna and Colette darting to and fro, instructing the eager learners in the rudimentary art of fine sewing.

In a very short time, Anna became especially attached to a young woman who was about her own age, though Sally already had two babes she brought with her each day. Sally was a quick learner with an even keener desire to secure a good job working for a dressmaker to fine ladies. Her stitches were neat and tiny, and she possessed a flair for matching color and pattern. She wore the same dress every day – one of Anna's castoffs – but Anna was pleased to note it was always clean.

"How long before I be good enough to earn me a livin' sewing, me lady?" she asked Anna.

"Though your progress is excellent," Anna said, "you must remember you will have to compete with those who have been sewing all their lives."

The thin blonde nodded knowingly. "How much do they make in a day?"

In truth, Anna had never given the matter a thought. What kind of daily wage did a seamstress make? "How much would you like to earn?" Anna asked.

"Enough to get me and me girls a nice little house with a garden."

"What about your husband?"

Sally colored. "I ain't got no husband."

"No one helps you provide for your babies?"

She shook her head. "I want them to have it better than I've had it."

Anna bent down and picked up the older of Sally's girls and held her close. She felt oddly jealous of the unfortunate Sally who possessed a world of wealth in her two lovely little girls.

But since lying with her husband last night, Anna felt less lonely. A flush of sweet fulfillment swept over her at the memory.

*　*　*

He'd be deuced glad when his mother's dinner was behind him, Haverstock thought as he directed his gig to Piccadilly. He only hoped they did not lose every single servant. Three had quit in tears this morning, and it was now his mission to secure some last-minute replacements at the agency.

Humming to himself and jostling the ribbons, he had to admit neither his abominable head nor the dowager's ill humor could diminish his good spirits today. An overwhelming tenderness washed over him at the thought of Anna. His lovely, wondrous, generous, loyal Anna. What a fool he had been to ever distrust her.

It was while he took his pleasure remembering the luxuriating feel of her beneath him that he thought he saw her from the corner of his eye. He turned to make sure and saw her, with Colette at her side, offering coins to a hackney driver.

Anger flushed his cheeks at what he saw next. Behind Anna and towering over her like a protective gargoyle was Jimmy.

When Anna was completely dressed that night, she dismissed Colette and waited for her husband to come escort her downstairs. She heard him speaking to his valet in the adjoining dressing room. Then she heard a door open and presumed Manors had left. But still, Haverstock did not come. After several minutes passed, she entered his dressing room. Her husband was not there.

She crossed that room and entered his sleeping

chamber. No one was there either. She glanced at the ormolu clock on his mantle. Guests would already be arriving. Surely he had not gone on without her. She waited five more minute – which seemed like an hour. Still, he did not come.

She returned to her room, opened the door to the hallway and heard a hum of voices from below. Fighting back tears of dejection, she squared her shoulders and glided downstairs.

Haverstock stood next to his mother in the receiving line. Swamped by the forlorn feeling of utter isolation, Anna fixed a smile on her face and regally strode to take her place at her husband's side.

"How lovely you look, my dear," he said coolly before introducing her to the guests at the head of the line, a Mr. and Mrs. Basil Fortesque.

After the Fortesques moved on, Anna found herself face-to-face with the prettiest woman she had ever seen. She was small and blond and fair with a filmy saffron dress.

"May I introduce you to my daughter-in-law, Lady Jane," the dowager said sweetly. "Anna this is Lady Jane Wyeth. I'm sure you've heard us speak of her."

The woman's name struck Anna like a fierce blow to the windpipe. She was the one the dowager had chosen to wed Charles. Anna trembled and could not find her voice, but somehow that ridiculous smile remained fixed on her face as she nodded at the gorgeous woman in yellow whose poise and assurance made Anna feel even more unworthy to be standing beside Charles as his marchioness.

Lady Jane dipped a graceful curtsey and offered Anna felicitations on her nuptials and compliments on her copper-colored gown.

Next, Anna was presented to Lady Jane's parents, the Earl and Countess of Langley, who gave every indication of doting upon their daughter.

After the 40 guests were seated at the huge dining table, Anna went cold when she saw Lady Jane at the opposite end of the table, to the right of Haverstock. No doubt, the dowager had placed Lady Jane there to underscore Anna's total inadequacy to be the Marchioness of Haverstock.

Dinner was interminable. Course after course and hour after hour, it went on. An ache in her stomach rid Anna of any appetite. She felt hot from all the candles, and started fanning herself. All that separated her from totally succumbing to a fit of embarrassing crying was the presence of Lydia on her right and Morgie on her left.

Early in the evening, Anna watched as Lydia gave a cold glance in the direction of Lady Jane.

"Lady Jane is very lovely," Anna said.

Lydia frowned. "She is exceedingly spoiled. Lord and Lady Langley lost three babes before she – their last – arrived. I fear they coddled her excessively. Her vocabulary is largely peppered with her two favorite words: *I* and *me*."

A gleam danced in Morgie's eyes. "What a devilishly wicked tongue you possess, Lady Lydia."

"I learned all my malicious ways from you," Lydia said. She returned her attention to Anna. "Of course, she is so lovely, I doubt the men ever listen to a word that issues from her beautiful face."

Every glance, every word that passed between her husband and Lady Jane sent tremors of fear and dejection through Anna. She could not help but recognize the fair lady of noble birth possessed the pedigree and confidence she herself lacked. And Anna felt more woefully inadequate than ever to be Charles's wife.

While a facade of carefully feigned civility cloaked Anna's agony, her sisters appeared in high spirits. Kate had arranged to have Mr. Reeves on her right and proceeded to dazzle the retiring man with her marked attentions. Cynthia, too, had persuaded her mother to seat Captain Smythe beside her, and the two spoke animatedly to one another.

Only Charlotte, with the rather handsome Mr. Churchdowne at her side, lacked gaiety. No doubt she pined for Mr. Hogart, whom her mother obviously found unworthy of an invitation.

After dinner, Anna sank into a seat at a whist table with Morgie and Lydia and found herself being introduced to Mr. Churchdowne, who would make a fourth at their table.

As she had throughout dinner, Anna once again found the man's clear blue eyes on her, and she felt uncomfortable. Lydia explained that Mr. Churchdowne had only this week come to town.

"I confess to having noticed you in the park with Mr. Morgan yesterday, Lady Haverstock," he said. "I was consumed with jealousy toward Mr. Morgan."

Shocked the man could speak thus to a married lady, Anna was at a loss for a reply.

He took the deck of cards in his long, slender hands and began to deal. "Might I hope to escort you one afternoon?"

"I am a married woman, Mr. Churchdowne. The reason my husband allows me to ride with

Mr. Morgan is that they are the dearest of friends, with Morgie being quite like one of the family." She gave a fake little laugh. "Also, my husband feels dreadfully guilty that he has no time for me."

"Your husband is an utter fool."

Anna attempted to treat his remark flippantly. "I beg you speak no ill of my husband. He is quite a dear."

Her husband's voice cut into Anna's circle. "How did you find dinner, my love?"

She looked up at Haverstock, handsome in his black silk coat and white knee breeches stretched across his muscled legs. "I am sure it was excellent."

"But you hardly touched your food, I noticed."

She was thankful he had noticed her at all. "I do not feel particularly well, Charles. I daresay I would retire early if this weren't my own house." The words stuck in her throat. This was not her house. She did not belong here. Nothing reinforced her unwelcomeness more than her exclusion from the receiving line tonight. Burned into her memory was the vision of her beaming mother-in-law standing proudly beside an amiable Charles, greeting their old friends.

The dowager cut into their conversation. "Oh, Charles, here you are. Some of the ladies are singing in the salon. I thought you could turn pages for Lady Jane while she plays the pianoforte."

"I should muddle it excessively if I tried," Haverstock said with finality, taking his leave from Anna but not going to the salon.

Somehow, Anna got through the night without embarrassing tears, but excused herself as soon as good manners permitted.

She allowed Colette to remove her gown and boast on how lovely she looked. "I peeked from the top of the third floor," Colette said. "No woman was a match for my Anna. You were most *joli* of all."

"Did you not see the lovely little blonde in yellow?" Anna asked.

"Very pretty," Colette said stiffly. "But her beauty, it paled next to that of you."

Anna held up her arms as Colette pulled the night gown over her head. "It is not a warm gown," Colette said, her eyes sparkling, "but with his lordship beside you, you will not be cold."

Colette knew every time Charles shared her bed, Anna thought. After the old abigail left, Anna climbed on the bed that only this morning swayed under their gentle lovemaking. What had gone so utterly wrong in so few hours? Anna wondered. What had she done to repulse him? These melancholy thoughts kept her from sleep. As time passed, she heard Charles in his dressing room and against all reason hoped profoundly he would come to her again.

Neither her desire for him nor her craving for sleep were to be realized.

# $\mathcal{C}$hapter 16

Still dressed in her riding habit, Lydia burst into Anna's room the following morning. "I was worried about you when you did not show up for your morning ride," she said, coming to sit at Anna's bedside. "Are you still unwell?"

Anna knew it was futile to be less than honest with her perceptive sister. "If you must know, I'm in rather low spirits. Did you not notice how Charles excluded me from the receiving line last night?"

Lydia nodded solemnly. "It was dreadfully inexcusable of him. It will never happen again. I've already spoken to him of it this morning, and he agrees it was thoroughly thoughtless of him. I don't know what has gotten into Charles lately. He's been his beastly old brooding self."

Anna sat up and flipped her hair from her face. "If you learn what troubles him, please share it with me."

Removing her riding hat and mindlessly twirling it in her hands, Lydia hesitated a moment, then said, "Speaking of sharing, would it be excessively rude of me to inquire where it is you and Colette go each afternoon?"

Anna leaned back into her pillows. "I suppose it does seem mysterious. Though it's not something I talk about, it's not anything I am ashamed of."

Anna told Lydia about her years of helping those in the East End and of the newly established sewing school. Lydia nodded knowingly when Anna disclosed that she chose not to take the Haverstock barouche on these forays.

When Anna finished, Lydia exclaimed, "What a delightful scheme! I would love to make whatever insignificant contribution I could at your school. Would you and Colette mind if I forced my company on you?"

"We would gratefully welcome the help."

* * *

His eyes strained and his hands ached from decoding messages from the Peninsula, but Haverstock still managed a fleeting rush of pride. The information he received from Monsieur Herbert had contributed to the French defeat at Salamanca. Haverstock had been very careful to personally dispatch the information himself to keep it from others in the London office.

This afternoon he would meet Pierre at their new meeting place. Poor Pierre suffered under the delusion that France would once again be what it was before the revolution. Before Pierre's wife and children had been slaughtered. To this end, he risked his life countless times on clandestine missions to France in the cause of Britannia. Because he still had friends in positions of importance, Pierre had been able to provide Haverstock with invaluable information. All for a few guineas and the satisfaction of knowing he hastened bringing peace to his native soil.

Haverstock, too, would do anything in his power to bring this devastating war to an end. For his own self, it could not be too soon to get his brother back in England. Every time he heard of casualties in the Light, his stomach did an odd flip, and he worried about James. God, but it would be good to see his little brother again.

He wondered what James would think of Anna. Of course, being a connoisseur of beauty, he would love her. And how would she feel toward him? Would she kiss him and flirt with him? He did not like to think of it.

At least she had not flirted with that insufferable Harry Churchdowne last night. How Haverstock longed to get in the ring with him at Jackson's. The man did not even have the decency to avert his gaze from Anna all night. Morgie had told Haverstock that Churchdowne had the audacity to ask Anna to ride with him in the park.

Now that he was thinking on it, Haverstock was not as receptive to her riding with Morgie as he once had been. And he really didn't like the idea of her kissing Morgie, either. Morgie was one of the juiciest prizes on the marriage mart. He was tolerably good looking, extremely well dressed, fun to be with and in possession of a vast fortune. Then, Haverstock remembered Anna knew Morgie before she knew him. And it was not Morgie she desired as a husband. She desired him. She had not sought to be his wife for love. Quite the opposite, he painfully reminded himself.

His breath caught. Did she still hate him? Had she feigned concern for him only to secretly go about wreaking havoc on his life? He thought back to all the times she had seemed so genuinely concerned over him. Especially two nights ago. He could still see her ashen face as she opened her chamber door and thanked God he was all right. He could almost feel her trembling beneath him as she gave him the greatest sexual pleasure he had ever experienced.

Was all that an act to conceal her lewd ways? She had willingly gone alone to Lord Wentworth's library with Sir Henry Vinson. She had gone alone to the stables where she had been rather intimate with Jimmy. And she and Jimmy had obviously gone off together in a rented hack. Why would the Marchioness of Haverstock, who had half a dozen conveyances at her disposal, rent a cab unless she was concealing her destination?

He put his head in his hands. He was better off before his marriage. He might not have been happy then, but he certainly was not happy now. That cursed wife of his was a constant source of consternation. Why just this morning he had to fight against his urge to check on Anna. When she did not show up for their morning ride he remembered she had not felt well the night before. Throughout the entire ride he worried foolishly about her.

That was the problem with a wife. Good or bad, they belonged to you. You had to take care of them. To care for them. And despite all the reasons why he should not care for Anna, he still cared for her and wanted to protect her. For her, he had said terrible things to his own mother.

Would that he had never laid eyes on Anna.

* * *

"Really, Lydia, your brother would be shocked if he knew you discussed such things with a man," Anna chided as they rode through Hyde Park in Morgie's curricle that afternoon. Lydia and Morgie had made a wager concerning the probability that Lady Rand, who was very much married, would meet with John Hancombe, her lover, in the park that afternoon.

"Morgie doesn't count as a man," Lydia said.

"Don't know that I like your line of reasoning, Lyddie," Morgie said.

A broad smile crossed Lydia's plain face. "I didn't mean it the way it sounded. What I meant is that you're like a brother, not a man with whom I have to act properly."

"Nice to know ladies don't have to act properly when I'm around," Morgie said mischievously.

"The fact is," Lydia continued, unflapped by his remark, "you're better than a brother. Charles has been an absolute ogre lately."

"I will accept that as a compliment, even if it is at the expense of my best friend."

"You must allow, Lydia," Anna said, "Charles is very tolerant of your wagering on horses even though it is not a ladylike pursuit."

"As well he should, since he led her down that unladylike road himself!" Morgie defended, nodding to an acquaintance who passed by.

"I have no complaint in Charles's treatment of me," Lydia said. "I could hope for him to be more amiable at home and to not stay away so much. When he's home, he's cross and tired and acts as if the weight of the world is on his shoulders."

"That he does," Anna lamented.

With smiling faces and a profusion of waves, they drove past Cynthia and Captain Smythe. When Captain Symthe's phaeton was well past them, Lydia turned to Morgie. "Has the expected union between my sister and Captain Smythe made it into the betting book at White's yet?"

"Indeed it has," he said, calmly reining in.

"Oh, please enter a wager for me, Morgie," Lydia said.

"'Pon my word, Lyddie, even your brother would draw the line at that."

She pouted. "But I know, as a gentleman, you will not disappoint me, Morgie."

"Very well, Lyddie. What bet do you wish me to place?"

"That Captain Smythe will make his offer by the end of the fortnight."

"It would not surprise me if Mr. Reeves did not offer for Kate by that time also," Anna said.

"Now I draw the line at betting for a marchioness," Morgie said. "Haverstock wouldn't like that one bit."

"I assure you, Morgie, I have no desire to wager."

Lydia's eyes narrowed. "I cannot like that match one bit. Kate positively detested the man two seasons ago, and now because she believes he will be duke, she welcomes his address with enthusiasm. It would serve her right if old Blassingame took a young wife and sired sons."

Anna refrained from commenting, though her thoughts matched Lydia's.

"Morgie," Lydia exclaimed, "you'll never guess where Anna and I were this afternoon."

"Let me think. Was it Bedlam?"

"No!" Lydia said with feigned irritation.

"Am I to enumerate all the sites in London, or do you enlighten me?"

"I shall enlighten. We went to Anna's sewing school in the East End."

"In the East End?" he queried, his gaze leaping to Lydia.

She nodded.

"On what street, pray tell?"

"Oh, a most unfashionable street, to be sure,"

Lydia answered.

"Whatever are you talking about? A sewing school?"

"Yes. Anna has founded a school to teach sewing skills to the unfortunate so that they can seek employment. She and her maid give instruction there every afternoon. They allowed me to come today, and I enjoyed it excessively. I found that I was able to make a small contribution, and it was most rewarding."

He pulled rein and shifted his gaze to Anna. "What does Haverstock have to say about this?"

"He doesn't know."

"She's not hiding it from him," Lydia added.

"Oh, no," Anna said. "I would tell him all about it if he were interested. It's just that we are seldom alone together to share a conversation."

"Well, I can tell you he would not at all countenance you two going to that part of town unescorted."

"Oh, but my groom comes along to keep a watch out for our safety."

He frowned. "I can't say that I like it – nor would Haverstock."

Lydia's eyes narrowed. "Well, we are not going to stop!"

"Then, I'll have to accompany you."

As they left the park, Lydia spotted Lady Rand's carriage heading down a little used path. And behind her, John Hancombe followed in his gig. "You owe me a crown," Lydia happily announced to Morgie.

* * *

Jimmy stood post outside the Whitehall building that lodged the Foreign Office. Day after day he had stood in watch for his master, but his lordship never left the building before dusk. On this day, however, Jimmy's heart quickened in anticipation when he saw his master skip down the marble steps just before two in the afternoon. He watched as Haverstock waited for his gig to be brought around, then Jimmy mounted his own horse and began to follow.

A hackney coach rounded the corner, cramming between Jimmy and the gig to obstruct his view of Haverstock. With a spurt of speed, Jimmy passed the coach just in time to see Haverstock turn onto Charing Cross. Holding back fifty yards, Jimmy also veered onto the busy Charing Cross, and within minutes followed his master when he turned onto The Strand, which was thick with pedestrians and every sort of conveyance. Before long, Haverstock pulled up in front of St. Clement Danes Church.

Unconsciously reciting a snatch of the nursery rhyme *Oranges Lemons say the bells of St. Clemens*, Jimmy watched as Haverstock tied up his gig and entered the church. Jimmy tied his horse around the corner and went back to the church's entrance, where he gently eased open one of its massive doors and slipped into the vestibule. Walking like a cat on soft paws, he edged toward the front of the vestibule and saw Haverstock sitting in a pew at the front of the darkened church where he was the only occupant.

A moment later, Jimmy heard the door squeak open and he darted into the shadows. A short, swarthy looking man who dressed like a gentleman strode down the center aisle of the church and sat next to Haverstock. They talked for a few minutes.

While they were talking, Jimmy quietly slipped from the church. He saw a black gelding tied up next to Haverstock's rig. Rounding the corner, he untied and mounted his horse and waited for the swarthy man to mount the black gelding.

A few minutes later, the man came out of the church and took off on the black horse, with Jimmy following at a discreet distance. The man rode to Billingsgate where he purchased fish. From there he rode through the bustling city, avoiding as many toll gates as he could, much to Jimmy's satisfaction.

After an hour, the man left his mount at a livery stable near Russell Square. Jimmy held back and watched as the man walked from the stable to a slender house in Bloomsbury. Number twenty-three.

# $\mathcal{C}$hapter 17

After Anna and Charlotte had walked through Green Park, Jimmy awaited at the foot of the steps to Haverstock House, begging a private word with Anna.

She watched Charlotte mount the steps before turning her attention to Jimmy. "Is his lordship all right?"

"Yes, me lady," he answered. "It is just that I followed him from that building in Whitehall, and he met with a man under what seems to me very suspicious circumstances."

Anna walked some distance away from the footmen, Jimmy at her side.

Jimmy told Anna of the secretive meeting at St. Clements and proudly announced that he followed the man to his lodgings at Number twenty-three Tavistock Place in Bloomsbury.

"What did the man look like?" Anna asked.

"'Bout forty years old. He was of dark complexion and medium size. Dressed like a gentleman but was not flush with money, if ye know what I mean. Made a big effort to avoid paying tolls."

Anna nodded and thanked Jimmy before returning to the house. She would finally have something to report to Sir Henry when she met with him the following day.

* * *

Instead of coming straight home that night, Haverstock chose to go to White's where he had the good fortune to meet Morgie.

The two men sat alone at a table and proceeded to consume a large quantity of port. Haverstock kept a watch over Harry Churchdowne, who sat with a group of young bloods on the other side of the room. "You would think with as many women who set their caps at him, the insufferable man would not have to dance attendance on married women," Haverstock said.

"What if the lady's husband has no desire for her company?" Morgie challenged.

Haverstock met his friend's quizzing gaze. "You have it all wrong, my dear fellow. I have a very great desire for my wife's company even if she vexes me to death."

"Strange way you have of showing it."

"I get so blasted angry with her. Do you know what she has done now?"

"Enlighten me."

"She and that maid of hers have been going off with that same old groom in a rented hack! I ask you, why would the Marchioness of Haverstock be renting a hack if she didn't have something to hide?"

"Have you asked her?"

"Course not. Can't let her think I've been spying on her."

"Nor can you let her know you care. Heaven forbid a man should care about his wife."

"Now, Morgie, blast it all! You make me sound like the one who needs to apologize."

"I believe you *are*, old chap. I do, in fact, know

why your wife rented a hack, and I assure you it was all perfectly innocent."

"Enlighten me, if you please."

Morgie shook his head. "I believe you and her ladyship need to talk. Ask her yourself."

Haverstock stiffened as he saw Churchdowne rise and walk toward him. "I will bloody well strike a blow to the man if he tells me one more time how fortunate I am to have wed Anna before the *ton* discovered her," he whispered to Morgie.

"Fancy finding you here, Haverstock, when I saw your wife not half an hour ago."

Haverstock raised a single brow.

"Yes, I had the good fortune to speak with Lady Haverstock at the entrance to Green Park. She was quite alone though she insisted she was meeting Lady Charlotte there. A pity. Were such a beautiful woman my wife, I would never let her out of my sight."

"I suppose you offered your services as her escort," Haverstock said.

"Yes, indeed, but she refused me again. You may be assured when the novelty of her marriage wears off, I will be first in line for her favors, Haverstock."

Haverstock leapt to his feet and crashed his fist into the smaller man's jaw, knocking Churchdowne to the floor. He was ready to assault the man again when Morgie restrained him and led him from the club.

* * *

When Haverstock arrived home, he found Mr. Reeves waiting for him.

"Ah, my lord, I beg a private word with you."

Haverstock, knowing very well what Reeves had come for, led the man to his library and offered him a chair near his desk. The man was a good ten years his senior, and Haverstock did not at all warm to the idea of having him for a brother-in-law. Especially since Kate herself had spurned him two seasons previously. He ran his eyes over Reeves. Though Haverstock was certainly no judge of what was considered handsome, he knew that no maiden could be attracted to this man who sat nervously before him. A circle of fat hung under his chin and on his waist, where one of the buttons of his waistcoat popped open. His coat, too, was much too tight. Had he gained so much weight of late or did he insist he was the same size he was decade earlier?

"You may have noticed my partiality toward Lady Kate," Reeves began.

Haverstock nodded.

"I have come to ask your permission to pay her my addresses."

"Have you spoken with her yet?"

"No, my lord, though I daresay she is aware of the constancy of my affection. I felt it proper to speak to you first. I am not a wealthy man, but I have grand prospects since I am the heir to my uncle, the Duke of Blassingame."

Was that all the poor man had to recommend him? "You most certainly have my permission to court Kate, but I cannot speak for her. If she welcomes your suit, you have my blessing."

A smile crossed Reeve's perspiring face.

"Glass of port?"

Reeves thankfully accepted.

* * *

When Reeves left, Haverstock hastened up the stairs and knocked on the door to Anna's chamber.

Her sore feet soaking in a pail of hot water when her husband entered her room, Anna looked up and smiled at him.

"I see your feet are no better than they were on the way home last night," he said.

"Oh, they do not hurt nearly as much," she said, removing them from the water and toweling them dry as she dismissed Colette.

"Did you speak with Mr. Reeves?" She walked barefoot to the settee and beckoned for him to join her.

"Did everyone in the house know of his call?"

"Of course."

"And, pray tell, what was my answer to be?"

"Kate said you would be delighted to have her a future duchess."

"And you?" he asked.

"I said you would tell the man you would abide by your sister's choice."

He lifted her hand and kissed it. "It seems my wife knows me better than my sister."

"I do not think she will be happy with the man, Charles."

"Nor do I, but it is a scheme of her own making."

She smelled the liquor on him, and knew it had loosened the rigidness that so often kept him from her. "Did you go to White's?"

"Yes. I met Morgie there."

"You seem more relaxed. While other wives complain about their husbands frequenting their clubs, I must welcome it if it brings you more often in my company."

He seemed unable to remove his eyes from her. "Where did you go in a hackney carriage?"

"How did you know about that?" she asked.

"I saw you paying the driver the day of Mother's dinner. You were with Colette and Jimmy."

Her mind spun. The day of the dinner. That night he had treated her so abominably! Could the two events be related? Why would he be so angry about her going somewhere with Colette and her groom unless he thought she had something wicked to hide? She burst out laughing. "Oh, Charles, why did you not speak to me? I have nothing to hide from you."

"I'm speaking now."

"All of my life I have done charity work in the East End. I do not like to take the Haverstock vehicles there for fear of attracting the attention of thieves – or worse. I did take Jimmy along for protection."

"What kind of charity work do you perform?"

"For years, I just took clothes I no longer needed, some food and coins. Recently, Colette and I started a sewing school so some of the women can learn a skill to seek employment. Lydia is now serving as one of the instructors."

"While I commend your intentions, I do not at all like you going there without more protection."

"You sound exactly like Morgie."

"He knows?"

"He found out just this week. He insisted on providing escort today, though my feet were too sore for me to go. I understand from Lydia he provided an impressive escort." She thought this would please her husband, but anger flashed in his eyes.

"Morgie has no business taking care of my wife and sister when I am perfectly capable of doing so. It displeases me that you hide these things from me, Anna."

"I have hidden nothing," she snapped. "It is difficult to talk with one's husband when the two are *never* together. And that is not my fault, either."

A slow smile curved his lip, and Anna found her own anger melting.

He drew her to him and whispered, "I do not think you should go out tonight, Lady Haverstock. Your feet are much too sore. I have plans that will not require you to be on your feet."

# $\mathcal{C}$hapter 18

For once Anna arrived at Hookam's before Sir Henry. She did not dare go straight to the Latin section for fear of attracting attention. What manner of woman would have knowledge of such? Even though there would be no privacy there, she walked to the corner which featured a rather large selection of poetry books. Her mood was so bleak she was drawn to morose verses. She swept past women reading Blake and men perusing Wordsworth, picked out a dust-covered volume of Donne and took it to another corner where a half dozen wooden chairs composed a makeshift reading room. No one else was there. She sat down, held her book with trembling hands and tried to read.

She had been unable to sleep the night before though Charles lay contentedly asleep at her side, an event that should have brought her great satisfaction. But the happiness was marred by the impending meeting with Sir Henry. The information she would pass to him could brand her husband a traitor. She wondered if a British peer could hang for treason. The thought horrified her. She would rather die.

She watched Sir Henry enter the shop. He saw her immediately but gave no sign of recognition. He quickly found a very large book and brought it to read in the chair next to Anna's.

Anna held her book and ran her eyes from left to right, whispering to Sir Henry as if she were reading a poem. "I have learned something, but before I share it with you, I must have your promise no harm will come to my husband." Why was it, she wondered, she was the one who felt like a traitor?

After a minute, Sir Henry held his opened book almost in front of his face and spoke. "Why would we harm someone as valuable as Haverstock? He will lead us to bigger fish across the channel."

"I believe I have a fish for you," Anna whispered. "Number twenty-three Tavistock Place. Bloomsbury."

"His name?"

She shrugged.

"What does he look like?"

"Small. Well dressed. Dark hair and skin. About forty years old."

"Your husband has met with him?"

"Secretly," she whispered.

A smile played at his thin lips as he got to his feet and left, leaving the book on his chair.

*  *  *

Mr. Reeves – now happily betrothed to Kate – stood near the marble mantle beaming at the morning callers who gathered in the parlor of Haverstock House. Anna detected a new proprietorial air about him in these surroundings. He acted as if *he* were welcoming the visitors.

"How very agreeable it is to see you today," he told Mr. Simpson, who danced attendance on Charlotte.

"Does Captain Smythe come today?" Anna asked Cynthia as she prepared the tea.

"I am sure I do not know," Cynthia answered with irritation before turning to Mr. Simpson and flirting.

Cynthia's normally sunny disposition had taken a decided turn for the worse since Kate had announced her engagement. Everyone at Haverstock House had expected that Captain Smythe would offer for Cynthia before Mr. Reeves entered into contracts for Kate. But still the captain had not discussed marriage.

Davis entered the room and announced Lady Langley with her daughter Lady Jane Wyeth. The two well dressed ladies glided into the room with unwavering smiles and courtly addresses. On this summer day Lady Jane wore a soft muslin dress the same blue as her eyes. It displayed to advantage her perfect figure and lovely skin. Anna felt pangs of jealousy. Had Charles possessed even the smallest fortune, he most likely would have married Lady Jane long ago, Anna surmised. She wondered if he regretted not marrying the petite blond.

Lady Jane, who sat in a chair near the sofa where Anna presided, glanced at Anna's pink dress. "How lovely you look, Lady Haverstock. Simply everyone in London talks of your exquisite taste in clothing. I must know who your modiste is."

Anna handed Lady Jane a cup and saucer. "I have never used anyone but Madam Devreaux."

"Of course!" Lady Jane exclaimed. "I should have known. The French are so clever with fashion. It stands to reason you being French would naturally select a French dressmaker."

"I really don't consider myself French," Anna said, holding back her annoyance. "I was born in

London, spent my entire life here, and though my mother was French, my father was thoroughly English."

Lady Jane tilted her head slightly, raising her brows. "Really? But was your name not de Mouchet?"

The room became suddenly lifeless before Lydia interjected, "Tell us, Kate, when do you plan to marry Mr. Reeves."

Anna was grateful for Lydia's intervention. Though she had lived every day of her life with the stigma of being illegitimate, she did not care to hold herself up to ridicule in her own drawing room. And she would never forgive Lady Jane for being so rude. Of course the woman – as indeed all of London – knew of Anna's background.

"We thought to marry at the end of the season here in London," Kate said, casting a sweet smile at Mr. Reeves.

"So much more convenient for all our family and friends than travelling to Haymore," Mr. Reeves said. "My uncle, the Duke of Blassingame, is in town, you know."

"Yes, we have had the good fortune to meet him," Lady Langley said.

Evans announced Mr. Hogart, and the room became lifeless again.

He entered, still wearing his ill-fitting black garments which Anna no longer noticed. She noted his freshly combed very blond hair and the look of sincerity on his angelic face and heartily welcomed him, scooting over and making room for him next to her on the sofa.

"Mr. Hogart studies to be a minister," Anna said as she prepared his tea. "Tell us, Mr. Hogart, are your beliefs centered more around God and the hereafter or on loving thy neighbor, thus entering the kingdom of heaven through good works?"

"Both actually," he said with animation. "Though I confess to being more earnest about the here and now and doing what I can for others in the here and now."

Charlotte fairly glowed with admiration. "I am given to understand he has helped all manner of wretched persons."

"My sister, Lady Haverstock, also directs much of her attention to helping the less fortunate," Lydia said.

Anna cast a disapproving glance at Lydia. "It is not something I speak of."

"How delightful!" Lady Jane said. "I did not know you were a Methodist."

"One does not have to be Methodist to help others," Anna said, giving Lady Jane a cold stare.

"Like her husband, Anna is Anglican," Lydia said.

Davis announced Mr. Harry Churchdowne, who strode into the room all elegance and good manners.

Anna was not pleased that he had come. She always felt terribly uncomfortable in his presence.

Mr. Reeves took it upon himself to greet the newcomer. "I say Churchdowne, bit of a surprise to see you here after the incident at White's and all."

Churchdowne gazed around the room. "Haverstock's not here?"

"Oh no, my good man, Lord Haverstock is seldom home at this hour," Mr. Reeves said.

"I had hoped to apologize to him for something I said at White's the other night."

"I will convey that to my husband," Anna offered. She had heard nothing of an incident at White's.

Churchdowne walked toward her, his eyes never leaving hers. "I beg that you don't, since you were the subject of our discussion."

The life was once again sucked from the room. Anna wondered if all the people in the room held their breath. Never had she felt more uncomfortable. What on earth could her husband and this man be discussing at White's that would concern her?

Before she could be forced to respond, Evans opened the door and announced Captain Smythe, who entered the room with jaunty grace. He swept into a bow before Anna, greeted her, then turned to Cynthia. "Lady Cynthia, you will be pleased to learn I bring a letter from your brother James."

Cynthia gave a cry of delight, then turned hopeful eyes to her elder sister.

Lydia took the letter from Captain Smythe and read it silently, tears springing to her eyes. When she finished she told those gathered about her brother's experiences at the Battle of Salmanca, and talk of the war occupied the remainder of the time.

* * *

It was a cool evening. Sir Henry wore a light coat and beaver hat as he stood beside a half dozen iron balustraded steps to a dark house on Tavistock Place. His eyes never left a slender red brick house across the street and down five houses: Number Twenty-Three. From his inquiries, Sir Henry had learned that Pierre Chassay, a once well-to-do Frenchman, occupied Number Twenty Three. Further inquiries with his friends in France netted Sir Henry the offer of ten-thousand pounds to silence the little Frenchman.

Never having earned his money by performing such a deed, Sir Henry had given the matter considerable thought before executing his plan. He did not give serious thought to the matter of accepting the offer. There was nothing he would not do for money. But having accepted, his thoughts now focused on how to perform the deed and get away with it.

The door to Number Twenty Three opened, and a short, dark-haired man emerged. He walked down the darkened sidewalk to the other end of the block from where Sir Henry stood.

Sir Henry pulled his hat down further on his forehead and set about following Monsieur Chassay. When the small man rounded the next corner, Sir Henry's long legs took broad strides to catch up. He barely turned the corner when he saw the Frenchman enter The Boar and Barrel public house.

From within the pub Sir Henry heard the raised voices of men happily whiling away an evening. Sir Henry would be careful not to come in on Monsieur Chassay's well-dressed heels. Standing in shadows a few doors down, he watched a number of modestly dressed men enter the establishment. After ten minutes, he entered. He had an immediate sense of Monsieur Chassay's presence without having to move his head in the Frenchman's direction. Sir Henry had known the Frenchman would be alone, standing by the bar and quietly observing those around him. Since Chassay was on the left side of the bar, Sir Henry went to the right. Not removing his hat, he ordered ale and drank it slowly, keeping his quarry within his sight.

Before long, Monsieur Chassay ordered more ale. He talked with no one save the employees of The Boar and Barrel.

Sir Henry nursed his drink to keep his mind clear and sharp.

In all, Monsieur Chassay drank four bumpers before donning his hat and coat and leaving.

Sir Henry set after him immediately. The street was empty at this late hour. Though his prey was just a few yards ahead, Sir Henry could barely see him for the fog which appeared to rise from the sidewalks. He hastened his step and soon came abreast of the Frenchman. Trying to sound inebriated, he said, "I say, lost my way around here. Could you direct me to Russell Square?"

Monsieur Chassay looked up kindly at the tall man whose hat was pulled all the way down to the tops of his eyebrows. He moved his shoulder and head in the direction of the square, then faced Sir Henry and gave directions in a thick French accent. Sir Henry moved closer, his hand in his pocket. Chassay's glance darted to the bulge in the Englishman's coat, fear flashing in his eyes.

In one swift move, Sir Henry withdrew his stiletto and thrust it into Chassay's heart. The Frenchman gasped, his hand grabbing Sir Henry's wrist. But his strength, like his blood, oozed from his body. His hand fell. His eyes went cold. And he slumped forward, groaning. The knife embedded in him, his blood spewing on his killer's hand.

Sir Henry put an arm around the smaller man and dragged him to the steps of the nearest house and released him.

The body of Pierre Chassay crumbled to the cold sidewalk, his blood pooling about him, the knife still protruding from his lower chest.

Sir Henry removed his own blood-stained gloves and put them in his pocket as he hurried away.

\* \* \*

Anna could scarcely believe her good fortune. Two nights in a row she would be able to enjoy a quiet evening at home with her husband. Three months ago she would never have believed she could be so bored by society and so desirous of solitude. Though being with Charles was hardly solitude. She watched him as he leaned back into the comfort of her settee and stretched his long legs in front of him. A lump came to her throat. To think that three months ago she did know of his existence. And now he occupied her thoughts every hour of the day and invaded her dreams at night.

May I hope that your feet are better tonight, Lady Haverstock?"

"Oh, yes indeed. I entertained a large number of morning callers today and still conducted the sewing lessons in the East End." She came to sit beside him.

His hand covered hers and gave it a squeeze. "I suppose Morgie provided escort."

She nodded. "You should never have need to worry over the safety of Lydia or me for Morgie absolutely smothers us with protectors." She noted a stray lock of black hair on his forehead and brushed it away. "I believe all his concern is for Lydia. They are as comfortable together as hand in glove."

"She's always been like a sister to him. They

practically grew up together, you know."

"Don't I! They are forever reminiscing about things they did as children at Haymore."

"Was Morgie one of the morning callers?"

"No, but Kate's intended and Cynthia and Charlotte's objects of affection were in attendance."

He stroked his chin. "Let me see, Captain Smythe was paying court to Cynthia. Who, pray tell, has Charlotte singled out?"

"Who is the only man she has ever spoken favorably of to you?"

"Surely you do not expect me to remember all the men who have stood up with my sisters these past weeks."

"Now, think on it, Charles."

"The shabbily dressed Methodist?"

She nodded.

"But he hasn't been around of late."

"I think not by choice. He seems excessively fond of Charlotte."

"You have talked with him?"

She nodded again. "He's very serious, very kind and, I believe, very much in love with Charlotte. I've made inquiries and learned he is of good family though he cut himself off some time ago because they did not support his decision to enter the church."

"A man of principle, then?"

She kissed his cheek. "I knew you would judge the inner man, not the outer."

"Far be it from me to be taken in by beauty," he said, smiling as his eyes appreciatively traveled her face and down the length of her.

"Were there other callers?"

"Oh, Mr. Simpson, who is smitten with

Charlotte. Lady Langley and her daughter and Mr. Churchdowne."

Her husband stiffened at Churchdowne's name. "Would that I had been here to *properly* dispatch the scheming Churchdowne," he said angrily.

"Actually, he said he was calling to apologize to you."

Haverstock's brows lifted. "Did he say what he was apologizing for?"

"Only that it concerned me. I felt so excessively uncomfortable, I did not wish to pursue the matter, but now I expect a full explanation from you."

"I struck the man."

"Oh, Charles, surely not at White's?"

He nodded.

"Had he. . .alluded to my parentage?"

Her husband nodded solemnly.

She swallowed, avoiding the scrutiny of his all-seeing eyes. "Oh, I almost forgot!" she said. "You've a letter from James." She walked to her desk and brought him the envelop.

He couldn't open it fast enough. As he read, his eyes moistened. He read it slowly once then reread it. When he finished he sighed and looked into Anna's eyes with a softness she had never seen there before. "We've been spared once again."

Until this moment Anna had never realized the depth of her husband's attachment to his younger brother. How could one brother daily jeopardize his life for his country while the other betrayed his country, thus betraying his brother? Oh, she did not at all understand this man she was in love with.

"May I read it?" she asked.

He handed her the letter.

James gave a brief but modest account of his role at Salmanca and with sadness told of the men he had lost at Badajos.

He inscribed a personal note to each member of his family. To his mother, he begged that she not worry about him and hoped she would be up attending balls with her beautiful daughters. To Lydia he wrote, "Oblige me by exercising Sultanna for me when you are at Haymore. I can trust you to give her a good romp." Not knowing about Charles's marriage, he reminded his brother that he was not getting any younger. "It is past time for you to chose your marchioness, you know," he wrote. "With your good looks and title, any beauty in London would be glad to have you – even with no fortune." Without having heard about Mr. Reeves, he kidded Kate that he fully expected her to be a duchess by the time he returned. He told Cynthia he hoped to be home in time to see her marry the man of her dreams, and he warned Charlotte against bringing home any more stray kittens.

Reading his letter brought James to life for Anna. She stiffened as she gazed at her husband and thought of his treasonous deeds. Wordlessly, she handed the letter back.

"I don't think my mind is ever free from worry over him," Haverstock said. "And since our marriage I've wondered countless times what he would think of you. How you would like him."

She realized the reason he did not look at her was because he spoke of deeply personal feelings. He even admitted that she occupied his thoughts a great number of times. The admission was something the oh-so-formal marquess never did.

And it one again made him dear to her. This time it was she who covered his big hand with her own slender one.

But it was her husband who initiated the intense lovemaking that followed.

$\mathcal{C}$hapter 19

She had enjoyed this morning's ride, Anna reflected as she reached for a hot scone. Charles and Lydia had invited her to race them, and although she did not catch up to the superior riders, she had managed to exhaust her thoroughly lathered mare and work up a decidedly healthy appetite herself. After washing and changing clothes and allowing Colette to repair the damage to her hair, she faced her husband across the breakfast table.

He appeared engrossed in perusing the *Morning Gazette*.

"Does you lordship find my appearance more tolerable than when you last saw me?" Anna asked.

The corner of his mouth lifted to a crooked smile. "I find your appearance last night the most agreeable of all. I like your body bare and your hair down."

Anna colored and glanced about the room to assure herself they were alone. "A Godiva fetish, I daresay."

The skin around Haverstock's eyes crinkled from his broad smile.

"Any news from the Peninsula?" she asked.

"Articles, yes. News, no," he answered, his glance skipping over the headlines.

In a matter of seconds, his mirth vanished. He stiffened and cried out, frightening Anna.

Her first thought was that something terrible had happened to James. She sprang from her chair and rushed to his side.

"What is it?" she asked. "Is it James?"

He ignored her, his eyes racing over the small print. She followed his gaze and saw that he read an account of a vicious murder in Bloomsbury.

When he finished reading, he flung the paper aside. "No, it's not James. A friend of mine has been murdered."

"How dreadful," she said, gently stroking his shoulder. "Who was it?"

"Pierre Chassay. A true friend to England – as well as to his native France."

"Does he have a wife and children?"

"No. They, too, were murdered. In the Terror."

Anna sank in a chair beside her husband in order to read for herself about the unfortunate Mr. Chassay. "Poor man. How was he murdered?"

"A dagger to the heart."

Anna winced.

Haverstock pushed his food away, got to his feet and curtly took his leave.

Anna picked up the paper and began to read the account of the murder. Her heart nearly stopped when she saw where the "deceased victim of this most heinous crime" resided.

He had lived at Number Twenty-three Tavistock Place.

The swarthy little man!

Her pulse drumming, she read on. The owner of the Boar and Barrel related that the little Frenchman came to his establishment every night. Though he was quiet, Mr. Chassay was well liked by everyone. "The gent couldn't of 'ad an enemy in the world," Mr. John Moore said. Mr. Moore went on to say there had been a suspicious man in his establishment the same night as the murder. The man kept his hat on the whole time he imbibed at Mr. Moore's, and he left as soon as Mr. Chassay did, although they sat on opposite sides of the pub and did not appear to be acquainted.

Mr. Moore described the suspicious man as speaking like a gentleman. He was tall and thin.

Had she driven the dagger into Mr. Chassay herself, Anna could not have felt more responsible for his death.

* * *

Haverstock had gone straight to his office and torn through the files. Just as he had known, there was no file on Pierre Chassay. Haverstock had taken care to protect the identity of those who supplied him with information. No one had known of Pierre except for Monsieur Hebert, and those two were life-long friends who would never betray one another.

From behind his broad walnut desk, Haverstock gazed out the window at the passing carts below, their drivers carrying hay and milk and coal throughout the hurried capital. His hollow insides churning, Haverstock keenly felt the demise of the little Frenchman, the patriot who had no one else to mourn him. He pictured Pierre proudly wearing his worn black coat of excellent cut and fabric every time the two men met. Haverstock remembered the wistful expression on Pierre's face when he spoke of restoring France to days of dazzling glory after the mad Corsican was annihilated.

Though he had died far from his native shores, Pierre would be buried in France, Haverstock vowed. And when the unspeakable horrors of this war were behind them, Haverstock would see to it that Pierre receive recognition from the country for which he gave his life as truly as a soldier on the battlefield.

He also vowed Pierre's death would not be in vain. If he had to die doing it, he would find the murderer and save England from his vile clutches.

He continued to stare out the window at the evidence of man's indifference to the life of one immigrant. Life went on though Pierre lay cold. The lad continued to hawk his newspapers, the old woman her posies. The hackney driver raced along with his fare.

As surely as he knew his name, Haverstock knew Pierre had been killed because of him. Someone had learned of their meetings. Someone knew that Pierre passed along valuable information about the French. But how?

God in heaven! Haverstock thought, a stabbing jolt to his already unsettled stomach, someone must have followed him to St. Clement's. What an utter fool he had been! He had violated one of the first strictures of foreign service agents. Feeling safe on British soil unmarred by war, he had not watched his back.

*Never again.*

\* \* \*

As he waited in front of the Foreign Office building for his mount to be brought around, Haverstock's gaze swept over the entire area, searching for anyone who looked suspicious. But it was too soon to tell.

Once on his horse, he took a circuitous route to The Strand, glancing over his shoulder as he rounded each corner. At some distance behind, he noted a lean young man on a roan gelding. With each turn, the man stayed behind him, though not close. By the time Haverstock reached The Strand, the gelding was still far behind him. In front of St. Clement's Haverstock came to a stop, but unlike usual, he did not dismount. He boldly waited until the gelding came near. With his hat shielding his eyes, he watched the gelding come closer, but as it neared St. Clement's, it turned a block short of the old church.

With an angry flick of his ribbons, Haverstock spurred his mount back over the distance they had just traveled. He turned on to the narrow lane where the young rider on the gelding had turned, and he saw the back of the man astride his now-stationary mount. Haverstock slowed and came to a complete stop beside him.

And he saw the rider was Jimmy.

Anger flared within him like blazing torch. His own groom had betrayed him!

His eyes met Jimmy's. "So it's you who's been following me."

Jimmy nodded.

"At whose behest?"

Jimmy swallowed. "Lady Haverstock."

Haverstock felt as if he had been slapped in the face. Unconsciously, he noted the knuckles of Jimmy's long, slender fingers whitening as he grasped the reins. Haverstock's eyes traveled over the groom's sturdy body and wondered why he could not recall watching the lad grow into a man.

"Don't try to tell me she wanted information about me meeting with another woman."

"I wouldn't lie to ye. 'er ladyship asked that I 'elp protect ye. She 'as a bee in 'er bonnet that someone means to 'arm ye."

"And, of course, she wished a full report on anyone I happened to meet under suspicious circumstances."

Jimmy nodded again.

"You told her about the small man who lived on Tavistock Place?"

"Yes, me lord."

The simmering anger he had felt over Pierre's death came to a full boil, and before he realized what he was doing, Haverstock delivered a blow to Jimmy's freckled face, nearly toppling the youth from his horse.

Shakily bringing himself astride, his back straight and proud, Jimmy said, "Neither me nor 'er ladyship would ever 'urt ye, me lord." He wiped a trickle of blood from his mouth.

A pity a lifetime of service to the Haverstocks had not warranted what Anna won in a fortnight. Haverstock felt doubly betrayed. "You are to leave my service this day," Haverstock ordered, swiping the gelding with his crop.

He shook as he watched Jimmy ride off. As mad as he was at the groom, he was angrier at his wife. God in heaven, he had married a French spy! If he had grieved over Pierre's death, he grieved tenfold over Anna's deception.

He had been betrayed by the woman he had given his name. And so much more. At the thought, a deep, gnawing feeling unlike anything he had ever experienced seared through him. Was Anna's deception of recent origin or had the entire marriage been hatched months ago by French conspirators? He groaned aloud. Had all her gentle innocence been feigned?

Had that first card game with Morgie been to gather him – not Morgie – into her vicious net? Morgie had never been her target. Always, he had known, it had been him. Something about the events of that day had long disturbed him, and now he knew why. He had been manipulated by a woman of cunning and skill. And someone of even greater cunning and skill must be manipulating her.

He remembered Monsieur Hebert's warning. Suddenly all the hazy pieces of the puzzle fit together in startling clarity. Sir Henry Vinson was the traitor. It had been Sir Henry who had introduced Anna to Morgie. Sir Henry who met Anna for a private tete-d-tete in a most public setting. And, most damaging of all, Sir Henry matched the description of the man who had been at the Boar and Barrel, the man who had murdered Pierre.

His heart drummed wildly when he realized Anna, his lovely, lovely wife, had been a party to the murder. He went numb at the memory of last night when his lips hungrily roamed over her extraordinary body. His breath grew short when he remembered her softness enfolded against him as she slept contentedly with her head burrowed into his chest. What an utter fool he had been!

As he began to ride along the narrow streets of The City, he planned how he would confront Anna. In his outrage, he wanted to hurry home and expose her. Send her to the Tower. Watch her head roll. Then his more reasonable, practical side took control and he realized he could use her to implicate Sir Henry and possibly others. As difficult as it would be for him, Haverstock would not reveal to Anna that he had learned the truth about her.

* * *

Dazed over the murder of the Frenchman, Anna was thankful it was Wednesday so she could meet Sir Henry face to face and sever their connection. The description in the newspaper left little doubt that he was Pierre Chassay's murderer. Would that she had never been spurred by misguided patriotism. She should never have trusted Sir Henry. His information had all seemed so plausible.

But now she did not know what was true or what was fiction. She knew Charles felt genuine remorse over the Frenchman's demise. He had called him a patriot to England. In his stricken state, he would not have fabricated such a description.

Could it be Sir Henry – not her husband – was the true traitor? Sweet heaven! That had to be nearer the mark. Hadn't Charles always been a man of honor? He was as dissimilar to his father as fire to ice, as good to evil.

Amidst such tumultuous thoughts, she donned her pelisse and bonnet and readied for the trip to the book store. She must wipe Sir Henry from her life.

She went early to Hookam's, as did Sir Henry. He stood in the Latin section examining a book, his eyes on her as she walked toward him. A quick glance assuring her no one else was near, Anna whispered, "I shall have nothing more to do with you. I would never have helped had I known you would murder the poor man."

His eyes went cold. "I won't deny it, Anna. I would do it again to save the lives of our men.

Pierre Chassay was Haverstock's messenger to the French."

She had no idea whom to trust, but she knew without doubt which man was more honorable. "I can help you no longer," she repeated in a clear voice.

"You have to. We must have the identity of the man Haverstock met in France."

She lifted a book and studied the meaningless title, her insides quaking, her mind numbed with confusion. "Perhaps you did not hear me. I said I can no longer work with you." She put the book back and swept from the store.

* * *

Drenched from the rain he had been oblivious to during his meandering ride through the old town, Haverstock entered his home, shedding his wet garments, and was immediately assaulted by the females who lived there.

"Charles! James is on his way home!" Lydia announced with delight.

"Squire Ainsley awaits you in the drawing room," Kate added.

"The head groom informs me you dismissed Jimmy," Anna said angrily. "How could you? He's been in your service his entire life."

"From whom did you receive the information about James?" Haverstock inquired of Lydia as he began to mount the stairs, divesting himself of his wet jacket.

Hurrying after her husband, Anna nearly slipped on water that puddled behind him.

"His entire regiment is coming home," Lydia said.

"Isn't it too, too wonderful!" Kate exclaimed.

Anna reached for the wet coat. "You will surely

take lung fever, Charles," she chided.

Ignoring her, he asked, "Squire Ainsley is here?"

"Indeed he is," Kate said. "He is acting most peculiarly. I believe he would like to speak to you privately."

"I daresay he's still grieving over Mary," Lydia said.

"Tell him I shall be down as soon as I change into dry clothes."

Midway up the stairs, he turned to Anna, who was by now beside him. "I will not speak to you of Jimmy, my lady. He displeased me excessively, and you cannot change my mind about sacking him."

Anna remained quiet, following her husband to his dressing room where Manors awaited. "Please close the window, Manors," Anna instructed. "I do not want his lordship to take a chill – if he hasn't already." She gave every indication of staying while Haverstock changed.

"Oblige me by leaving the room, Anna," he said sternly.

# $\mathcal{C}$hapter 20

His hair still wet but displaying no signs of receiving the contents of a rain cloud, Haverstock strolled into the library.

Its lone occupant, Squire Ainsley, rose and bowed.

"How good it is to see you are no longer in mourning," Haverstock greeted.

Though a widower might be expected to take on a solemn look and bow his head gravely at the mention of his deceased wife, Ainsley did not. He smiled at his old neighbor, his eyes crinkling at the edges. "As Mary always said, 'Life goes on.'"

Haverstock poured port for each of them, and both men sat down in broad, comfortable chairs.

Having known Ainsley all his life – though the squire was eight years his senior – Haverstock knew the man felt his wife's loss keenly. However, Ainsley's face wore a perpetual smile. Were he to be the bearer of tragic news, Ainsley would likely grin as he conveyed the morbid details.

"Your children are well?" Haverstock inquired.

"Quite well, thank you, though the girls sorely need a mother's guidance."

It suddenly occurred to Haverstock that Ainsley had traveled to London to seek Kate or Cynthia or Charlotte for a bride. "I forget now. How many children have you?"

"Six. Meg, the oldest, is twelve."

"All are girls, are they not?"

"Actually, the babe Mary lost her life bearing *was* a boy. Little John's a year old now."

"And I thought *I* was cursed to have five *younger* sisters."

Ainsley began to laugh hardily. "I am given to understand your home has added yet another female, my lord."

Haverstock's eyes narrowed. "Ah yes. Lady Haverstock."

"My felicitations. I look forward to meeting her ladyship."

"You must dine with us tonight."

"Oh, I couldn't impose on your hospitality."

"It would be a pleasure, not an imposition."

Still smiling, Ainsley looked nervous. "I have come to London, Haverstock, because I particularly wanted to speak with you."

So he was right, Haverstock thought. The man wanted to offer for one of the girls. It was really too bad for the poor fellow that all three of them had engaged their affections elsewhere. He truly needed a wife. But, then, his sisters would poorly fit into Mary Ainsley's broad shoes. Haverstock thought of the plump matron who had totally dominated her small, cowering, doting husband. Haverstock raised a brow.

"I beg permission to call upon Lady Lydia with serious intentions."

Lydia! Her astonished brother reeled from the shock. Why, the man could not seriously want to claim Lydia for his wife. No man had ever courted her. But as he thought on it, Haverstock realized she was imminently qualified to preside over Greenley Manor. Add to that her love of children and her life-long friendship with John Ainsley, and there was really no surprise at all. Except that the decision to offer for Lydia seemed too wise to have been hatched by the agreeable squire, who held few thoughts in his head that had not been put there by someone else.

"I must admit your proposal has taken me quite by surprise, Ainsley," Haverstock replied.

"I daresay you long ago accepted that Lady Lydia would not marry, despite all her superior qualities. I remember well Mary telling me what a shame Lady Lydia was not blessed with beauty for she would make some gentleman a fine wife."

"Your wife was extremely wise."

"Oh, that she was. But so is Lydia. She always was so much smarter than the other girls. I like that."

*And you need that.* "Of course, it would give me great pleasure if my sister would entertain your suit, but that truly lies out of my hands. I give you permission to call on her, but any decision will have to be my sister's."

The slim man nervously smoothed a hand over his wavy hair. "Yes, yes, of course."

Haverstock stood. "We will look forward to seeing you at dinner, then."

As Haverstock gazed after the departing Ainsley, he wondered if Lydia would favor the man's suit. Would a woman who had been raised as the daughter of a marquess settle for marriage to a country squire? Would she give serious consideration to Ainsley's proposal, in light of the fact he had overlooked her eligibility the first time he selected a bride?

\* \* \*

"Before you know it, Mr. Ainsley, your girls will

be having their season in London," the dowager said.

The squire, who sat across from the dowager Lady Haverstock at the long dining table, gave a funny little laugh. "I daresay you're right. Time does march on."

"How old is Meg now?" asked Lydia.

He finished chewing his peas before answering. "Twelve."

Anna had been watching Ainsley's behavior toward Lydia with interest. Before they had come down to dinner, Haverstock had asked Anna to see to it Lydia sat next to the squire, but her husband would divulge no more information.

In fact, Charles had been quite abrupt with her. When she asked him if she should wear the Haverstock Jewels, he had acted indecisive before nodding, and when she asked him to clasp the jewels about her neck he had done so with considerable coolness. His behavior was in marked contrast to what it had been just this morning when he pulled her back into bed every time she tried to rise. He had murmured endearments and nuzzled soft kisses to places that made her blush now.

But tonight he treated her with no more familiarity than he would a charwoman. Her loving partner of the past two nights was as far removed from the cool host opposite her as day to night.

Once more she had angered him, and once more she knew not why. He was understandably upset over his friend's murder, but she sensed that for some odd reason his anger was directed at her.

If only she could push aside her hurt feelings

and act as gay as Kate and Mr. Reeves. Instead she forced down her food and barely kept up the civilities of polite conversation. She longed for the solitude of her room where she could nurse her grief. Such a horrid day it had been. First, she learned poor Mr. Chassay had been murdered, and it had all been her fault. Then sweet Jimmy had been sacked. Now, her husband gave every indication of loathing her.

She must learn where Jimmy was and at least give him a character and some money to tide him over. He had been such a dear, doing her bidding as if he'd been in *her* service all his life. A jolting thought caused her to nearly spill her wine. Could Jimmy's allegiance to her have something to do with Charles booting the poor lad? For some reason, Charles had acted resentful of Jimmy. He had even acted as if he were jealous of the gap-toothed youth.

A knot twisted in her already upset stomach. Sweet heaven! What if Charles learned Jimmy had been following him? Had he learned that she and Jimmy were responsible for the death of Pierre Chassay?

If that were the case, Charles had every reason to treat her with the utmost hatred.

She must find Jimmy.

As she watched Lydia and the squire, Anna became convinced the man had come to London to win Lydia's hand. He deferred to Lydia with his every comment.

Obviously unaware of his intentions, Lydia treated him as she would any neighbor. There was no flirtation, no coyness in her manner, only sincere friendship and solicitations for his children. Lydia would be the ideal wife for the widower.

But Squire Ainsley was in no way the man for Lydia, Anna realized as she watched the good-natured fellow. The topic of Lydia's new horse seemed the only one over which the two shared an interest. The only subject on which he could converse at length was farming, a subject which caused Lydia to turn her attention to Anna while he regaled her brother with the merits of his new reaper. Anna could only imagine the poor man's disapproval of Lydia's witty criticisms of lesser mortals. The two would never suit.

Anna turned her attention to her mother-in-law. "You must be overjoyed that James is coming home, Mother."

A wistful smile swept across the dowager's face. "That I am. Sons are a woman's greatest blessing."

\* \* \*

Acting upon her mother-in-law's mellow mood, Anna begged the woman to be her partner at whist after dinner. Not liking to lose, the dowager accepted Anna's offer. Lydia readily made a third, against her brother's suggestion that she entertain the squire.

"I would far rather play cards," Lydia said, "but I welcome the squire as my partner."

The sun-darkened skin crinkled around Ainsley's hazel eyes as he chuckled. "I thank you for the invitation, Lady Lydia, but I've never been able to master the game. I would be most happy to watch you and your brother. Perhaps I can learn."

\* \* \*

Haverstock muttered under his breath as he took a seat at the card table. A very poor host indeed he was to John Ainsley, claiming Lydia for his own partner and depriving Ainsley of a chance to speak privately with her.

He dealt the cards and was surprised that Ainsley still stood behind Lydia's chair, studying how she arranged her hand. Ainsley was a good man. He would treat Lydia well. And most importantly, tonight he had completely ignored a table full of beauties – two of them quite eligible – to direct his every attention on Lydia.

Lydia deserved that kind of devotion. By God, he hoped the man succeeded in his suit. Even though Haverstock would dreadfully miss Lydia. He had been closer to her than he had ever been to any woman. Until Anna.

Just as he was discovering his complete satisfaction with the married state, he realized his bride was a French spy.

A quick glance at his hand revealed that he would be able to control trump. It wasn't matrimony he had come to enjoy. It was Anna. Not just her great beauty. The sound of her sweet voice, her gentle yet passionate lovemaking that had completely enslaved him. And most of all, he had rather liked the heady feeling of possession Anna solicited in him. He enjoyed worrying about her and feeling protective toward her.

Now, he had to forget any affection he held for the harpy. Because of her, Pierre Chassay was dead.

He felt the brush of Anna's leg against his, and involuntarily in took a deep breath. He would have to avoid being close to her. Her very touch weakened him.

Anna and his mother won the first hand, which increased his mother's good humor.

Ainsley still stood directly behind Lydia's chair.

"Have you been to Hyde Park?" Anna asked the squire.

The corner of Haverstock's mouth lifted to a smile. So his wife was going to do her best to promote a courtship between Lydia and Ainsley.

"No, I haven't yet, though I would beg to claim Lady Lydia to ride with me tomorrow afternoon." He smiled down at the top of her black hair.

Lydia did not even look up. "I'm afraid I've promised to chaperon Anna and Morgie tomorrow."

"What she means," Haverstock explained, "is that my friend Ralph Morgan has kindly agreed to take my wife to the park because I am much too busy. Lydia accompanies them for propriety. However, I find that I am able to take Anna myself tomorrow, so you are free to ride with John, Lydia."

Now, Lydia bestowed a smile on her old neighbor.

Haverstock tossed out the wrong card and silently cursed himself. Not only was he playing foolishly, now when he least wanted her company, he had promised to take Anna to the park.

\* \* \*

Allowing her husband to assist her onto the gig, Anna hoped he did not notice the dark half moons under her eyes. She had lain awake all night, longing to take the few steps that would bring her to his room, to his strong arms. Not only was her heart bruised, but she physically ached to be held in her husband's solid embrace. There was nothing she wouldn't do to earn his affection. Except go to his room like a beggar.

They followed the rig Ainsley had profusely

made excuses for. "I know it's not as grand as you're used to," he had said apologetically while Lydia had assured him of its suitability.

During the silent ride Anna watched the grim set to her husband's face.

She was unable to chide him for his coolness toward her. If her suspicions about why Jimmy was sacked were correct, she had truly earned her husband's loathing.

This morning she had endeavored to learn Jimmy's address, but the head groom had informed her Jimmy had gone to his cousin's in Kent. Apparently, Jimmy had an open offer of employment at the establishment where his cousin was employed. However, the head groom had no idea the name of the establishment. Anna was thankful she had pressed a handful of coins on Jimmy, supposedly for tolls, the day before he received the ax.

"You know," Anna said to her husband, "Lydia and the squire will not suit."

He turned surprised eyes on her. "My wife is not only an expert at cards, dancing, and fashion, but she is also clairvoyant."

Anna laughed. "One does not have to be clairvoyant to see what's as plain as the nose on your face."

"Then you must know John Ainsley would make Lydia a worthy husband," Haverstock said.

"Oh, I will not deny that. And I am sure he would be pleased with her performance as his wife."

Haverstock turned on to the most heavily traveled lane. "But?"

"I think he would bore Lydia excessively. Think on it."

Her husband apparently took her advice, for he remained silent for several minutes.

"Before we married," Anna said, trying to topple the wall that had erected between them, "did you bring young ladies here?"

He did not answer for a moment. "I suppose I did."

"I shall be very jealous," she said, her lips forming a pout.

"Would that I had married one of them and saved myself from an almond-eyed vixen," he muttered ruefully.

Anna felt as if her heart had been torn from her chest.

She watched as Ainsley turned his curricle on to a little traveled lane and knew that was where he had chosen to propose to Lydia.

"To mimic my sister Lydia," Anna said flippantly, "shall we take wagers on Lydia's answer?"

"Five quid says she accepts," he said.

"It's a bet!"

# $\mathcal{C}$hapter 21

Lydia came early to Anna's room the next afternoon.

"Morgie won't be here for half an hour," Anna said, motioning for Lydia to sit beside her. "Let's talk."

"I confess I desire private conversation with you," Lydia confided.

"You've asked Mr. Ainsley for time to consider his offer?"

Lydia's black eyes clouded. "You know?"

"Of course," Anna said, smiling. "Being ever-so-proper, the amiable Mr. Ainsley first solicited your brother's permission to call upon you. And besides, anyone with eyes in their head could see how besotted Mr. Ainsley was over you at dinner the other night."

"Then I must have very poor eyes, indeed," Lydia said in a low voice. "He quite surprised me with his offer."

"Have you decided when you will give him an answer?"

Lydia nodded. "I will tell him tonight."

"Then – -then, you've decided?"

"Oh, yes. I shall have to accept. You see, it's my first proposal. I shan't be able to wait thirty more years for another, and I should very much like to be married, to be mistress of my own home, to have children."

"You are on good terms with the squire's children?"

"Very good. I am flattered that he would entrust their care to me, for he's a very devoted father."

"He will make a dutiful husband."

"To be sure," Lydia said, her eyelids downcast, her voice scratchy.

"Of course, you're not in love with him."

"Perhaps that will come," Lydia said, trying to sound cheerful. "And even if it doesn't, I will have far more than I ever thought to have." She straightened her shoulders and forced a smile. "What does Charles think of the offer?"

"He thinks Mr. Ainsley's judgment most superior, and he is determined the man will treat you like a princess."

Lydia threw back her head and laughed. "Bless Charles!"

Anna took Lydia's hand. "There is no one else, is there, Lydia?"

"Why, of course not." She did not sound convincing.

"You've never fancied yourself in love?"

"If you know me as well as you think you do, dear sister, then you know I am much too practical to go about swooning over unattainable men. My eyes are good enough that I know the woman who faces me in the looking glass is not close to being tolerably attractive."

Anna could not argue with Lydia's assessment of her appearance. "It is true that your stature is somewhat larger than the accepted mode, but you have many fine features."

"Pray, enlighten me."

"Your hair is a rich black, like a rook in sunshine. If you took more pains with its styling, I believe you could look like a Grecian goddess."

Lydia laughed out loud.

"Do take me seriously. You also have very fine eyes. I ought to know. They're exactly like Charles's. One look into his eyes, and I'm his slave." Only to Lydia could Anna be completely honest.

"What a fine notion! Do you think Ainsley will be my slave?"

"I can not imagine the two of you being anything more than amiable. Can you see yourself sharing your innermost thoughts with the squire?"

"Goodness no! The man is far too polite. How wicked he would think me if he heard my sharp-tongued musings on half the people to whom I am acquainted."

Anna appraised Lydia's figure, what could be seen of it in the brown serge gown that did a thorough job of covering it. "It is my opinion, he admires your body."

Lydia blushed crimson. Though low cut dresses were in vogue, she avoided wearing them, tending to dress like someone's maiden aunt or gentlewoman's companion.

"You do possess a bosom any woman would covet. You should divulge more of it."

"I should feel like a doxy!"

"No one will ever take you for a doxy, Lydia."

"If I'm going to be betrothed, I suppose I am going to have to allow you to help me select a suitable trousseau."

"With pleasure. Now, before we go to the East End, I would like you to allow Colette to arrange your hair fashionably."

* * *

Anna knew Charles would not come to her chamber when he came home. He would go to his dressing room and don fresh clothing for the Taylors' ball, avoiding any private conversation with her.

When she heard him talking with Manors in the adjoining chamber, she quietly opened the door, greeted both gentlemen, then walked up and placed five pounds in her husband's hand. "It seems you won the wager, my lord."

Wearing a freshly ironed shirt and gray breeches, Haverstock looked from his hand to his wife's face, realization dawning. "So our loss will be Ainsley's gain."

Anna nodded.

His mouth set in a grim line, he said, "I will make the announcement at dinner."

Before dinner, Lydia met with Ainsley in her brother's library, freeing Haverstock to announce the nuptials over the dining table where the newly betrothed couple stood somewhat awkwardly while the family toasted them.

Even in his enthusiastic toast, Haverstock's face bore no sign of happiness. Indeed, none of the family showed signs of elation over Lydia's engagement. Cynthia burst into tears. "What are we going to do without Lydia?" she asked, her voice muffled with sobs. "This is so sudden."

Anna suspected Captain Smythe's failure to make Cynthia an offer brought on her tears as much as attachment to Lydia.

"Wouldn't it have been nice to have had a double wedding?" Kate asked, placing a bejeweled hand on Mr. Reeves' arm. "But we'll be wed before your bans are posted."

Now two of Charles's sisters were embarking on misalliances, Anna thought with sadness. She shot a glance to the end of the table where her own husband sat, and her heart constricted. It wasn't just his size that gave Haverstock commanding presence. Everything in his dark good looks – the stern cut of his square jaw, the wisdom in his black eyes, the strength of his magnificent body – exuded authority. Anna realized she had no right to judge anyone's choice of husbands. She certainly had not married for love. And for all she knew, her husband still could be a French spy. More the pity. For now she would probably love him were he a homicidal maniac – though she could not seriously imagine him doing anything that was not honorable.

If only she could prove that Sir Henry – and not her husband – was the French spy.

But the truth was no more attainable than Charles's love, she lamented.

Anna noticed the dowager's disposition had taken a marked turn for the better in the past two days. Was it because James was coming home? A contented smile softened her black eyes at the announcement Lydia would be taken down off the shelf.

"I must say, Lydia," Kate offered, "your hair looks uncommonly good tonight."

Lydia beamed at Anna. "Anna's Colette arranged it for me."

"They will do well by you, Lydia," Haverstock said.

"Tomorrow Anna and I will go to Madam Devreaux's for my trousseau."

"Do you mean Anna knew about the

engagement before your very own mother?" the dowager demanded.

"I am afraid, Mother," Haverstock intervened, "the close friendship between Anna and Lydia excludes most of us. The two share many things we are not privy to."

The dowager gave a snort. "Like those afternoon romps. One would think they were going to a leper colony."

"I feel so very fortunate Anna has come into our family," Lydia said.

Squire Ainsley lifted Lydia's hand and placed a kiss on it. "Not nearly so fortunate as I that you are coming to mine."

Color rose to Lydia's cheeks.

Following dinner, they rode in two carriages to the Taylors' ball. Lydia and the squire rode in Haverstock's, and Kate, Cynthia and Charlotte rode in Mr. Reeve's.

"I beg that you not ask me to stand up with you, squire," Lydia said on the way to the ball. "I am a most deplorable dancer."

Taking her hand in his, the squire said, "Please, call me John. And I am pleased you are not partial to dancing because I fear I have two left feet."

Looking at the pair across from her in the dimly lit carriage, Anna wished Lydia wore a more lovely dress. The drab green was serviceable, but a special night like this called for an elegant dress.

"I wonder if Captain Smythe will be at the ball," Lydia said.

"One wonders if he will ever come up to scratch with Cynthia," Anna said. "What do you think, Charles?"

In his brooding mood again, Haverstock
hugged the side of the carriage, not even allowing
his leg to touch her skirts. He met her gaze.
"Pardon?"

"Do you think Captain Smythe will offer for
Cynthia?"

"I don't know that I've ever given it a thought,"
he said stiffly. "I daresay the matter is between
Cynthia and the captain."

"I think he's behaved shamefully," Lydia said.
"All these weeks he's been leading Cynthia on.
Everyone expects a declaration any day. As pretty
as she is, no other man will even come close to
her. And now the captain's become conspicuously
absent."

"Shameful, indeed," the squire uttered.

* * *

Though it was late in the Season, the crowd at
the Taylors' was the largest Anna had seen.
Haverstock and Anna led the newly betrothed
couple around, introducing the squire to everyone
as Lydia's fiancé.

After spending over an hour on introductions,
the gentlemen settled Anna and Lydia at chairs
against a wall in the ballroom and went to
procure refreshments.

Vigorously fanning herself against the room's
stifling heat, Anna did not notice Sir Henry had
walked up to claim her for a dance. A frown on
her face, she slowly closed her fan and rose to her
feet, stiffly offering him her hand.

"How delightful it is to see you tonight, Lady
Haverstock," Sir Henry said, leading her on to the
dance floor.

Anna did not respond.

Since the dance was a waltz, he gathered her

into his arms and whispered, "Have you found out the information we need so desperately?"

"My husband tells me nothing, and if he did, I would not tell you."

"What about Ralph Morgan? I see you two together every afternoon at Hyde Park. I think you could get anything you want from the man."

"You mistake the matter," Anna said with vehemence. "Mr. Morgan escorts me out of friendship to my husband."

"Mr. Morgan is noted for having an eye for beautiful women, Anna. And in case you have not looked in your glass lately, you are incredibly beautiful."

"I assure you Mr. Morgan is completely oblivious to any beauty I might possess." Anna saw her husband return to where she had been sitting, holding two drinks. He scanned the dance floor until he saw her. Then he stiffened.

At that moment Lady Jane, wearing a heavily embroidered ivory gown, walked up to him, bowed low to say something to Lydia, then straightened up again and spoke to Haverstock, an angelic smile on her face. Anna's stomach plummeted when she saw her husband give Lady Jane the drink he had brought for her.

The dance seemed interminably long, and Anna discouraged conversation with Sir Henry. She could not take her eyes off Haverstock and Lady Jane. Why wouldn't the woman leave? Now she was fanning herself. The next thing Anna knew, Lady Jane acted as if she were going to swoon. Only Anna was sure it was feigned to solicit Haverstock's interest.

He gently took the slim blond by her elbow and led her from the crowded ballroom.

"I see your husband's marriage has done nothing to cool his feelings toward the lovely Lady Jane," Sir Henry said.

So Lady Jane did have a claim on Charles's feelings, Anna thought morosely, unable to respond to Sir Henry.

When the dance was over and Sir Henry restored Anna to her seat by Lydia, Lydia greeted Anna wryly. "Would that I'd had a banana peel to throw at Lady Jane's delicate feet."

A smile crossed Anna's face. "How wicked you are."

"Not as wicked as she. I have never seen a more unbelievable attempt at fainting."

"So I'm not the only one who thought so," Anna said.

"I hope my fool of a brother can see through her."

Anna felt a tap at her shoulder. She turned and saw Mr. Churchdowne.

"May I have the pleasure of this dance, Lady Haverstock?"

Anna gracefully rose.

* * *

He knew that she didn't love him. He knew that she never had. He knew she was responsible for Pierre Chassay's death. And she was an enemy of his country. So why did it hurt so badly to see her in the arms of Sir Henry and Harry Churchdowne?

Haverstock smirked at Jane. She had always fancied herself a marchioness. His marchioness. And she had always annoyed him. She was no more faint than he was. After giving her a suitable amount of time to cool off, he asked, "Do you feel up to standing up with me for the next set?"

Something in his pride made him want to show Anna other women could be attracted to him.

"Oh, I'm quite refreshed now, my lord," she said, setting a possessive hand on his arm as he led her to the dance floor.

He swept by Anna, ignoring her while giving a curt nod to Churchdowne. He gave his full attention to acting as if Jane were the most important person in the room. He made a great deal of seriously looking into her eyes. He laughed and smiled at everything she said. He squeezed her hand. All the while he watched Anna from the corner of his eye.

It was as if there were no one else on the dance floor except his beautiful wife. He watched her lovely body moving gracefully beneath the soft drape of her sky blue gown. And with a bitter rage, he watched Churchdowne's face as his earnest eyes caressed Anna.

Damn that Churchdowne! Haverstock kept thinking. Did he have to hold Anna so close? And how dare he dance with Anna after the scene at White's. It might give Anna a bad name.

"Since you've gone and married," Lady Jane said, "I have decided to marry, too."

"And who is the fortunate man?"

"I cannot tell you since I have not yet received the offer, but I expect it within the week. I will say that he outranks you."

Haverstock raised a brow.

"And he's quite old, so I may have to take pleasure with a younger man like you, Charles."

Somehow, with all her faults, Haverstock could not imagine Anna speaking as Jane just did. Jane of the impeccable lineage, he thought disgustedly.

# $\mathcal{C}$hapter 22

Madam Devreaux ran her discerning eyes along the sizable length of Lydia and spoke to Anna. "I have not seen this sister before, no?"

Anna shook her head. "This sister's tastes run to riding habits more than ball gowns, but now she will need a trousseau."

Within minutes, the modiste's assistants scurried around Lydia, measuring her, holding lengths of various shades about her face. All the while Madam Devreaux exuded excitement.

Anna realized the dressmaker extraordinaire was not just counting the generous sums she would receive for the commissions, but she was also being challenged creatively to transform Lydia from the ugly duckling into the beautiful swan.

"Do you not agree, Madam Devreaux, that Lydia's breasts are one of her best assets and should not be covered?" Anna asked.

"To be sure," the woman said, leading Lydia into a dressing room. There, Lydia disrobed, and Madam Devreaux draped a bright white sarcenet from just over her bosom to the floor.

Anna stood back and gazed. Lydia looked almost pretty. Certainly striking. "You are a positive genius, Madam. Lydia looks quite lovely."

Lydia gave a skeptical glance into the glass.

"Do you not think the bodice is too low?"

"Not at all!" the modiste said. "We only see the top of what promises to be exquisite endowments. Your husband-to-be, he will be enraptured."

Lydia's face clouded.

Madam Devreaux had undoubtedly said the wrong thing, Anna thought. The idea of intimacy with the squire was not welcome to Lydia. Anna remembered with deep longing every torturing touch from her own husband. Despite the pain of losing him, she would do it all over again. Better the pain than going to her grave never having experienced their magical blending.

Anna watched the young assistants work. "Tell me, Madam Devreaux, are your helpers good needlewomen?"

"But of course. Only the best." The dressmaker wrote some measurements down on paper.

"What kind of wage do they receive?"

"I pay a generous wage," she defended, not mentioning a sum.

"Have you need for another employee?"

The woman nodded. "This season we have been so terribly busy. My poor girls, they work into the night. I could undoubtedly use another."

"Sally!" Lydia exclaimed.

Anna's eyes danced with delight. "Exactly."

"You have someone?" the modiste asked.

"She has no great experience," Anna said, "but her work is good, and she is an excellent learner. To compensate for her lack of experience, I propose to pay her wages during her apprentice period – without her knowledge, of course."

Madam Devreaux smiled broadly. "Of course."

"Oh, Anna, what a delightful plan," Lydia said. "I cannot wait to see her face when we tell her."

"I say, Lyddie," Morgie said on the way to the East End that afternoon, "you look different."

"It's her hair," Anna said.

"Oh, yes. Quite becoming," he said.

"Lydia is to acquire a new wardrobe for her trousseau," Anna announced.

With shaking hands, Morgie reined his horse, pulling to a complete stop, then turned wide eyes on Lydia. "Your what?"

"My trousseau," she answered. "Did you not know I am to be wed?"

"I did not!" he snapped. "By all that's holy, I see you twice every day, and you don't even have the consideration to tell me something as momentous as your wedding plans. Just who in the bloody hell is it you're marrying?"

Anna's gaze shifted from Morgie to Lydia, and her long-standing belief in their affection for each other was confirmed. A pity Morgie did not realize the depth of his feeling for Lydia.

"Squire John Ainsley," Lydia said.

Morgie took up the ribbons and began to canter, avoiding Lydia's gaze. "Never heard of the man."

"He lives quite near Haymore. He's a widower," Lydia said.

"I am sure you don't have to explain the man to me," Morgie said, his lips compressed.

An uncomfortable silence filled the carriage. Unconsciously, Anna listened to the clopping of hooves, the cracking of whips, children at play. A fog horn on the Thames.

Presently, Morgie said. "This is the second cannonball wedding betrothal I've heard of today. You'll never guess the other one."

"Enlighten us," Lydia said dryly.

"Blassingame has offered for Lady Jane Wyeth."

"But the old duke must be eighty years old!" Lydia said.

"He is but five and seventy," Morgie corrected.

"Do you realize how this could affect Kate's plans?" Anna asked.

Lydia's hand flew to her mouth. "Goodness! If the duke and Jane have a son, poor Mr. Reeves will have no prospects, and Kate will never be a duchess!"

"Delicate subject, I know," Morgie stammered, "But the babe might not even have to be the duke's, if you know what I mean. Men of a certain age have difficulties with that sort of thing, I am told. He'd be pleased as punch to have everyone think him capable."

Lydia blushed and purposefully looked away from Morgie's direction.

A throbbing torment raged through Anna as she remembered her husband with Lady Jane the night before. Had they been planning to become lovers once Jane married the old duke? As much as she could picture Jane scheming behind her husband's back, Anna could never imagine Charles denying Kate her heart's desire.

"Anna," Lydia said, "Kate's wedding's only two days off. I fear she will stop it if she learns the duke's plans."

"That might not be a bad thing," Anna said.

"But Kate deserves to be miserable. She's such a schemer. It's either her being miserable or poor Mr. Reeves – whose only mistake is falling in love with Kate." Lydia set her chin forward. "I shall not tell her about Blassingame."

Anna hated to see Kate locked in a loveless marriage, but it was of her own choosing. Whether or not Mr. Reeves became a duke really had nothing to do with winning Kate's love. That he would never be able to do. Perhaps Lydia was right to keep the news of Blassingame's plans from Kate.

Morgie ran a skeptical eye over Lydia but said nothing.

At the sewing school, Morgie stayed with his equipage, as he usually did. Anna, Lydia and Colette divided themselves among the students. Sally sat at the end of one of the tables with her two little girls, who wore patched dresses. She was putting the finishing touches on a new dress for her eldest girl.

"I think the dress will be the very thing to show your new employer," Anna said.

Sally's blue eyes lifted hopefully, a slow smile coming to her lean face. "You mean I'll 'ave a proper job?"

Anna nodded.

By now Lydia had come, all smiles.

"You will be an assistant to Lady Haverstock's dressmaker," Lydia said. "The most fashionable women in London are patrons of Madam Devreaux."

Sally reached down to her toddler, swept back the little one's blond ringlets and hugged her, tears brimming in her eyes. "I don't know what to say, me lady. I'm so excited."

"During your apprentice, you will earn two shillings a week."

The young mother's eyes nearly popped from their sockets. "Oh, I can't thank you enough!"

"No thanks are needed. It is your own skill and

determination that have won you the position," Anna said.

A dreamy smile on her face, Sally said, "Some girls may have wanted to be a princess, but all I've ever wanted was to be a fine dressmaker."

"That you are," Anna said.

When they met Morgie outside, he introduced a skinny lad who could not have been over nine years old. His body was bruised, and his hair and tattered clothes were dirty. It actually surprised Anna that Morgie of the meticulous dress would allow himself so near the urchin. Most men of his station would not.

"This is Andy," Morgie said, placing a hand on the boy's scrawny shoulders. "Got a fancy over horses."

"Master Morgan's been letting me work with 'is 'orses," Andy said.

"In fact," Morgie announced, "he's going to become my groom."

Andy hopped on back the coach, the others got inside, and it took off.

Lydia lifted approving eyes to Morgie. "How wonderful of you to take in the boy, Morgie."

He shrugged off her praise. "He'll make a fine groom. Loves animals."

"What of his parents? Isn't he awfully young to leave them?" Lydia asked.

"Poor lad has no family," Morgie said. "I've been throwing coins at him from time to time for helping with my mounts, and I believe that has been his only means of survival."

"That is so good of you," Lydia said, admiration in her eyes that swept over his pensive face. "I do not understand how a young child like that could not have a family."

"Too many mouths to feed. No home. No known father and a faithless mother. Any number of reasons," Anna said lowly. "And though we cannot repair the problem, we can lift the load from a few to make their lives easier. Hopefully, others will do so also."

"Mr. Hogart and Charlotte, I do believe, mean to do good works in their lives – that is if Charles will allow them to marry," Lydia said.

"You must know Charles sets no store over rank and riches," Anna chided. "And besides, Mr. Hogart has failed to ask the question."

"He's not going to," Lydia said. "He is much too gallant to ask Charlotte to share a life of poverty."

"They will not have to be poor, I assure you," Anna said. "I will make a settlement on them. It would please me to see them continue his work."

Lydia hugged Anna. "I *will* say it once more. We are so very fortunate to have you for a sister."

"Pooh," Anna said.

"When do I meet this squire of yours?" Morgie asked.

"Come to Haverstock House tonight. We're staying home. I would love you as my whist partner, since the squire – I mean, John – does not play," Lydia said.

"What kind of man doesn't play whist?" Morgie murmured crossly.

* * *

In a small family ceremony at St. George's Hanover Square, a sobbing Kate became the wife of Mr. Reeves. Anna observed the ceremony from the front pew, her attention focused almost entirely on her very handsome husband standing beside the nervous bridegroom. Haverstock wore gray pantaloons with a rich black coat adorned with diamond buttons that matched his spurs. His very virility made Anna catch her breath.

She remembered their own wedding. How differently she had felt toward him then. As her thoughts wandered thus, he caught her eye, and she smiled at him.

But he turned his glance away quickly.

The Duke of Blassingame attended, balancing his thin frame on a silver-handled cane. There was no sign of Lady Jane, and no announcement of their forthcoming nuptials had yet appeared in the newspapers. But Anna knew that Kate knew.

Following the ceremony, a wedding breakfast was served at Haverstock House. By this time Kate had quit crying and graciously met with each guest, including the duke's five middle-aged daughters – his progeny from his now-deceased wife.

But it was Lydia who drew the most praise on Kate's wedding day. For this was the first time she had worn one of the dresses fashioned by Madam Devreaux. The gown was of the palest violet, its neckline plunging extremely low, the soft gathering of the slender dress making her appear statuesque, almost slender.

Colette had arranged her hair in the Grecian style, and a lavender ostrich plume swept from her black locks.

Morgie could not take his eyes off her.

Anna detected that he was intimidated by the woman with whom he had always enjoyed an easy intimacy. Under normal circumstances, he would be sitting beside Lydia at this moment, the two of them delivering tongue lashings over some of the pompous guests.

But today, he stood alone, swallowing hard as

he watched Squire Ainsley devote himself to Lydia.

Anna walked up to Morgie. "Despite that he cannot play whist, how did you find Squire Ainsley?"

"Dull witted."

"But you must admit he is very amiable, and quite devoted to Lydia."

"He will bore her to death."

"But he does enjoy riding, and I am told his stable is well equipped. That should make Lydia happy."

"It's not right, you know, asking her to come in as mother to six children who are not her own."

"Lydia loves children."

"Deserves her own."

"The squire will most likely be happy to oblige in that."

Morgie heaved an impatient sigh.

Anna changed the subject. "How does little Andy do?"

"Happy as a lark. My housekeeper bathed the lad and found some clean clothes that aren't too big on his skinny little frame. We'll have him fattened up in no time. Wonderfully good appetite he's got." He looked around. "Mary did not come?"

"Did you not know she is about to present the dowager with her first grandchild?"

"None of you ever tell me anything anymore," he snapped.

"What do we never tell you?" Haverstock asked Morgie, walking up and slipping an arm around Anna's waist, causing her knees to feel cottony.

"First, not a word about the squire fellow dancing attendance on Lyddie. Then, no one tells me Mary is increasing. And you always said I was like one of the family."

"You must perceive that you are the only person here who is not related to the happy couple," Haverstock said, clasping a firm hand on his friend's shoulder. "Actually, I find you quite superior to most members of my family. Come, let us find the champagne."

They left Anna alone. She wondered if she were one of the members of her husband's family whom he found lacking. Of course she was. If only she were more like Lady Jane, Anna thought.

# $\mathcal{C}$hapter 23

"These ladies bloody well need her," Morgie said crossly, flicking his ribbons on the way to the East End. "Don't know why Lyddie has to gallivant 'round with that squire fellow this afternoon. He sees her every blasted night."

Anna laid a gentle hand on his arm. "It's just for this one afternoon. The poor man has scarcely had a moment alone with his fiancé their betrothal. Besides, I am particularly desirous of speaking to you today on a very private matter."

He lowered his eyes. "Your most obedient servant, my lady."

Though she knew they were quite alone, save the tiger at the rear, Anna glanced around the darkened, narrow street they traveled to assure herself no one could hear. No other carriage was near. Not even Colette had come today, so Anna's conversation would reach only Morgie's ears.

"I know how close you are to Charles," she began. "He shares with you what he shares with no one else. I am aware – though not from him – that you accompanied him to France. What I do not know is if Charles is working for or against England."

"How could you doubt him?" Morgie snapped, cracking his whip against the horse and casting a suspicious glance at Anna.

"In my heart, I know he's good. However, a man I fear may be working against Britain persuaded me that Charles was a traitor."

Morgie nearly collided with a passing hay cart. "Tis insanity, I vow! There's no finer man than Haverstock."

"I very much want to believe that," Anna assured. "I want you, too, to believe that I have absolutely no sympathies for the French. That's part of what makes everything so terribly difficult for me. If I had to choose between my country or my husband, I don't know which I'd choose. For I care for Charles very much."

Morgie's eyes softened and he lowered his voice. "You shouldn't have to choose. Haverstock's as English as the king."

"Then I need you to help me prove it."

"How do I do that?"

"I'm not quite sure." Anna felt a refreshing burst of cool air off the Thames as Morgie's curricle plunged on to the wider Strand. "I thought perhaps you could help me trap the man I suspect."

"And, pray, who is this man?"

"Sir Henry Vinson."

"Never cared for the worm."

"Neither do I, if the truth be known."

"Tell me about him," Morgie commanded, rounding the next corner at a brisk pace.

Anna disclosed that Sir Henry had used her to spy against Haverstock by convincing her Haverstock was a French loyalist. "He has been scheming to learn the identity of Charles's contact in France – the one you two visited."

Morgie nodded but said nothing.

By the time they reached the old building that

housed the sewing school, he turned to Anna, a stern look on his narrow face. "Leave it to me. I know how to smoke out varmint."

\* \* \*

"Allow me to buy you a drink, Almshouse," Morgie said, settling in a leather chair in a darkened corner of White's and getting the attention of a passing waiter.

Theodore Almshouse, whose once-fine coat was now well worn, sat next to him. "Good of you, old chap, considering I still owe you that five-hundred quid. Regret to say it will be the next quarter before I can pay up. My luck's been devilishly bad of late."

Morgie leveled his gaze at his old school chum, displaying neither satisfaction nor scorn, but a controlled power. "You may not have to pay up," Morgie announced cheerfully. "I have a proposal for you."

Almshouse leaned closer, his ears perked.

The waiter brought a full bottle of port with two glasses. Morgie watched as Almshouse took his glass with shaking hand. "What with your rotten luck and all," Morgie said, "it shouldn't be too difficult for you to actually play to lose."

"You are proposing to pay me to lose?"

Morgie nodded.

"To whom, pray tell?"

"To Sir Henry Vinson."

\* \* \*

As she demonstrated a daisy stitch to a middle-aged woman who stank of onions, Anna sensed someone standing over her shoulder and turned to face Mr. Hogart.

He wore an impish smile, which she affectionately returned.

"I suspected I would find you here," he said, bowing.

Anna gave him her hand. "How did you know?"

"I happen to spend a good deal of time in this neighborhood myself. It took no great intellect to surmise the fine lady who had set up the sewing school was none other than the Marchioness of Haverstock. Tell me, does his lordship know about this?"

Anna nodded as she led him away from the students.

"And he has no objections?"

"His only objection is to our safety. I'm not even sure he fully trusts Mr. Morgan."

"He should have no worries about you. You're worshipped as a saint here. No hand will be ever be raised against you."

"You know these people well."

"I do, and I know I'm doing good. Not just spiritually." His voice held hope, his eyes excitement. Then, he sighed and lowered his voice. "But Haverstock could not be expected to welcome the idea of his lovely sister spending her life toiling for the ignorant masses. She deserves a life of privilege and ease."

Their feet struck the stone floors as they moved further away from the students. So this visit was not just a social call, Anna realized. The pulls of prospective matrimony must be tugging quite firmly at Mr. Hogart's heart. "You underestimate both Charlotte and my husband. Charles has a very generous heart. And he's not given to feeling superior to others. Take his choice of a wife. You know of my background?"

Mr. Hogart nodded, averting his gaze from her. "Charlotte tells me the two of you wish to marry."

"More than anything."

"Then you must seek permission."

"I cannot do that. I have no money. No home to offer."

"I have set aside dowries for all of Charles's sisters. Charlotte's is a modest one, but you should be able to have a little home and an income of two-hundred a year. And it's not as if you won't come into money of your own one day."

"I cannot accept your generosity."

"Oh, but it's not for you. The dowries were set up before I ever knew of your existence."

His face cleared. His eyes shone. "I could kiss you, Lady Haverstock!"

"Save that for Lady Charlotte."

* * *

There was no pleasure in winning from Almshouse, Sir Henry thought. The man was no more skilled at hazard than at handling his liquor. And now Sir Henry would pocket another worthless IOU from the blasted man. Almshouse owed everyone in town.

"Just one more hand," Almshouse said, his words slurred from brandy. "I feel my luck is changing."

Sir Henry went to rise. "You've no more money."

"Sit down, my good man," Almshouse said, his eyes casting about the opulent room at Mrs. Chambers' establishment. None of the other players in the large parlor were within hearing distance, but Almshouse still lowered his voice and leaned toward Sir Henry. "I have information which is worth a goodly sum."

"I cannot imagine myself being interested in

purchasing information."

"Are you not associated with the Foreign Office?" Almshouse asked.

Sir Henry raised a brow and moved his chair somewhat closer to Almshouse.

"There is a certain high-ranking Frenchman who can be useful to you, I understand." Almshouse lifted his glass and slowly took a drink, his eyes watching Sir Henry. "That is, if you knew his identity."

Though his heart leapt at the prospect of learning who the Frenchman was, Sir Henry attempted to remain calm. He must not appear too interested. His only sign of eagerness was a slow swallow that accentuated his prominent Adam's apple. "I may have heard something about the fellow," Sir Henry said casually. "But how is it you know of the man?"

"My friend Ralph Morgan – when in his cups one night – was talking about meeting the chap in France."

Morgie's trip to France had been secret. Almshouse really knew what he was talking about. "Tell me, when did this meeting occur?" Sir Henry asked.

Almshouse shrugged. "Maybe three months ago. Maybe six. Around the time Haverstock married."

Sir Henry nodded. It was all he could do not to burst out smiling. The wildest good fortune had finally smiled upon him. The ten-thousand pounds he received for dispatching Monsieur Chassay would be a paltry sum indeed compared to the fee for revealing France's highest-ranking traitor. However, Sir Henry knew he must not seem too eager. He pulled out his timepiece and gave it a glance. "Suppose I could manage another game. What say you the stakes?"

"If I win, I get my markers back. If I lose, you receive the Frenchman's name."

Sir Henry handed the dice to Almshouse.

* * *

Except for speaking of the morning nuptial announcement between the Duke of Blassingame and Lady Jane Wyeth, Morgie and Lydia were markedly quiet on the way to the East End. Anna found herself trying to keep up the entire conversation, remarking on how well Kate was taking the duke's marriage announcement, asking Lydia about her outing with the squire the previous day, commenting on the day's heat.

Once they arrived at the sewing school, Morgie asked Anna to stay back for a private word.

"I believe our plan has worked, my lady," he said. "Your suspicions about Sir Henry appear to be completely accurate."

Her eyes danced. "You can prove it?"

He nodded. "A near do well fr – er, acquaintance of mine played right into Sir Henry's hand, it seems. In exchange for money, the acquaintance offered Sir Henry the name of the French official."

"And he positively jumped at the chance to get it, did he not?"

"Quite correct. I knew it wouldn't do to make up a name, so we furnished Sir Henry with the real name, then I hired Bow Street runners to watch Sir Henry round the clock. They were to indefinitely detain – without Sir Henry's knowledge – anyone with whom he secretly met." Morgie rather cockily said, "We now have in custody a certain Mr. Thomas Brouget, who was hastening to Dover after meeting with Sir Henry at St. Paul's this morning."

Sweet heaven! Charles was innocent! Anna felt as if she'd been released from a cage. Now she could be rid of the odious Sir Henry Vinson.

\* \* \*

What Anna hoped would be her final assignation with Sir Henry was brought about by a note from Anna requesting Sir Henry meet her at the British Museum.

Anna was quite alone among grim glass cases when Sir Henry entered.

He coolly appraised a mummy. "I have finally realized you can be of no service to me."

"Then we are of like minds," Anna said. "I do not trust you. And I believe you, and not my husband, betray England."

His eyes turned cold. "You don't know of what you speak."

"Oh, but I do. I'm just sorry it has taken me so long to see the truth."

"The truth is that your husband works for the French."

"You're a liar."

"You know he was meeting Pierre Chassay."

"Because Monsieur Chassay was working with the British, and you couldn't allow that, could you, Sir Henry?"

He glared at her.

"I bitterly regret I was very stupid to have trusted you, but that will happen no more. If you value your skin, you'll leave the country before I inform my husband of your activities."

"How dare you threaten me!"

She shot him a frosty glance before turning on her heel. "I'll give you two days."

* * *

It was difficult for Haverstock to concentrate on the codes. He kept thinking of Anna's treachery. Of Pierre's death. Of that disgusting Harry Churchdowne who was so obviously besotted over Anna. Of Sir Henry Vinson's role in this business.

He took out the miniature of Anna and gazed at her likeness. Laughter licked at her rich brown eyes and a mischievous smile played at her lovely mouth. He could almost hear her sweet voice and smell her rose water. Even knowing all he knew of her, the sight of that flawless face grabbed at his heart. It was a sign of disgusting weakness. His foolishness over her had cost Pierre his life.

For the first time ever, Haverstock longed to be like his father – not to care for any woman. They only destroyed. He was testament to that.

A knock sounded at his door, and his secretary announced a Mr. Cook.

Haverstock's heart quickened. Mr. Cook was one of the Bow Street runners he had hired to follow Anna since he had fired Jimmy.

Haverstock asked the man to sit down. Before Mr. Cook said anything, Haverstock knew Anna had met with Sir Henry.

"You have a report on my wife's activities?" Haverstock asked.

Mr. Cook nodded grimly, and took a small ledger from his shabby coat. "Lady Haverstock met with a tall, thin bloke, I'd say about fifty years of age, this morning at the British Museum. They spoke for about ten minutes. Then the gent came to this very building – we've learned his name is – -"

"Sir Henry Vinson."

"Just so."

Now Haverstock knew with certainty Anna was indeed meeting the man who matched the description of Pierre's killer.

Haverstock pounded his fist against his desk. He wondered if he had the stomach to see Anna's slender neck with a noose around it.

# $\mathcal{C}$hapter 24

Sir Henry would be damned before he would let that scheming female dictate to him! And just when things were going so very well. Thomas was on the way to France with the minister's name. In all likelihood, Sir Henry would be considerably richer within a fortnight. He had a nice little niche here in London, especially now that he had capital to spare.

If only he had not encouraged Anna to marry the blasted Haverstock. That had been his undoing. He had not counted on their falling in love with one another. It simply wasn't done. Haverstock had previously been content with any number of mistresses, but he had not taken one since Anna came to his bed. Sir Henry thought of her mother, Annette de Mouchet, and how satisfied Steffington had been with her. Any man could have luxuriated in her loveliness, Sir Henry thought with bittersweet remorse.

Perhaps he should have taken Anna for his own mistress. But he'd grown so bloody tired of demanding females. He had thought he could control Anna without relinquishing his autonomy. In the beginning she had seemed so fertile for his endeavors. Her hatred for the House of Haverstock had been Sir Henry's leg up. But he had failed to recognize the attraction of a powerfully muscled body, of black eyes that held a woman as powerfully as chains and of a head of thick hair the color of freshly turned earth.

Damn the bloody bitch! Giving him two days! Just three months ago he would have been pleased to flee to Paris, to take up residence in the promised Palais Vendome. To become reacquainted with friends he had not seen in over a decade of war. To take his rightful place at the highest echelons of the world's most brilliant society.

But now he was strangely reluctant to go. Paris most assuredly had changed since he was last there. The nobles were no more.

A vision of Anna gracefully presiding over a Parisian gaming table, dressed in lavish gowns, crowded into his mind. Ah! With Anna at his side, he would have Paris at his feet.

But how could he manage that? An idea suddenly occurred to him. He could play to her weakness.

Her weakness for the Marquess of Haverstock.

\* \* \*

After breakfast Anna listened to the quiet voices coming from her husband's dressing room. And when Manors left, she entered. It pained her that the only way she could be alone with her husband was to force her company on him.

She noted the flicker of anger that singed his face when he looked up and saw her. Did she repulse him so greatly? Was there no hope for a reconciliation?

He was fully dressed in rich grays and lifted his gloves while his eyes darted toward the door as if he were in a great hurry to be gone.

Her voice gentle, her step graceful despite the

tumult within her breast, Anna walked toward Haverstock and spoke. "I thought I had best warn you yet another man shall beg the hand of yet another sister."

His eyes traveled lazily over her. "The chap who wears black?"

She nodded.

"Correct me if I'm wrong. Is he not the one who has no money?"

"While he has no money at the present, Charlotte has a tidy little dowry coming from her sister-in-law."

"That is very kind of you," he said coolly. "When does the fellow seek my permission?"

"He dines here tonight."

"You think it a good match?"

Her eyes glittered. "Very much so. They are both so very good. And I am so happy for them." She walked toward the window. "I am sorry you were denied what Charlotte will receive."

"Which is?"

She turned to face him, anguish on her face. "A chance to marry whom you choose. I thought I was doing the right thing at the time," she whispered. "I never meant to harm you – or anyone."

He swallowed hard. "I must go," he said, turning away from her.

* * *

Dressed in a new coat – though still a drab black – Mr. Hogart met privately with Haverstock before dinner to solicit Lady Charlotte's hand in marriage. Since the discussion with his wife that morning, Haverstock had prepared his affirmative response.

Throughout the day he had been unable to do

anything but remember every word that passed between him and Anna that morning. God, but it was difficult to hold a conversation with her when she stood before him, her voice soft and her sentiments always on the mark. It seemed impossible she could be the same woman who had schemed to marry him, to spy against the country that had provided her mother and her with refuge and prosperity.

Undeniably, Anna had many good qualities. It was a fine thing for her to dower his sisters, especially sweet Charlotte so she could marry Hogart. He was a good man. He would treat Charlotte well. From what Anna had told him, Charlotte would have happily given up everything to be Hogart's lifelong helpmate. Haverstock smiled to himself over his little sister. She had always had a soft place in her heart for the downtrodden. To think of all the mangy dogs she had taken in and nursed to glowing good health. He was rather proud of her and her desire to devote herself to the less fortunate.

He had been proud, too, of Anna – before Pierre had been murdered.

At dinner, Charlotte's wedding announcement was made. Kate and Mr. Reeves were there, their solemn faces looking nothing like happy newlyweds.

"My uncle weds next week," Mr. Reeves announced gloomily.

"Never have I seen so many engagements in so short a time," Charlotte mused happily. "First Kate, then Lydia, then Lady Jane – and now me! Isn't it just too thrilling?"

Haverstock glanced at Cynthia, who looked quite wan. She neither touched her turtle soup nor spoke. Once again, Captain Smythe was absent. They had all been taken in by the captain. Haverstock wondered if he should speak to the man about Cynthia. Of course, Smythe had never made any promises. But an honorable man simply did not use a lady as Smythe used Cynthia.

"Soon, I'll be all alone," the dowager complained.

"No, Mama, I am sure I will never wed," Cynthia declared, a distinct note of martyrdom in her voice.

"A lovely girl like you must have had countless offers," Ainsley said.

"Not a single one this season," Cynthia lamented. "I fear I am getting too old."

"Nonsense!" the squire countered. "Look at Lydia. She's thirty."

Lydia colored.

"I don't know what I'll do without Lydia to run things for me," the dowager said.

Haverstock glanced to the opposite end of the table where Anna sat, her face bathed in soft candlelight. "You'll have Anna."

The dowager ignored her son's remark, babbling on as if to herself. "That is if I choose not to take up residence in the dowager house. I may very well want a place of my own."

"And you, my love, do you enjoy presiding over your own establishment?" Haverstock asked Anna mockingly.

"It is not the place one grows attached to but the people in it, I have found," Anna said. "I will be happy wherever I am as long as loved ones are near. And like Mother, I shall dreadfully miss Lydia."

"Then you shall have to spend more time at Haymore," the squire said.

Anna threw a challenging look at Haverstock. "Exactly what I have been telling my husband."

Haverstock frowned. He would never be taking Anna to Haymore. He had no right to continue living with a spy. Nor could he turn her over to the authorities. He knew now what he would do with her.

And damned but it hurt to know he would never see her again. A silly, romantic verse came to mind. He'd never cared for such drivel, but these lines kept repeating in his brain. *Better it would be to be a rock or tree and never feel the pangs of love for thee.*

Such sentimental nonsense, he scolded himself. He was not in love with Anna. Love had never been part of their marriage.

* * *

Sir Henry did not trust Anna not to have him followed. Even his page could be followed. Therefore, he had to be particularly cautious and rely on the cunning that had held him in good steed for fifty years.

He rang for his secretary. "I say, Whitestone, I seem to have mistakenly received a message sent to Lord Haverstock. See to it that it gets delivered to him."

As the drably dressed man left the room, Sir Henry casually said, "By the way, since it's of a private nature, I'd prefer that Lord Haverstock not know his letter came across my desk, if you know what I mean."

Within minutes, the office boy carried a letter to Haverstock's secretary, who in turn put it on top a stack of papers on his master's desk.

Haverstock put down his pen and crossed the room to open the window. Another beastly warm day. A coach passing below with outriders reminded him very much of Morgie's. In fact, this was the very time of day Morgie escorted Anna, Lydia and Colette to the East End. Haverstock smiled to himself. Whatever would his father have said if he knew the Marchioness of Haverstock and his own daughter were willingly associating with the uncivilized who populated the East End? And the late marquess had thought the graceful, accomplished Anna de Mouchet beneath his family!

He turned back to his work, not really wanting to be indoors on so sunny a day. He longed to feel a horse beneath him as he galloped along a country road. He picked up the letter his secretary had placed on his desk.

It was addressed in an unfamiliar hand. A hurried masculine hand. It had been posted from Bordeaux. As he read it, Haverstock's heart raced. *Your brother, Lieutenant James Upton, has been gravely injured by a sniper's musket ball just a few scant miles from his company's point of embarkation. He needs special care in getting back to England. Could you possibly cross the channel and make arrangements to care for him? As soon as possible. And do not breathe a word to anyone because the French are not to know of the change in our position.* The letter was signed by Colonel Jacob Cole.

Haverstock looked for a date on the letter, but there was none. It was impossible for him to guess how long ago James had been injured or when the letter had been posted. All he knew was that it was urgent he get to James as soon as possible.

He had no time to change into riding clothes. It was best not to go home where he might be questioned. This way he could scribble a note to Anna informing her he would be out of touch for some time. No explanation needed.

With that missive dispatched, Haverstock went to his bank where he withdrew a goodly sum as well as letters of credit. Then he mounted his horse and took the road for Dover, the sun hitting his back, and the sooty skies of London behind him.

# $\mathcal{C}$hapter 25

The sewing lessons were almost over when Mrs. McCollum, one of Lydia's most promising pupils, showed up.

"Sorry I am to be late," she said hurriedly, removing a squashed straw hat from her silver hair. "A right good 'anging there was today. Had me a prime seat on top of me brother-in-law's 'earse. Ye shoulda seen the fine lady danglin' there like a spider!"

Anna's eyes widened and her chest tightened. She raised a hand to protest Mrs. McCollum's morbid conversation.

"Lady Haverstock has no stomach for such talk," Lydia said kindly to her student. "Here, I've selected a new piece for you, Mrs. McCollum." She gave the woman a length of royal blue velvet.

Anna felt hot and flushed. She hastened across the stone floors to gasp fresh air from outdoors. She kept thinking about the gentlewoman dangling from a hangman's rope. *It could be me.* Her hand grasped the smooth column of her throat.

Morgie, who had been keeping an eye on his horses, shot a concerned look at her and rushed to her side. "Are you all right, my lady?"

She nodded. "I just need a breath of fresh air."

"You'll not find it here," he said, taking hold of

her arm. "Perhaps a ride to Greenwich when we finish."

Lydia, her new lilac gown billowing behind her, came rushing after Anna. "Is she all right, Morgie?" she asked.

"I believe she got overheated."

"We had best get her home." Lydia headed back into the building to gather their things.

They rode home in Morgie's coach and four, with Colette and a pale Anna facing Morgie and Lydia.

"I say, Lyddie," Morgie said cheerfully, "becoming new dress you're wearing."

She glanced down at the soft muslin and colored. "It's a new one for my trousseau."

He folded his mouth into a grim line and did not speak again until they reached Haverstock House.

While Colette and Lydia were making a great fuss over directing Anna to her chamber to rest, the butler presented Anna a letter from her husband.

Puzzled, she took it, dismissed her well meaning companions and mounted the stairs. In her room she broke the seal and read: *My dear Anna, I have been called away on sudden business and shall not return for a number of days. Yours, Haverstock.*

When the dinner hour approached, Anna had no desire to dine without her husband. The house seemed strangely empty without him. And grim. She took a tray in her room and spent a restless night wondering and worrying about Charles.

* * *

Before the fashionable hour for morning callers, Davis announced Sir Henry Vinson begged an audience with her ladyship. Anna threw a glance of distress at her mother-in-law and Lydia. Her first instinct was to refuse the man's request. Charles would be outraged if he knew Sir Henry visited her. Then, too, there was the certain knowledge Sir Henry was a vile turncoat against his country. If only she could simply turn him over to the officials. It was extremely distasteful to welcome him into her husband's home, but what else could she do in front of the dowager? "Show him in," Anna said in an unsteady voice.

Sir Henry came strolling into the drawing room, all smiles for Anna until he saw she was not alone. Then he regained his authoritative command and swept into a deep bow before the dowager. "How very agreeable it is to see you looking so well, my lady," he told her. He moved next to Lydia, bent into a bow and felicitated her on her upcoming nuptials. With a sparkle in his eyes and a flicker of a nod toward Anna, Sir Henry came to sit by her.

For the next several minutes, he was all that was amiable. He congratulated the dowager on her good fortune to be getting her younger son home. He queried Lydia about her plans for life at Greenley Manor. And he completely avoided turning his attention toward Anna.

As the other sisters began to fill the drawing room and welcome morning callers – including the long-absent Captain Smythe – Sir Henry took his leave. But as he reached the door, he turned to Anna. "Lady Haverstock, your husband helped select my new gray. He said you would very much like her. Would you care to see her? She's right outside."

Anna shot a dubious glance at her mother-in-law, then slowly rose and followed Sir Henry.

The gray was hitched to a stylish phaeton. Sir Henry ignored the horse, stooping to let down the steps. "Get in, Anna," he sneered. "We must take a little ride, you and I."

The sound of his voice scared her. She glanced at her footmen.

"I promise I shall have you back inside an hour," he said, loud enough for the footman to hear.

She could not possibly go off riding with Sir Henry. Charles had never been angrier than the night she had met Sir Henry alone in Lord Wentworth's study. She did not have to get burned twice to learn when something was hot. "My husband has expressly forbidden me to be alone with you, Sir Henry."

His eyes held menace. "My dear Anna, though my two days are up, you are in no position to dictate to me. Not when your husband's life is in danger."

Anna grabbed at her breast. All through the long night, she had known something was wrong with Charles. And now, Sir Henry's expression confirmed her fears.

With resignation, she allowed Sir Henry to assist her into the carriage.

She took her place and angrily watched him take the reigns. "What have you done to my husband?" she demanded.

"The question is what have *you* done to your husband?" He flicked a sinister glance at her.

"What do you mean?" She could barely control the tremor in her voice.

"As we speak, Haverstock is being detained as

a suspected enemy of the crown."

"God in heaven, no! There is no truer patriot."

He shrugged. "Alas, but there is the fact he is wed to a French spy – though I daresay he would likely substitute his own honorable neck to spare yours."

"That is completely out of the question."

"Just as I thought you would see it."

"And what do you propose?"

"Don't worry over your lovely neck, Anna. You will keep it intact if you do as I say. You have merely to write a confession that will effectively clear Haverstock, and you will then accompany me to Paris where you'll be the toast of the town."

"I despise you," Anna said. "And I cannot possibly believe a word you say."

"But you really have very little choice, my dear."

\* \* \*

Her room was still dark when she rose the next morning. She had packed the night before. She had written the confession that would exonerate Charles. *I, Lady Haverstock, am writing this to admit my own unintentional role in the death of Pierre Chassay, whom I understand was working with my husband and the English government to thwart the French. My husband had no knowledge whatsoever that I was having his every move scrutinized. He is guilty of nothing save a deep devotion to his country.* Sir Henry insisted he would channel her letter to the proper authorities. She had fought back the urge to write a farewell letter to Charles. There was nothing she could say that could repair the irreversible damage to their marriage.

If it was a marriage, she thought sadly. So

much harm she had caused Charles. At least he would be free of her now. Though she could never be free of him. Through her misguided hatred, she had found and destroyed her heart's desire.

She dressed herself in a comfortable traveling garb of soft green with a darker green pelisse and tied on a green and gold bonnet. She had hoped never to have come this far. As soon as she had spoken with Sir Henry the day before, she had gone directly to Morgie, having finally learned not to blindly believe the words of the contemptible Sir Henry Vinson. She told Morgie of Haverstock's absence.

"I will make inquiries," Morgie promised her.

Late last night Morgie had come round to Haverstock House, begging to speak privately with Anna.

Shaking his head grimly, he informed her no one in London nor anyone at the Foreign Office knew Haverstock's direction.

Still in the morning's darkness, she walked to the settee that was placed before the cold fireplace. She gently fingered its raised silk pattern, remembering how many nights she and Charles had sat there nestled within its warmth, sharing confidences, taking pleasure in the intoxicating feel of one another. She could almost see his powerful shoulders outlined in flickering flames, a hungry look on his handsome face as he held his arms out to her and she had taken bliss beyond measure in his comforting embrace.

So many tender moments had passed between them in this very room. She swallowed over the huge lump in her throat. Never again would she feel his arms around her or run her hands through his dark hair.

With tears clouding her vision, she turned away from the settee – their settee – and wondered if another woman would ever share this room with him.

Though she could not write to Haverstock, she felt obliged to write to Colette. It pained her that Sir Henry forbid her to bring Colette on the journey. Or to tell anyone good-bye. But she could not just leave Colette. She would take the coward's way out by writing to Colette instead of speaking to her.

She walked to her desk, sat down, picked up her quill and began to write, in French. *Dearest Colette, By the time you read this I will be gone. I have gone to Paris with Sir Henry in order to spare my husband from the misdeeds I have orchestrated against him. I am leaving you enough money to get by until I send for you. I hope that shall be very soon, cheri.*

She addressed it and propped it on the table beside her bed where Colette would find it when she brought Anna's morning tea.

Lifting her valise, Anna quietly left the room. It was too early even for the servants, except those below in the kitchen beginning the day's baking. She tiptoed down the broad staircase, along the marbled foyer and through the towering entry doors.

The quiet street was so dark and foggy she could barely see the nearest lamp pole, much less Sir Henry's traveling chaise. Not that he would be there yet. She was quite sure she was early. Hugging herself against the chill, she walked to the end of the street and waited.

Within minutes his coach pulled up, and the coachman jumped down from the box, relieved

Anna of her case and let down the carriage steps for her. Sir Henry had not moved a muscle. He sat in the middle of his comfortable seat, a rug thrown over his lap. "Let us hope you are as good a traveler as you are with the pasteboards," he said.

She glared at him, climbed in and sat down opposite him.

"You have the confession?" he asked.

She nodded, took it from her reticule and handed it to him.

He put it inside his coat pocket, yawned and settled back into his soft leather squabs. "May I suggest you try to get some sleep. It's a long journey ahead for us, my dear."

# $\mathcal{C}$hapter 26

Haverstock had gained no advantage in his journey by leaving in the afternoon. Darkness that made the roads untravelable forced him to put up at a posting inn along the way. It was late the following afternoon before he arrived in the busy port city of Dover. How war had changed the sleepy little seaside town from what it was when he had been a child! Now soldiers resplendent in red coats, colorfully plumed ladies of bordellos and legions of injured paraded through the streets.

The waning sun at his back, Haverstock went straight away to book passage on the first packet out, but his luck had failed him again. The last ship of the day had just sailed, and he would not be able to get another until morning.

Another deuced night in a noisy inn. After leaving his mount at the livery stable, he walked the short distance to the Plank and Plow, a three-storied gabled building noted for good food and clean rooms. There, he bespoke a bed for the night only to be told there was not a vacancy in the entire city.

"Damn near entire regiment of the Light landed in town this hour past," the apologetic innkeeper said. "'Tis sorry I am to refuse you, your lordship."

His spirits low, his worry over James mounting, Haverstock followed the sound of raucous voices and found himself in the inn's public rooms that were filled with cheerful soldiers raising mugs of ale and saluting bonny England. He ordered ale from a buxom serving maid who promptly offered to share her bed with him that night. Taking no pleasure in lying with a woman still wet from another man, he kindly declined her generous offer and tossed her a coin.

He was impatient to get to James. He did not even know the extent of his brother's injuries. The colonel had not said what kind of wounds James had sustained or when they had been incurred. Perhaps one of the soldiers in this very room knew something of the situation. Surely one of them would know of Lieutenant Upton. Haverstock ran his eyes over the mostly youthful faces when his attention was caught by a young blond officer moving into the room. The blond was the very color of James' hair. Was his imagination playing tricks on him? The man *looked* remarkably like James. Of course, it had been five years since Haverstock had seen his brother. James' appearance would be bound to be greatly altered. Especially if he had been wounded.

Haverstock could not remove his eyes from the man, who strode into the room with a commanding presence, a gathering of other young officers around him. Damned but it looked like James. Older, of course. His fair skin now bronzed by Iberian skies. The leanness of youth now banded with sturdy muscles, the hollow planes of his youthful face weighted heavy with command.

God, but it was James! And he was perfectly all

right. Haverstock rushed toward his brother.

The blond officer was talking to a man next to him when he looked up and saw Haverstock. "Charles?" he said, his voice tentative.

It was James' voice! Older, too. Haverstock stopped just short of taking his little brother in his embrace. His eyes traveled the length of James before he met his gaze once more, satisfaction on his face. "I perceive you are unharmed."

A smile broke across James' face as he clasped two strong arms around his older brother. "Blasted good it is to see you."

"But what of the sniper? What of Colonel Cole's letter?"

"I have not been under Cole's command these six months past." Turning back to his companions, James said, "May I present to you my brother, the Marquess of Haverstock."

Haverstock bought rounds for all.

James took a long drink. "Now, about the sniper."

Exactly what Haverstock had been wondering. He had obviously been duped. But by whom? And why? It was not a subject he cared to bridge in a public tap room. "I think we need to talk."

"In my room." James' eyes lifted skyward.

"You have a room?"

"Apparently a lieutenant carries more rank around here than a marquess."

A smile creased Haverstock's scruffy face. "A hazard of war, I expect."

It was already quite dark when they mounted the narrow staircase to James' second-floor room. A chambermaid who led the way left a single taper on the wooden table beside the turned-down feather bed, curtsied and left the brothers alone.

Haverstock pulled from his pocket the letter from Colonel Cole and handed it to James.

Hunched down within the room's dormer, James held the letter toward the candlelight and read. When he finished, he turned to his brother. "It appears someone badly wanted you away from London."

Haverstock nodded grimly. He felt like a fool. Why had he never been suspicious when the letter had been delivered to the Foreign Office instead of to Haverstock House? His work at the Foreign Office was not widely known. All personal correspondence came to his home.

Of course, Sir Henry was the culprit. He easily had access to information about James' troop movements and commanding officers. And getting the letter put on Haverstock's desk at the Foreign Office would pose no problem for Sir Henry.

The man was clearly squirming. He must be feeling the noose tightening about his skinny neck.

"I say, are you still rather running the Foreign Office?" James asked.

"Nothing as important as that though I endeavor to assist where I'm needed."

"That is not the story imparted to me by Wellesley. Treated me as if I were the king himself when he learned I was your brother. Said you'd done more than all the admirals and generals bundled together to win the war."

"The man is given to exaggeration, I daresay."

James looked back at the letter again. "You trust those who work with you?"

"Of course not."

"Now you sound like Papa."

"It has struck me that the apple does not fall far from the tree."

"In your case, I'd say a veritable hurricane swept Papa's seed quite far away."

"A reassuring thought."

"You have a very good idea who is behind this – -" James flung the letter on the table. "Do you not?"

Haverstock nodded. Thanks to Mr. Cook.

"Then I suggest you and I apprehend the swine." James cradled his hand over the hilt of his gleaming sword. "It seems my fighting days are not behind me after all."

"You know I am married." Haverstock stated it simply. The thought brought pain.

James searched his brother's face. "She is very beautiful, my sister-in-law, is she not?"

Haverstock swallowed. "Very."

"And her name?"

"Anna."

* * *

The two brothers left Dover before dawn and rode hard all day to make London by nightfall. During the ride, Haverstock revealed to James his suspicions about Sir Henry Vinson. He told him about Pierre's death and the description of his killer. He disclosed that he had hired Bow Street runners who saw Sir Henry meeting with a French – a French sympathizer.

But he could not bring himself to tell James about Anna's treachery.

"We will go to Sir Henry's before you see Mama and the girls," Haverstock said.

"One wonders why he so desperately wanted you from London," James mused aloud.

When they arrived at Sir Henry's house on

Curzon Street, not a single light shone from any window. The brothers dismounted, climbed the steps and rapped at the darkened door. But there was no answer. They walked around to the stables and learned Sir Henry had gone away in his travelling coach at dawn for an undisclosed destination.

"He'll be in France tomorrow," James said.

"I believe you are right," Haverstock said grimly.

At Haverstock House, the cool reception James received was somewhat puzzling to the marquess.

His sisters flew into James' arms, exclaiming boisterously, but their faces were sad, their eyes red. Haverstock himself was the recipient of pitying glances.

With great ceremony, the dowager descended the staircase to welcome home her youngest son. She spread her arms around him and pulled him into her bosom. Their shoulders were of identical height. "It is good to have you home, son," she said solemnly.

Then, she turned to her eldest son. "Anna is gone." There was no triumph in her voice.

His mother was not merely mentioning that Anna was from home at present. Her expression conveyed far more than her simple words. Anna had left him.

All at once, Haverstock knew she had run off with Sir Henry Vinson.

# $\mathcal{C}$hapter 27

Anna thought nothing could be worse than the stifling carriage ride staring across into the face of the detestable Sir Henry. But the channel crossing in the dark, cramped quarters of the dipping schooner was undoubtedly the most discomfort she had ever endured in her life. She emptied the contents of her stomach many times over in a cracked chamber pot as rivulets of perspiration flowed down her face. She wrenched off her damp pelisse and used it as a pillow between her swimming head and the cabin's hewn pine wall. If only she could get used to the steady sway beneath her, she kept thinking. Perhaps then her stomach could settle.

But her stomach did not settle, though she became resigned to the sheer physical misery. This she could endure. But what pleasure could life hold without Charles?

Her only consolation lay in the fact her letter would exonerate him. He would be free and could resume the activities which had restored honor to his family. She wondered who would receive her letter. She vividly pictured Sir Henry slipping it inside his coat. Until they got on the ship, Sir Henry had not left her side. He had not posted the letter nor sent it by a messenger. Her heart caught. Sir Henry had no intention of sending the letter.

Her body shaking in rage, she rose to unsteady feet, and gripping hold of the wall, hastened to the door of her cabin. She tried the knob.

The door was locked from the outside.

\* \* \*

James cast a disapproving glance at his brother twenty feet away. Haverstock, his cravat loosened, his face showing signs of needing a shave, sat rather slumped at White's highest-stakes table, a near-empty bottle of Madeira at his elbow.

"I fear my brother has vastly changed in five years," James remarked to Morgie. "While I should be the one hell bent on excesses, it seems Charles cannot get too much liquor."

"Not Haverstock!" Morgie protested. "Why, I've never known him to – well, not since Oxford, anyway."

"Then these changes have not accrued over five years?"

"Two days, more likely," Morgie said.

James lifted a brow. "This sudden disregard for life must be tied to the actions of his faithless wife."

Morgie stiffened. "You obviously do not know the marchioness," he said coolly, his eyes narrowed. "And what do you mean 'disregard for life'?"

"He damned near got us killed this afternoon with his reckless riding. And he has not stopped drinking since we arrived in London last night, not to mention his losses at the tables!"

"What does his wife say to all this?"

James' face reddened. "The vixen must be the very cause of it. She left him, you know."

Morgie's mouth dropped open. "Davis merely told me that Lady Haverstock was not in yesterday when I called. I had no idea she was gone."

"Haverstock House is like a tomb. All those normally prattling females, and not a one of them will tell me anything."

"It doesn't make sense," Morgie said. "Her ladyship is thoroughly besotted over Haverstock."

"A wife does not leave a man she is besotted over."

"Unless. . ." Morgie spun away from James. "We cannot allow Haverstock to go home like that. He must stay at my place tonight."

* * *

Morgie barely lifted his aching head from the pillow. "My good man, must you open the draperies? Devilishly bright outside. What hour is it?"

"It is one o'clock, sir, and a lady awaits you downstairs."

"A lady?" Morgie sat straight up. "For me?"

"Yes, sir." The valet walked to Morgie's bedside and assisted his master from the bed.

Placing a hand to his head, Morgie asked, "Pray, who is she?"

"I couldn't say, sir. She is quality."

"Tell the lady I will be down presently."

For a man given to meticulous appearances, presently translated to nearly an hour, after which Morgie – freshly shaven with a newly ironed shirt and a dapper morning ensemble, regally strode into his drawing room to find Lydia sitting stiffly in a French chair, looking quite fetching herself in a soft yellow summer dress.

A troubled look swept over his face. "I say,

Lyddie, not at all the thing for you to be here unaccompanied. Where's your maid?"

"I am thirty years old and engaged to be married. I hardly need worry about propriety."

"You most certainly do. I will not have your reputation bandied about! You must leave at once."

"Rubbish!" She got up from the damask chair and walked toward the window. "Everyone knows you're rather an extension of our family. You don't count at all as a man." She saw the hurt look cross his face. Her voice softened and she moved to him. "What I mean is, of course you're really quite a dashing man and all, but . . ." She turned away.

"But since your affections are engaged elsewhere, I simply don't count."

She gave him a puzzled look, then fingered her gloves, her eyes downcast. "I need your help, Morgie. We must find Anna. I just know something is dreadfully wrong."

"What does Haverstock say?"

"He won't discuss it. I've never seen him so distraught. He seems to believe Anna has run off with another man – which is preposterous."

"I should say so! And who is the *other* man supposed to be?"

"The odious Sir Henry Vinson."

"The hell you say!" Morgie's hand flew to his mouth. "Beg your pardon."

She turned large brown eyes on him and nodded sadly. "Anna would never willingly leave Charles. She positively adores him. And I don't believe she cares for Sir Henry."

"I know for a fact she detests the man," Morgie grumbled.

"She's confided in you?"

"Yes, she confided in me. I should have told Haverstock straight away."

"Told him what, Morgie?"

He refused to meet her gaze. "Cannot tell you, Lyddie."

"You offend me greatly."

"I would if I could, really, but it's a matter of national secrecy and all that, you know."

A sparkle leaped to her eyes. "You mean you are contributing to the war effort in a clandestine nature, Morgie?"

"Wouldn't exactly put it that way."

"Then how would you put it? Pray, tell me what you know about Anna and Sir Henry."

He shook his head emphatically. "Cannot do it."

"Cannot do what?" Haverstock asked. He strolled into the sunny room and kissed his sister's hand.

"Mother is excessively vexed with you, Charles," Lydia snapped. "Not one night since Anna left have you slept in your own bed. She even went so far as to say you were better off with the daughter of the horrid French woman."

Morgie cast a warning glance at his friend. "I need to have a word with you, Haverstock. Should have spoken with you two days ago. It's quite important."

"You can speak in front of Lydia."

"Bloody well cannot. She ain't to know about. . .about your duties."

James now strolled into the drawing room. "You mean Charles's work at the Foreign Office?"

Morgie looked from James to Haverstock to Lydia.

"Oh, I know Charles toils away with cloak and dagger activities all in the name of the crown," Lydia said.

Morgie plopped into the nearest chair and sighed.

James took a seat near Morgie and poured himself a cup of tea from the tea table. "He's quite good at it, I am told."

Haverstock ran his hands through his disheveled hair. "Not so good that I didn't marry a French spy."

"That, my dear lord, you did *not* do," Morgie snapped. "The wretched Vinson played upon Anna's patriotism for England to make her think *you* were the French spy."

Would that he could believe his old friend, Haverstock thought wistfully, his eyes fixed on Morgie hopefully.

"She came to me the other day," Morgie continued. "It was – indeed always has been – obvious that she's devoted to you. She had come to realize Vinson had been duping her, that you were the one on the right side, not him. That's when we set a trap for him."

Three pair of eyes immediately attached themselves to Morgie. Not a sound could be heard in the room.

Morgie told them about Almshouse's play with Sir Henry and finished by telling about nabbing the French courier, who was even now in custody.

A gush of relief washed over Haverstock. Certainly what Morgie told him about the trap for Sir Henry vindicated Anna of wrong-doing. Or at least of intentional wrong-doing. "I must talk with the man," he said.

"Yes, I should have told you day before

yesterday." Morgie grumbled. "Daresay Anna would still be here if I had. I can tell you she positively loathes Vinson. No way she would go off with him."

"That's not true," Lydia said. "She would go off with him if she thought she were protecting Charles."

Morgie steepled his hands in thought. "How could he make her think that?"

"It has to have something to do with Charles being called away from London," James interjected.

"Why *did* you leave?" Lydia asked Haverstock.

He proceeded to tell them about the hoax he was sure had been perpetrated by Sir Henry.

"Oh course!" Lydia exclaimed. "If he had you out of the way, he could persuade Anna that you were being blamed for whatever activities he was responsible for, and the only way she could clear your name was to admit her guilt and flee with him. Now I understand her letter to Colette." Lydia withdrew the letter from her reticule.

"She wrote to Colette?" Haverstock asked.

Lydia nodded and handed the letter to him.

He read it solemnly.

Damn! Once again he had done Anna an unpardonable injustice. With a vigilante madness, he'd blindly blamed her for outrageous deeds: seduction, treason, murder – even adultery. Even while his heart proclaimed her goodness, he sought fault with Anna.

A bitter self-anger raged within him. He had driven away the most precious person in his life. Never had he given consideration to her feelings. Was it possible that Morgie and Lydia were right about Anna's feelings for him? Her affection was not something he had ever allowed himself the luxury of presuming.

Whether she loved him or not, Haverstock could not allow her to be whisked off to France by Sir Henry. By God, she was his wife. And he would kill the man who took her away. The thought of Sir Henry forcing himself on Anna made Haverstock want to skewer the man on his sword.

Haverstock stalked toward the door. "I'm going after my wife." *My wife.* The words conveyed a heady rush of possession. His Anna. His love. If only he weren't too late.

James leaped to his feet. "*We're* going after her."

# $\mathcal{C}$hapter 28

Anna's stomach no longer rocked. The ship was moored, its passengers long gone. The cabin's heat had been replaced by a night chill. But still Sir Henry had not come for her. What game was he playing?

She had decided she would go along with whatever he wanted. Until she could free herself and rush back to London. For Charles's life depended on her. She must clear him.

Even if it meant her own death.

She heard footsteps, then the turn of a key in the lock.

Sir Henry opened the narrow wood door. "Feeling better, my dear?"

A barely perceptible nod tilted her head. She swept her hair back from her face and squared her shoulders, lifting her wrinkled pelisse. Then, she soundlessly followed him up a wood ladder to the deck.

"You'll find we're quite alone," he said. "I should not want to leave a warm trail for anyone desirous of following us."

"And who, pray tell, would choose to chase us to French soil?"

He tightly took hold of her elbow. "One cannot be too careful." He continued to grasp her arm as they walked down the gangway.

Anna saw the hired chaise waiting and knew her only chance of escape must be attempted before they reached the carriage. Off to the right the dim lights of a tavern shone. She would run there.

The instant she felt solid ground beneath her feet, Anna shoved Sir Henry and lunged forward.

"Stop her!" Sir Henry yelled.

She ran as hard as she could toward the tavern lights. From the corner of her eye she saw the coachman spring toward her. Sir Henry's footsteps pounded behind her.

She sprinted, propelled by fear and determination.

The stout coachman was able to get an angle on her and use his body between Anna and her destination. As she slowed to go around him, Sir Henry caught her from behind. He grabbed her with both his hands, the pressure so strong he dug into her flesh.

She struggled to break free, but his long fingers encircled her wrists, digging into her very bones. She fell down, and before she could stand up, he began to drag her as if she were a sack of grain. Her dress tore, and she stung from the dock's weathered wood scraping her raw flesh.

The coachman walked ahead and opened the carriage door. Sir Henry shoved Anna inside, keeping one hand banded tightly about her slender arm.

"To Paris?" the coachman asked.

"No," Sir Henry replied. "My wife and I go to Chateau Montreaux."

* * *

At the foot of the Haverstock House staircase, Morgie planted his booted feet on the marble floor and greeted the brothers. Then he cast a wary glance at Lydia, who sailed down the stairs in a dark green riding habit. "I say, bit late in the day for you to go riding, is it not, Lyddie?"

"Oh, I shall ride as far as Dover with you," she said casually. "I shan't be any trouble. I plan to visit an old friend there. I'll not take any trunks to slow us down."

Haverstock gave his sister a sideways glance. "She does ride as well as any man, Morgie."

"But what will the squire chap say about his betrothed traipsing around the country like that?" Morgie asked, hands on his hips as his eyes raked over Lydia.

"The squire has been obliged to return to Greenley Manor," Lydia informed him. "So he need never know how utterly unfeminine I am."

"Now, I wouldn't say that," Morgie said apologetically.

"Just who is this friend you plan to visit in Dover?" Haverstock asked, fetching his hat from the footman.

Lydia twirled her brown bonnet, suddenly quite interested in it. "Oh, dear me, this will never do." Running back up the stairs, she called, "I believe I'll get my green. I'll just be a minute."

Haverstock cast a suspicious look at his sister, but his worry over Anna quickly pushed Lydia's uncharacteristic coyness from his mind.

* * *

"Now, Morgie, I am quite concerned about you," Lydia pronounced, mounting the gangplank to the schooner. "I remember well how dreadfully sick you were back at Haymore just fishing from the placid little rowboat on our lake." She placed a booted foot on the deck, linked her arm through his and led the way onto the sailing vessel. "I have determined you need a place directly in the center of the boat. Less sway."

She swept by the profusely male passengers, Morgie silent at her side. "You must keep up your strength if you are to be of help to Anna. After all, she is our chief concern."

"Undoubtedly." His eyes darted from James to Haverstock – who were standing at the rail deep in conversation – to the plank, which was being raised. "I say, Lyddie, you had best depart now. The ship's about to sail."

"Another thing I've been concerned about," she said, ignoring his comment, "is your deplorable French. They'll take you for an Englishman straight away if you open your mouth. And that will certainly not help us find Anna."

"Us?"

"I think perhaps I should accompany you." She did not meet his gaze. "I could pretend to be your wife. That way I could do the talking. My French, you know, is uncommonly good."

"You can't go into France with us! It's far too dangerous."

"Pooh, I'll blend in with the natives." She stopped and faced him.

"Now see here," Morgie said, watching the ship inch away from the dock. "Haverstock!" he shouted.

The marquess, turning and seeing his sister still on the boat, rushed to her side. "What the deuce are you doing onboard?"

"I've decided to accompany you," Lydia stated.

"This is no trip for a woman," he said scathingly.

"Nothing will happen to me with my two

brothers and dear Morgie to protect me."

"Got to do something with her, Haverstock," Morgie uttered.

Her brother watched the distance between the boat and dock widen. "What she needs is a good spanking." His mouth tightened into a grim line, then he met James at the stern. He had to remove himself from Lydia's presence lest he do something vulgar like shake her senseless.

"At least we're on the right track," James said hopefully. "Even if it is two days cold. We would have been mistakenly on our way to Bordeaux if you hadn't found that fisherman who remembered Anna and the *proper* English gentleman on the Calais boat."

The fisherman's words still haunted Haverstock. "The lovely lady looked as if she were scared to death of something," he had said.

Haverstock seethed with a rage toward Sir Henry. Any harm the man meted against Anna would visit him tenfold, Haverstock vowed.

He watched the waves lap against the sides of the ship and felt the spray of salt water in his face. Each knot forward seemed endless. If only he weren't two full days behind! Not only were they at the disadvantage of two days' start, but they had no idea which direction Sir Henry would have taken.

What could he do to gain on them, Haverstock wondered. Sir Henry was sure to be hiring a traveling coach, so riding horseback should make up some of the distance. Provided they could determine Sir Henry's destination. Haverstock could make up additional time by not stopping for meals.

"Lydia's not being her usual practical self at all,

it seems," James remarked.

"Lydia's fortunate to still have her neck intact."

"What do you plan to do with her?"

"Lydia has no part in my plans. Nothing will come between me and finding Anna. Lydia will have to take the first boat back to Dover."

"You know that won't be until tomorrow morning."

Haverstock nodded. "And I'll bloody well not wait. Morgie can take care of her."

"But – -"

"But she will be compromised by being forced to spend a night in Calais with him."

"Yes."

"My dear brother, has it not occurred to you that is the very thing Lydia wants?"

* * *

Before Dover's white cliffs were out of sight, Morgie's face turned a decidedly raw shade of green, his brow grew moist and he looked as if he were about to expire. At Lydia's insistence, he had plopped down on the wooden deck, dead in the center of the boat, putting his head between his drawn-up knees.

Pulling her skirts beneath her, she sat along side of him and stroked his sweaty brow. "Poor Morgie," she soothed.

As wretched as he felt, the touch of Lydia's hand brought him an almost settling feeling. That was the thing about Lyddie. She was settling. No wonder that squire fellow wanted her. What a fine home she would make for him and his brood. Perhaps it was because she was the first-born female. She had a way about her of completely taking charge. Of making things always run smoothly.

Quite surprising, actually, that she hadn't been snatched up earlier by some lucky chap. But, then, she was not a beauty. His eyes traveled slowly over her. She had removed her hat, and her black hair glistened in the fading sun, the salt air whipping it away from her face. She was the same size as he was – a size he had never considered very feminine. But now, it seemed a very agreeable size. Like Lydia herself. Solid. Dependable. It wasn't as if she were fat or anything. And her breasts really were quite spectacular. She had a very fine posture, too, and looked most becoming in her new dresses. Actually she had an elegance about her.

That squire was a lucky chap indeed.

Morgie shook his head and rued his own plight. He was going to be sick. Very sick.

Lydia sensed it. She got up, walked a short distance away and came back with a small wooden barrel. "Here."

He gratefully accepted it and proceeded to heave the contents of his stomach into it.

At first he was too sick to be concerned over the embarrassment of his situation. Then, when it occurred to him Lydia was sharing a rather unpleasant intimacy with him, he seemed not at all to care. He rather fancied sharing intimacies with her.

\* \* \*

"We'll use the last vestiges of daylight to try to learn their direction," Haverstock told those gathered about him on the Calais dock. "Check the stage," he told Morgie, who had made a remarkable recovery as soon as his feet touched the firm soil of Calais.

"I'll see what I can find out at the livery stable,"

James said.

Haverstock nodded. "I'll go up to the tavern and see what I can learn."

Hands on her hips, Lydia said, "I plan to make myself agreeable to all the ship's hands I can. Maybe I'll find one who remembers Anna."

"Now see here, Lydia," Morgie said. "You can't be wandering about those ships unescorted."

"Then you'll just have to accompany me," she challenged.

* * *

Haverstock swallowed hard. "It's as if they were never here," he said a half hour later as their discouraged group gathered in front of the now-empty schooner.

No one matching the description of Sir Henry and Anna had boarded a public stage, Lydia and Morgie learned.

No horses had been hired by an English gentleman two days earlier, James determined.

Not a soul at the tavern saw an English lady the day before yesterday.

Even Lydia's queries of the deck hands yielded no information.

"You'll just have to put yourself in Sir Henry's position," Lydia said. "What would he do?"

"He would take Anna to Paris," Haverstock said bitterly. He put a firm hand on his brother's shoulder. "Come, James. We'll take the road to Paris."

"What about us?" Morgie asked.

"My dear friend," Haverstock said, "you are responsible for escorting my troublesome sister back to London."

"But – -there's no boat tonight," Morgie said.

Striding toward the stables, Haverstock threw

a glance over his shoulder to Morgie. "I have full confidence in your sound judgment."

# $\mathcal{C}$hapter 29

As soon as the brothers left, Morgie engaged a private dining parlor for Lydia and himself. What he was going to do after dinner, he did not know. He watched her as he moved toward their table near the hearth where a low fire was laid. But someone else was watching, too. He turned and saw a woman standing in the doorway, outlined by the cloudless night sky. Dressed in peasant clothing, she was of an age near his own and carried a babe in her arms. She looked straight at him and mumbled something in French.

"What's she saying?" he asked Lydia.

Lydia sprang to her feet, walked up to the woman and began a conversation in rapid French.

"She's worried about her husband. He hired out his carriage two days ago for a short ride to the Chateau Montreaux and has not returned yet." Lydia questioned the young mother some more. "She says an English gentleman hired her husband, but she doesn't know if there was a woman with him. The man matches the description of Sir Henry."

Morgie pressed a coin into the woman's hand and instructed Lydia to get the directions to Chateau Montreaux. "Assure the woman we'll do everything we can to restore her husband to her. And find out who in this town owns the fastest horses. I intend to make an offer that cannot be refused."

\* \* \*

The hemp which bound her hands together cut into Anna's wrists. This was the second day she sat in the shabby drawing room on a faded damask sofa looking at a torn Aubusson carpet. Once a sparkling testimony to French aristocracy, the chateau now served as headquarters for espionage activities, though only a handful of minor French officials remained. And each of them – thankfully not in this room now – held Anna in contempt.

"You know you can untie me," Anna told Sir Henry, who stood beside the marble mantle dressed impeccably in pale blue silk. "I daresay it would be impossible for me to escape with your spies about."

A devilish smile played at his lips. He moved across the fragile carpet, withdrew a knife from beneath his waistcoat and cut the rope.

"You'll have no need to try to run away again, Anna."

"Oh, but I have a need. I must clear my husband's name since you have no intention of releasing my confession."

"What a fool you are. You do not have to end your life to preserve his. The marquess is perfectly safe. He has not been arrested. It was only a lie I devised to get you to come with me."

Swept up in a savage rage, Anna stormed across the worn carpet, raised back her arm and slapped him as hard as she could.

Sir Henry's expression flitted from stun to controlled anger. "You will regret that," he said, stroking his reddened cheek.

"Where is my husband?" Anna demanded.

"He is probably at Haverstock House thoroughly furious with you for running off with me."

Her eyes flashed. "I hate you!"

"And if you're wondering about your confession, I can assure you it is in a perfectly safe place. It will ensure I have your cooperation in whatever endeavors I choose. The letter clearly discloses your French sympathies. So it is to your advantage to live in France now. With me."

She had been an utter fool. And of course Sir Henry was right. She could never go back to England and never again see Charles.

At least she had the consolation of knowing her misdeeds had not ensnared her husband.

Anna nodded reluctantly. She still wore the same tattered dress she had worn two nights ago when she had tried to run away. "Allow me to dress more presentably if we are to go to Paris."

* * *

Monsieur Le Fleur, who owned a most profitable vineyard, also possessed the fastest horses on the entire coast, but they were not for hire, Morgie was told. Fortunately, Monsieur Le Fleur's winery was on the road to Paris, and fortunately for Morgie, Monsieur Le Fleur was most agreeable to accepting one-thousand gold sovereigns for his two best horses.

Morgie's good fortune, however, did not include a moon-lit sky. His and Lydia's ride was painfully slow at times while they slowed for curves and ruts and cursed the darkness that impeded their progress.

"My brothers face the same obstacles," Lydia said reassuringly. "And do not forget they will be checking every posting inn along the way. We will easily make up their hour's head start."

As the road left the coast, it straightened, and they could ride much faster. Lydia's prophecy was fulfilled within two hours when she and Morgie raced over a hill only to ride up on Haverstock and James.

Haverstock turned sharply when the riders came abreast. "What the deuce?"

Morgie reined in. "Wrong road," he gasped.

Haverstock and James came to a complete stop.

"You know where Anna is?" Haverstock asked hopefully.

Morgie nodded. "A place called Chateau Montreaux."

"Damned if I don't know the place!" James said. "Not far from Calais."

Lydia nodded.

"Bloody hard to get in, though," James added.

"I've been thinking," Lydia said.

Morgie slapped his forehead. "We're in for it now."

"Hear me out," Lydia urged. "Whoever is manning the gatehouse at Chateau Montreaux would hardly be able to refuse admittance to a single female."

"Meaning you?" Haverstock asked.

"Yes. I plan to tell him I have been retained as a companion to the English lady. The fellow who works the gate would hardly know that wasn't the truth."

"Capital idea," Haverstock said sarcastically. "My very English sister just waltzes herself into a chateau teeming with Frenchmen and single-handedly rescues my wife while I preserve my hide on the safe side of the chateau walls."

"He's wise to dislike your plan, Lyddie," Morgie said.

"I wasn't finished," Lydia snapped. "I thought you could sneak in while I distract the gatekeeper."

"She's right," James said. "We could sneak in while she's talking to the fellow. As dark as it is tonight, we'll never be seen."

Morgie stroked his chin. "Not bad."

Haverstock nodded thoughtfully.

* * *

It was midnight when they tied their horses to a tree several hundred yards from the Chateau Montreaux gatehouse. "The less you know of our whereabouts, the better you will be," Haverstock told Lydia. "Just concentrate on your part. We'll get in."

Lydia nodded, then rode her horse all the way to the gate where she called out, announcing herself in flawless French.

The door squeaked open and a gray haired man rubbing his eyes directed an impatient gaze at Lydia.

She gently stroked her horse's mane and walked to where her face was illuminated from the glow of the lantern which hung beside the gate. "Pardon for waking you, sir. I daresay you looked for me hours ago," Lydia said. "I was beset by highwaymen who took my bags as well as the very carriage I was riding in. But I'm finally here. By the way, I am the companion to the English lady."

Shaking himself into a shirt, he ambled toward the gate. "You are alone?"

"Yes, quite." She saw no sign of her brothers or

Morgie and became alarmed. But she remembered Haverstock's words. *We'll get in.* She just had to do her part.

She decided to mount her horse to draw the gatekeeper's eye to a higher level. He began to pull the gate open. She heard it scraping against the hard earth as he walked forward, his back to her.

Then she saw them. Three of them lying on the ground, shimmying through the opening. She kicked the horse and it spurted forward, coming abreast of the gray haired main. She must think of something to say to him to keep him from looking back.

"Are many people here now?"

"Besides the English couple, there's just four others."

"I do wish you'd do something about your bandits. I'm at a dreadful disadvantage without my personal belongings." She trotted in, the gloomy chateau at the end of the lane now capturing her attention.

As prearranged, she dismounted half way up the drive and waited for her companions though she was so impatient, she retraced her last several yards.

She did not hear them until James greeted her. "Well done, Lyddie."

She asked excitedly: "Did you hear how many – or should I say how few – are here?"

"Only four?" James said.

"That gives us even odds," Lydia said.

"No, it doesn't," Haverstock said firmly. "You have no part from here on out, Lydia. In fact, I plan to walk in quite alone. James can be my backup."

He strode off purposefully toward the big

house. It was in darkness except for one lighted room on the first floor. Setting his feet carefully on the cracked ground, he followed the light spilling from a French window. As he got close, he heard muffled voices. One of them was Anna's. He edged closer and peered through the panes. His heart caught at the sight of Anna. Dressed in a low-cut gown of ivory silk, she sat at a marquetry game table. Her hair was swept away from her face, accentuating the elegance of her slender neck. Sir Henry sat opposite her. No one else was in the room.

The sight of Anna unhurt and in possession of her faculties flooded him with relief. "My wife plays vingt-un," Haverstock whispered to James as he placed his ear closer to the window.

Sir Henry dealt. "The man I had hoped to meet here, my dear, has not come. We will go to Paris in the morning. That fool coachman is driving me quite mad in his impatience to visit the capital."

Haverstock tried the knob. It opened, and he strolled into the salon. "I've come for my wife, Vinson."

Sir Henry flung down his cards and bolted to a standing position, feeling for a sword at his side that was not there. His jade eyes flashed with anger.

"Charles!" Anna gasped. A flicker of emotion – was it pleasure? – danced in her soulful eyes.

"Are you all right, my dear?" Haverstock asked as he walked to her.

He held her in his gaze as she slowly nodded. His eyes trailed over her. She appeared physically unharmed, but there was something in her demeanor, a moroseness, he had not seen there before.

The thought of Sir Henry forcing himself on Anna was almost as frightening to Haverstock as physical harm. "If you have violated my wife in any way, Vinson, I will kill you here and now."

"Please tell your brute of a husband that I have not forced my attentions on you, Anna," Sir Henry said.

She took a long look at her husband. "I am guilty of many wretched things, Charles, but not of adultery."

It was all Haverstock could do not to cradle her in his arms that very minute. Sir Henry took a few cocky steps toward Haverstock. "That is not to say Anna did not choose to leave with me of her own free will."

"I have no reason to believe you," Haverstock said. "You are a traitor, a murderer – and now an abductor."

"Tell him, my dear," Sir Henry instructed.

Haverstock confidently watched Anna. Hadn't she just assured him she was not an adultress?

There was raw pain in her face as she lowered her lashes and spoke softly. "I. . .I belong in Paris."

Her words were a kick in his stomach and a knife in his heart at the same time. "But. . .you can't mean it. The man's a murderer. I know you loathe him."

She nodded but refused to meet her husband's gaze. "I can no longer live in England."

Haverstock swallowed hard. "Even if I vow to accord you the love and honor you deserve?"

Now she met his gaze, her eyes brimming with tears and an unbearable sadness on her lovely face. "It would make no difference, Charles."

Grief as acute as death numbed him. Drawing

his lips into a tight line, Haverstock said, "It seems I've come here for nothing." He swept into a bow. "Good evening, madam."

# $\mathcal{C}$hapter 30

"I can't believe it, even if I did hear her with my very own ears." Lydia strode through the overgrown grass. "I tell you, Charles, Anna's madly in love with you."

"And she loathes Vinson," Morgie added.

"We did hear her, and she made her wishes quite clear," Haverstock said bitterly.

He followed Lydia, his thoughts incoherent. Anna had been the stars in his heaven, and now there was only utter darkness.

For a second back at the chateau he had thought she loved him. Was it not a painful heart that bespoke her fidelity? But then her duplicity twisted her words into barbed dejection.

Lydia veered from the direction of the path which would have taken them back to the lane.

"Where are you going, Lyddie?" Morgie asked.

"To the mews."

"And why might that be?"

"Because we have to see if the hired chaise is here. We did promise the coachman's wife we would find out about her husband."

"So we did," Morgie said, trotting off after Lydia, with the brothers following him.

In the stables, they found a traveling chaise, then woke the coachman, who slept in a small room overhead.

He immediately set about a recitation of the indignities he had suffered at the hands of the arrogant Englishman. Why, he had not received a single franc from the man, yet. And while the Englishman kept saying they would be going to Paris, the coachman was losing many fares in the meantime. And he didn't for one minute believe that woman was the Englishman's wife. True, she did want to run away from the insufferable man. He felt ashamed of himself for watching idly as the poor woman's hands were tied behind her. That was no way to treat a lady. Especially one as beautiful as the mademoiselle.

On hearing this, a raw, bitter anger boiled within Haverstock. He grabbed the man by his shirt and spoke through clenched teeth. "When did this happen?"

"Two nights ago. When they left the ship in Calais. The mademoiselle, she tried to run away, but the miserable Englishman caught her and dragged her to the coach. And when they arrived here at the chateau, her hands were bound."

"I'll kill him!" Haverstock vowed, shoving the coachman and stalking off toward the house.

As he approached the chateau, the drawing room now lay in darkness. His gaze swept to the second floor where light spilled onto an upper balcony. He could reach the balcony by climbing a huge oak. He took off his jacket and began to climb. He straddled a branch which extended to the balcony and feared it would not bear his weight. But it did. He leapt down to the balcony and looked through the window.

It was Anna's room. She lay weeping on the bed. The sight tore at his heart.

He opened the window and stepped into her

room.

She jerked into an upright position, clutching her lace handkerchief to her eyes. "Charles!"

He stopped short of the bed. "I'm taking you home, Anna."

"But. . ." Her voice faltered. "But I'll only hurt you. There. . .there is a letter."

"There's only one way to hurt me, Anna." He stepped closer to her. "That's by leaving me. I find I cannot seem to live without you."

She hurled herself into his arms. "Oh, Charles, I do love you so!"

He gathered her into his chest. Her arms circled his waist, her face cradled in the hollow of his chest. He reveled in the exquisite feel of her. His wife. His love.

"When you went away," she said, "he told me you had been arrested. I thought to clear you by writing a confession – which, of course, he is using against me now. It will ruin you."

He laughed and pulled her even closer. "There you are wrong. If I have you, I have everything." He lifted her face with a gentle finger. "Besides, your confession can hardly be terribly incriminating. You are guilty of nothing more than having my own groom follow me. Hardly the material for your death warrant."

The chamber door snapped open, and Haverstock looked up to see Sir Henry standing there, leveling a pistol at them. "I thought I heard voices."

Haverstock pushed Anna aside and stepped in front of her.

"I was afraid you'd come back for her," Sir Henry said, kicking the door shut behind him. "But I must insist on keeping her. I need her more than you do, Haverstock. You derive a great deal of satisfaction from your work. My lifeline has always been the glitter of society. And I'm not a young man any more. I need Anna's beauty and talent to assure my place at the best houses in Paris."

"You will not be welcomed in Paris, Vinson," Haverstock said ruthlessly. "Does the name Thomas Brouget mean anything to you?"

Sir Henry's eyes widened. "So that's why he's never shown up here."

"He never left London. You will get no reward from Boney. In fact, I daresay Monsieur Hebert has a hefty price on your head as we speak. Going to Paris is out of the question for you."

"Why, you..." Sir Henry raised the pistol.

The French window burst open. James poised on the threshold, his drawn sword gleaming under the light of the torchieries. "Here, Vinson," he called in an effort to detract Sir Henry's attentions from his unarmed brother.

Sir Henry threw a panicked glance at James. In less than a heartbeat, Sir Henry aimed his pistol at James and fired.

The smell of gun powder, the hiss of his brother's gasp, the patch of blood on James' sleeve spurred Haverstock into motion. He dove at Sir Henry, but not before the older man flung the smoking pistol to the floor and grabbed a knife from his waistcoat. Haverstock lunged and pinned him against the cracked plaster wall, grasping his knife hand.

Haverstock's huge hand covered Sir Henry's bony wrist and repeatedly slammed it into the wall.

Though he cried out in pain, Sir Henry would

not let go of the knife.

Haverstock next sent his fist crashing into Sir Henry's face. But still Sir Henry held the knife firmly, even as the two men fell to the floor. They rolled like a lopsided windmill. Haverstock wound up on top his adversary. He watched as the blood pooled around Sir Henry's head, and the life stilled from his ashen face. The knife, still in his hand, had sliced Sir Henry's throat.

Haverstock sprang to his feet and turned sharply toward his brother. "James?"

James let the sword drop to the floor as his fingers spread across his wound. Blood oozed down his arm. "Nothing but a scratch."

Lydia leaped onto the balcony, took one look at James, who had fallen back through the open French doors, and she swooned.

Morgie sprang to the balcony next, took one look at Lydia and fell to her side, taking her hand in his. "Oh, my poor Lyddie. I'll never forgive myself if something's happened to you."

"Nothing's happened to her," Haverstock said, walking to the balcony where the rapid pounding of hooves below drew his attention. Four horsemen hurriedly rode off from the direction of the mews down the main road to the gatehouse. "Despite my sister's propensity for controlling most situations, she seems not to be able to tolerate the sight of blood." Still watching the lane, Haverstock added, "It seems the Frenchmen who were here have no desire for a fight."

He turned to Anna. "My dearest, how do you tolerate the sight of blood? Will you be able to give me a hand with my brother?"

Anna, flinching from Sir Henry's grim death scene, directed her gaze to James. "This is

James?"

James made a half bow. "Your most obedient servant, my lady."

"Oh, but you're hurt. This is too terrible. Charles! Help me get his coat off," Anna cried.

Haverstock removed his brother's coat and determined James had not been far from the mark when he said he only sustained a scratch. The bullet singed his coat but entered only the fleshy part of his arm. They wrapped it in strips of lawn from Anna's undergarments.

Turning her attention to Lydia, Anna fetched vinaigrette from her reticule and held it under Lydia's nose until she stirred. Morgie helped lift her upper torso.

"Gave me the fright of my life, Lyddie," he said. "Thought you'd been shot."

She turned the most wistful smile on him. "You cared, then?"

"Of course I cared. You're like a sister."

"I already have two brothers, Morgie. I do not need another."

"Well, you certainly don't need a fiancé, either, since you've already got one of those, too."

"A pity," she said.

"Why is it a pity?"

"If you were. . .well, there is something so romantic about the idea of marrying in France."

Her words rendered him speechless for a full minute. Then he said, "As you've pointed out, my French is very poor. I might not understand the clergyman."

"Can you say yes?" she asked.

He squeezed her hand. "*Oui.*"

"It's about time you two realized you belong together," Haverstock said.

"If that isn't the pot calling the kettle black," Lydia said, looking affectionately at Haverstock.

He smiled at his sister, then walked to Anna and took both her hands in his and dropped to one knee. "If I had been in possession of half a brain those months ago I took you for my wife, I would have begged for your hand and told you there was no other woman on earth I would rather have."

A troubled look crossed her face. "But I've done such terrible things."

He stood and gently set his palms on her cheeks. "Like cheating at cards?"

"You knew?" she asked, her eyes widening.

"Of course. It was the luckiest night of my life."

"You don't think I'm awful?"

"You're not awful, except when you leave me. You are actually quite wonderful, Lady Haverstock."

She threw her arms around him, melting into him. "And to think, we both thought we were sacrificing ourselves for England."

He held her tightly against him, dropping a soft kiss on top her head. "Ah, sweet sacrifice."

# $\mathcal{C}$hapter 31

*Haymore, three months later*

Divesting themselves of their pelisses and bonnets, Anna and Lydia entered Haymore through the French windows that faced the terrace.

Standing in the salon, Haverstock met his wife and took her pelisse, handing it to the butler. "I do not like you wandering about the countryside in your condition," he told her, hooking an arm around her and gently patting her stomach. "We mustn't endanger the little earl."

She stood on her toes to brush her lips across his. "I keep telling you our baby could very well be a she."

"A pity. I suppose I would have to force myself to continue trying for a son."

Lydia swept past her brother and kissed Morgie on the cheek. "Did you two succeed in arranging Mother's portraits to suit her at the dowager house?"

Morgie threw a questioning glance at Haverstock.

Haverstock closed the doors. "Morgie has yet to understand that Mother is never quite satisfied with anything," Haverstock said.

Lydia smiled. "At least she won't admit it when she is. Like with Anna. Morgie and I positively begged her to live with us, but she insisted on moving to the dowager house at Haymore, saying she had to assure the future marquess was brought up correctly. When, of course, we all know how much she has come to regard Anna."

Haverstock looked at Anna with pride. "Mother can't bring herself to admit how pleased she is to be here, nor how fine a wife Anna is."

"How was your outing?" Morgie asked his bride as they strolled across the broad room.

"Oh, Morgie, the most wonderful thing! Mr. Archer has died and his heir has decided to sell the abbey."

"What's wonderful about the fellow dying?" he asked.

"You could buy the abbey, and we could be neighbors with Charles and Anna."

He came to a halt, turned to his wife and scowled. "Won't live so close to that damned squire."

She lovingly stroked the thin planes of his face. "You goose. Haven't we told you the squire plans to wed the vicar's widow?"

His face brightened. "Don't see how he could have gotten over you that quickly."

"Because I am persuaded he realized how utterly unsuited we were." She linked her arm through his. "With his deep sense of propriety, he must count himself fortunate to be rid of a woman who had no more sensibilities than to elope – and on foreign soil at that."

"Then he's the fool I've always said he was."

"He's a fine man, really, Morgie," Haverstock interjected. "By the way, I received a letter today from Captain Smythe. From The Peninsula. He apologized for not coming up to scratch with

Cynthia. Said he wanted nothing more than to make her his wife, but with his future so uncertain he had no desire to make her a widow."

"How sad," Anna said. "It sounds as if both of them are now miserable."

"I respect him for it. It would hardly be fair to bring a child into the world, then not be there for *him*," Haverstock said, giving Anna a mischievous sideways glance.

"Or her," Anna countered with mock defiance.

"I believe Cynthia will wait for the captain," Lydia said.

Anna frowned. "Would that Kate's love were that constant."

"Kate never loved Reeves," Haverstock said, pausing at the doorway. "The news of her London *affairs* comes as no surprise."

"A pity everyone cannot be as happy as the four of us," Lydia said.

"Charlotte and Hogart appear to be," Morgie added. He opened the door and led Lydia into the expansive marble hallway.

"As well they ought with your fortune behind the sewing school and their other ministries," Lydia said.

Anna addressed Morgie. "Speaking of your fortune, I really do think you should buy the abbey for Lydia."

"I can't seem to refuse the vixen."

Lydia winked at him. "Come, let me beat you at billiards. I sense my brother and Anna want to be alone."

After they left, Anna closed the door and said, "I don't for a moment believe they're playing billiards."

He lowered his face to hers. "I've trained you

well."

She wrapped her arms around him. "I've always credited you with being a gifted teacher."

He cradled her face within his hands. "Not so adept as you, my dearest love. Because of you I have learned the infinite depths of my once-cold heart." His face came so close to hers he could feel her warm breath. "Your love has fed me as sunshine and rain sustain a mighty tree."

"And my life began the day I married you."

He drew her into his chest and nestled his face in her scented hair. "The day you became my lady by chance."

## The End

# Author's Biography

A former journalist and English teacher, Cheryl Bolen sold her first book to Harlequin Historical in 1997. That book, *A Duke Deceived*, was a finalist for the Holt Medallion for Best First Book, and it netted her the title Notable New Author. Since then she has published more than 20 books with Kensington/Zebra, Love Inspired Historical and was Montlake launch author for Kindle Serials. As an independent author, she has broken into the top 5 on the *New York Times* and top 20 on the *USA Today* best-seller lists.

Her 2005 book *One Golden Ring* won the Holt Medallion for Best Historical, and her 2011 gothic historical *My Lord Wicked* was awarded Best Historical in the International Digital Awards, the same year one of her Christmas novellas was chosen as Best Historical Novella by Hearts Through History. Her books have been finalists for other awards, including the Daphne du Maurier, and have been translated into eight languages.

She invites readers to www.CherylBolen.com, or her blog, www.cherylsregencyramblings.wordpress.co or Facebook at https://www.facebook.com/pages/Cheryl-Bolen-Books/146842652076424.

Printed in Great Britain
by Amazon